BROWN-EYED
DEVIL

EVAN GILBERT

Dreamspinner Press

Published by
Dreamspinner Press
5032 Capital Circle SW
Ste 2, PMB# 279
Tallahassee, FL 32305-7886
USA
http://www.dreamspinnerpress.com/

Brown-eyed Devil

Cover Art by Justin James
dare.empire@gmail.com

ISBN: 978-1-62380-228-8

Printed in the United States of America
First Edition
December 2012

eBook edition available
eBook ISBN: 978-1-62380-229-5

For Robert DeWayne.
You would've have liked this one, kid.

CHAPTER
ONE

"GOD. Who is *that*?" I stopped in the middle of the crosswalk, staring.

Garrett Chess sighed and stopped too. Although we were both eighteen, puberty had only hit me about seven months ago. Since then, just about any human body with XY chromosomes made my mouth water. Garrett had zero patience with my boy-watching because he wasn't gay and because it didn't take much, in his opinion, to catch my attention. But when his gaze fell on the latest object of my desire, he gave me an understanding pat on the back.

The dude was tall, buff, and bronze-skinned, a bit older than Garrett and me—twenty, maybe twenty-one. Dressed in blue jeans, yellow T-shirt, and white sneakers, he had straight, glossy black hair hanging just about down to his waist. He wasn't carrying a backpack, and his thumbs were hooked casually in his front pockets. He was way good-looking, and he didn't even glance my way, of course. But he had none of that I-look-so-good-you-can't-stand-it attitude some of the beauty kings and queens at school threw. His eyes were oddly vacant, the way a person looks when daydreams have taken over the brain. There was sadness deep in his face that he didn't seem to be aware of, and it made me want to wrap my arms tight around him.

Or maybe it was the wonderful, heavenly way those jeans hung on his slender waist and gorgeous ass that fired the impulse in me.

A horn blared, breaking the spell. To our right, a car making the turn from Alabama Avenue had jerked to a stop. Behind the wheel, the snarling driver shook a fist at us. I've got no particular skill at lip-reading, but it was easy to make out the warm and fuzzy request the man mouthed for us to get out of the street. By way of reply, I shot him the one-finger salute, double-handed.

Garrett swatted me across the back of the head. "Move it," he snapped, shoving me forward. He'd always had this thing about respecting adults, even ones who didn't feed and clothe him. He was wiry but nearly half a foot taller than me. I looked, and sometimes felt, like a twelve-year-old next to him.

We made it to the sidewalk, and my eyes immediately went after that long-haired dude. He was half a block away now, his back to us, hair swaying gently back and forth as he walked. He looked good from any angle.

"Must be new in town," said Garrett, watching him too.

"I gotta go talk to him," I blurted.

"Yeah, right." Garrett knew me. I was the guy who found fine dudes great to look at but scary to talk to.

"I *gotta*." The urge felt strange, like a surge of electricity in my head, and so strong I actually took a step in the dude's direction.

Garrett grabbed my backpack and pulled, halting me in my tracks. "Uh-uh. You're not making us late, Myron. Come on, you'll see him in school."

Only the guy was heading in the *opposite* direction. And he looked as if he was in college, not high school. "But—"

"Come on," Garrett repeated. He headed down the street, tugging me along after him. I walked backward, staring, until the guy rounded the corner at the end of the block and disappeared.

I sighed. Deeply.

"Man." Garrett laughed. "You sound like a kid who just got a scoop of some damned good ice cream and dropped it in the dirt."

Suddenly, I was pissed. I jerked away, freeing myself from Garrett's grip, then turned and marched off, leaving him behind.

He caught up in two strides. "Aww. Like your scared runt ass had a chance with him."

"Shut up!"

He laughed again, which made me want to smack him one in the mouth. Of course, he would probably punch me back, and he could hit a lot harder than I could. So I swallowed the urge and kept walking.

Garrett was a good-looking black guy with a strapping build, but I'd never felt any kind of attraction to him. I'd known him since we were seven, and he was the closest thing in my life to the brother my parents always promised but never gave me. In addition to being a faggot, I was, in the vernacular of the town bigots, a mutt because my father was black and my mother was white. With my straight black hair trimmed close and combed forward, as I usually wore it, I looked like a white guy with a really good tan (or so I'd been told).

It was an unseasonably warm morning in the middle of October. So far, it seemed that summer had no intention of packing it in, with the mid-South still getting daytime temps in the upper seventies. Garrett and I were both silent as we made our way toward the high school.

Killebrew High and Killebrew the town have two things in common: they are small and they are dull. The town is wedged between Bartlett and Millington in west Tennessee. A hundred or so years ago, it was just a stretch of dirt roads connecting a bunch of farms. Now, Killebrew's streets are paved, and there's a business core with peculiar, fancy boutiques, a movie multiplex, professional suites, government offices, and such. Surrounding that are clusters of simple brick houses, the kind you find in just about any suburb, with a few tiny churches scattered among them. But northeast of town there are still farms with mind-numbing rows of corn, cotton, and soybeans sprawling like gigantic patchwork quilts across endless fields.

Yawn.

The high school is on the west side of town, at the dead end of Macon Street. The building's got no style. It's just a two-story rectangular block squatting atop a low hill. The architect behind this place really got one over on the town council. A monkey with a sharp stick and a smooth patch of dry dirt would've come up with a more imaginative design for the price of a mango. The sight of the mud-brown brick facade looming ahead made my sour mood even worse, which was strange because I actually liked my senior-year classes. I shoved my hands into my front pockets and grouchily hunched my shoulders.

Garrett, laid-back as ever, wasn't bothered by my foul attitude. He casually nudged my arm with his fist. "Hey, we got ten minutes before the bell," he piped cheerily. "Let's swing by the cafeteria and grab some donuts." Half an hour ago, when I got to his house, Garrett was sucking down a tower of pancakes topped with sliced bananas and strawberry syrup. If you think that meant he couldn't possibly be hungry now, think again. The guy has the metabolism of a Kansas tornado.

Once more, I pulled away from Garrett, but he didn't notice. We'd begun to blend into the wave of kids hiking toward school, and he shouted at Coop and LaVelle, who had just now shifted into view ahead of us.

"Hey, it's the B Team," LaVelle said when he turned back and spotted us.

"Yo, wannabes," said Coop with a grin so wide it looked as if his face had split in half.

Coop and LaVelle were on the basketball team. I'd tried out for my third and final time at the beginning of the school year but, as before, didn't make the cut. At five foot four, I'm a bit shorter than average, but I'm faster than just about any guy in school, and Coach Wilson says I move like a cat on the court. Unfortunately, I couldn't sink a shot if somebody paid me in cash. Graduation was barely seven months away. I suppose any chance I had of landing a basketball scholarship at some Big Ten Conference university was pretty much dead, huh?

Personally, I think the fact that some of the guys had "concerns" about sharing the showers with me had a lot to do with the coach's latest decision. Around the time of the tryouts, I drew a picture of myself lip-locking Brian Grady, a tall, hot white guy from the football team with a mustache that had more hair than I have on my entire body. I was stupid enough to even put our names on the picture, with an arrow helpfully pointing to the figure that was me and another one pointing to the figure that was Brian. And of course, a big goon who already hated me got his hands on the picture, and that was my blast out of the closet. In PE, the coach lets me use his own personal shower now, supposedly to keep me from getting bullied by the other guys. But there would have been no such accommodations on away games if I'd made the basketball team. When I mentioned my suspicions to Garrett, he said I should go to the ACLU and file suit. But I didn't want to be anybody's gay poster boy, because I was trying to survive high school, not get myself chased out of town by gun-waving mobs.

Garrett was a good all-around player, and given the fact that the coach had been urging him since freshman year to try out, he could easily have made the basketball team. But he was shooting for an academic scholarship to spare his financially strapped father the burden of funding his college education. He figured being on the team would eat up time that he should be putting into the books. That was not something his dad forced on him, either. He made that decision totally on his own.

Yeah, I know. Garrett's weird.

Stanley "Coop" Cooper was tall like Garrett, but thicker, sporting short, bristly brown hair on his big head and skin that looked permanently sunburned. LaVelle Spears was shorter and leaner than Garrett and Coop, but still bigger than me. He reached up to hook an arm around Garrett's neck. He tried to wrestle Garrett into a headlock, but Garrett jabbed an elbow into his ribs and LaVelle broke away, laughing. The four of us have been friends, like, forever. They couldn't understand my attraction to guys any more than I could understand their attraction to girls, but they stuck by me after I was forced out of the closet. And that's saying a lot, considering that for the first few days after my outing, they got called fags almost as much as I did. The fact that they weren't ashamed to be seen with me was the main reason the whole thing blew over as quickly as it did. And it made our friendship stronger.

But now I found myself hanging back from them.

LaVelle grinned over his shoulder at me, his dark face shiny in the sunlight. "What's the matter, pee wee? Can't ya keep up on them stubby little legs?"

We'd been ribbing each other that way since first grade, laughing it up. Today, I didn't even smile. Instead, a stream of curse words bubbled up into my throat like bile. Tucking my head, swallowing hard to keep the words to myself, I veered off.

"Myron, where're you going?" Garrett called after me.

"Gym," I snapped, not looking back.

"See ya in homeroom."

My eyes got so narrow with anger, I could barely see.

THE gymnasium was behind the school, every bit as squat and bland as the main building, only smaller. I found myself counting my steps as I went, something my dad used to make me do when I lost my preschool temper. Just when I reached the gym's south entrance, the door flew open, and I jumped back as Bette Herron came barreling outside.

"Oh, sorry," she said when she saw the outrage in my gawking eyes. With an embarrassed, apologetic smile, she flashed the cigarette tucked between the first two fingers of her right hand. "Emergency situation here." She promptly tugged a green disposable lighter from her pocket, lit up, and inhaled so deeply I feared her face would cave in.

I shook my head but didn't chide her about the smoking. Been there, done that with her, and it didn't make a lick of difference, except to get me told, in very colorful terms, to mind my own business. "I was just coming to see you," I said.

Bette eyed me suspiciously as she tilted her head back and spewed a stream of white smoke through her pursed lips. "Don't waste my time. I'll die if I don't get some nicotine in me, and the bell's about to ring." Seventeen, she'd been a good friend of mine for almost nine years. In that time, I'd never seen her dress in anything but ragged jeans and oversized T-shirts. She was in all gray this morning, which made her look even dumpier than usual. Her short, dirty-blonde hair was pulled back and tied into a little ponytail at the base of her neck. Bette put in an hour a day at the school office as one of the principal's six hand-picked student assistants.

"Any new guys register in school lately?" I asked, on the highly improbable chance that the totally hot, muscular guy I'd just lusted after wasn't already out of high school, as well as out of my league.

She shook her head, taking another puff off the cig. "No, why?"

"I saw this way fine dude at the corner of Alabama and Macon this morning. Looks like he's new to town. Just wondering if he'd registered in school."

"What makes this guy so special that you're trying to track him down?"

"Well, for one thing, he doesn't smell like burnt wood," I sneered.

"Eat this," Bette replied, flicking the ash off the end of her cig at me. "If you're in the mood to track people down, you ought to try and find Coach Frieda."

Frieda Blevins, Bette's homeroom and PE teacher, coached all of the girls' sports teams at school. I was in her health and hygiene class last year. Coach Frieda made a running joke out of the fact that I couldn't say "penis" in class without stuttering. I liked her, even if she embarrassed the hell out of me. "Something happen to Coach Frieda?"

"She hasn't been to school in six days."

"Wow. She must've picked up one really nasty bug." The backpack was making my shoulders ache. I leaned against the brick wall for support.

"She's not sick, she's missing." Bette grabbed my collar and pulled me forward, peering down at me over her wide nose. She lowered her voice to a whisper, puffing smoke in my face as she spoke. "I overheard the principal on the phone yesterday. He went by the coach's house because nobody here has heard from her since last Thursday. He saw a plate of food on a tray in the living room and her TV was on, but there was no sign of her."

"Maybe she had a family emergency. She's from Birmingham, you know. Maybe she had to drive back down there."

"Except her car's in the driveway at her house." Bette released my collar and stepped back.

"Then maybe she went off with a friend, in the friend's car."

"Maybe. But then, why didn't she call the school? Teachers are supposed to call if they can't come in so the office can get a substitute to cover the classes. And why didn't she take her purse, her credit cards, her cell phone? The cops say all that stuff was still in her house."

I didn't know what to say to that, so I just stared at Bette.

Bette took another long drag off her cig. In her eyes, there was a flicker of unease, and that was enough to make me nervous. It took a lot to rattle Bette.

"You think somebody kidnapped her?" I asked, my voice hushed.

Bette opened her mouth, letting a little cloud of smoke drift free. She shrugged. "I don't know. I don't know what to think. I just know that the coach is gone and something's not right. The cops say there was no sign of a break-in at her place. The doors were all locked from the inside. But there were signs of a struggle in her kitchen. The table had been pushed up against the fridge, the chairs were overturned, and a pot of boiled corn had spilled on the stove. And there was straw all over the floor too."

"Straw?"

"Yeah, like the kind that comes out of a broom. Only thicker, and choppier."

Bette looked at me again, and this time something in my face seemed to puzzle her. She frowned. Immediately, I wondered if I was sprouting another zit. Last month, I had one in the center of my forehead that got so big you could've used it for a coat hook. "What?" I asked testily, fingers probing at my forehead.

Instead of answering, Bette looked at her watch. "Damn. One minute 'til the bell." She threw down the cig and ground it into the turf with the heel of her sneaker. "Better run. See ya later, Ron."

She yanked the door open and disappeared into the gym. After she'd gone, I stood there for what felt like hours, feeling peeved, confused, and on edge, all at the same time.

The bell rang, a loud, grating pulse that jangled through the air and made me shiver. I was now officially late, my fourth tardy this month. My homeroom teacher, Mrs. Perkins, had promised me detention if that happened. And my parents would go off like a nuke when they found out. But thoughts of punishment barely registered in my head.

As I walked slowly toward the main building, I wondered if Coach Frieda was lying hurt somewhere. Or dead.

CHAPTER
TWO

"DAMN, Myron. What's the matter?" Coop looked at me across the Formica tabletop. His face had an expression of honest-to-goodness concern. "You look like you just swallowed a hunk of charcoal."

We were seated, along with Garrett and LaVelle, at our usual corner table on the east side of the noisy, crowded, and brightly lit cafeteria. A group of ninth graders had staked it out on the first day of the school year, but it was a prime spot, close to the serving line yet kind of secluded, so we chased them off and took it over. I'd just wolfed down a bite out of my steaming bacon cheeseburger, one of the few dishes the cafeteria served that I actually liked. I would scarf those suckers down in less than two minutes; they were *that* good. But today, the first bite stuck in my throat like... well, a hunk of charcoal. I thumped my fist twice against my chest, almost gagging as I forced the stuff down. "Shit. The cook must've dozed off back there. Burger's kinda dry today."

"Really? Let's see." LaVelle reached over, grabbed the burger from me, and chomped off a mouthful. "Hmm." He rolled his eyes thoughtfully, chewing. He swallowed. "Tastes juicy to me," he said. He offered the remainder to Coop. "What do you think, man?"

Coop stuffed the rest of the sandwich into his mouth. He spoke around a mass of mangled bread and meat, crumbs spraying liberally. "I quite agree," he garbled in a horribly fake British accent. "Excellent juiciosity, and plenty of flavornoids to please the tongue." He gulped noisily as the food went down, and he followed up by mooing out a long, loud, rumbling burp.

I saw kids on the opposite side of the cafeteria turning, grossed-out looks on their faces, trying to figure out where the truck-like sound had come from.

"Real funny," said Garrett. He was reading some chapter in his chemistry textbook while he munched chicken nuggets, and he didn't bother to look up as he spoke. "Now why don't you clowns go buy the man another burger."

It was not a request, and Coop and LaVelle knew it. Chuckling, LaVelle shrugged good-naturedly and started to get up.

"No, that's okay," I said quickly. "I'm cool." The idea of more charred meat was suddenly disgusting. I was starving, but I couldn't think of a single thing on the day's menu that would satisfy me. I wanted something hot... fresh... *juicy*.... Sighing, I pushed my tray away from me. Coop snatched up my plate of untouched fries, and LaVelle helped himself to my carton of apple juice.

Garrett looked at me. "You okay?"

"Yeah." I rocked my chair back onto the two rear legs, bracing my knees against the underside of the table for balance, trying for nonchalance. Garrett kept staring at me. Finally, I turned to him, annoyed. "What?"

"You know what's up, man," said LaVelle, using a straw to stir apple juice into his glass of root beer. "You got Daddy Garrett all worried now. He must be as dumb as Old Lady Perkins."

I hadn't pulled detention when I walked into homeroom this morning, five minutes late. Mrs. Perkins had taken one look at me and tried to send me to the nurse's office. I'd told her I was fine. I was still somewhat shaken at the time from my conversation with Bette, but overall I just had this detached, unconcerned attitude about everything. I'd slumped at my desk and put my head down. Mrs. Perkins had stared worriedly at me while she finished taking attendance and went through her announcements for the day. When it came time to move on to first period, she'd caught me on my way out the door and suggested that I go home. I'd told her again that I was fine and drifted off into the hall, heading for Spanish.

"That was a cool move, though, playing sick," LaVelle continued. "The lady didn't say a word about you walking in late."

"That never worked for me," Coop said with just a touch of bitterness. He huffed out a laugh and added, "Old Lady Perk must have a thing for runts." The smile dropped suddenly from his face, and he reached down, slapping his hands against the pockets of his jeans. "Oh, damn."

"What?" LaVelle asked.

"I forgot my insulin pen again."

"Shoot. That's the third time this week. The doctor oughta just stick a pump in you and forget about it."

Garrett ignored them. He looked into my eyes. My mom could read me like a book, just by looking into my eyes. With most folks, I could put up a good bluff, but my mom was able to see past all that and pick out the very thing I was trying to keep to myself. Garrett was nowhere near that good at reading me, but he could sometimes tell when I was lying. With our gazes locked, he asked again, pointedly, "You okay?"

For several seconds, I kept silent. When Mom and Dad sat me down for the old birds-and-bees discussion two days after my twelfth birthday, they said I could expect emotional changes as I made my "progression to manhood." (Dad and I had both cracked up when Mom quoted that one. I'd already read it on the 4parentsofboys.gov website, which she kept bookmarked on the computer.) Maybe that was why I felt so weird today. Pubescent emotional changes. I couldn't say that, however, to Garrett. Coop and LaVelle would have a field day with it. The fact that I was just going through at eighteen what they'd gone through at twelve was already fucked up and embarrassing enough. I coughed and said, "Got a headache. That's all."

That would have never worked with my mom, but it did the trick with Garrett. "I've got a bottle of aspirin in my locker. You want some?" he offered.

"Nah. I'll be okay."

"Daaang," LaVelle said, grinning at Garrett. "You really are dumb, man."

I won't repeat what Garrett told LaVelle to do with that observation. But it made me laugh for the first time that day.

IN PE, it was basketball. I was on the Shirts team, and Coop was with the Skins. Coop kept up the usual running commentary on my skills as we went up and down the court. Was it getting under my skin? You bet. But it was one of his teammates who really got me steamed.

Aldo Farmer was this big redheaded dude with freckles as dark as old pennies sprinkled over his face, neck, and upper torso. In addition to PE, we were in the same American history and algebra classes, and we didn't like each other. Aldo was a jerk, the kind of guy who wasn't ashamed of throwing his weight around with guys who were smaller. I'd been his favorite target since he transferred to Killebrew from a finicky prep school in Nashville. He was the one who noticed how the crotch of my jeans filled up every time I scoped out Brian Grady's fine, slender body, and who snatched the drawing of my fantasy kiss with Brian, promptly turning around and broadcasting the news to the world. He got even more hateful toward me after that. Word was that his mom and dad had beaucoup dinero, although nobody at Killebrew had a clue as to what they did for a living. No one knew why Aldo had left the finicky prep school, either, but we figured he must have done something really bad to get himself banished to our little Podunk public institution.

Aldo was as tall as Coach Wilson, a few inches over six feet, and his body was bulky, flabby with muscles that weren't toned but strong just the same. As a basketball player, he didn't have any speed, nor could he jump, but his long arms gave him a nasty reach, and he had a hook shot that was deadly accurate from as far away as half-court. I ran rings around him, confusing the hell out of him, and sometimes I managed to steal the ball or force him to lose control of it. I'd been doing a lot of that in this particular game. He, in turn, hit me with all manner of cheap shots every chance he got, elbowing me in the back, clipping me with those planks he called feet, shoving me off balance.

Coach Wilson saw none of it. Neither did any of the guys on my team. That's how slick Aldo was. I protested at first, but with no witnesses to back me up, I stopped wasting my breath and just fumed.

The game wasn't broken down into the standard quarters in PE class; there wasn't enough time. We just went at it, and whichever team was up at the end of the twenty-minute session was the winner. This game was down to, like, five minutes, and the Shirts were up by twelve points, despite the star power of Coop and Raymond Stern, another guy from the basketball team. I snagged the ball from a Skin driving for our basket and zipped straight down the court with guys from both teams scrambling after me. I just had to keep control of the ball until another Shirt got himself set up under the Skins' basket, then pass off to him so he could score.

But there was Aldo, waiting at center court like one of those big stone Greek statues that stood guard outside the town library. I spotted him at the last second and veered left, trying to steer wide of him, but he was too close. He stomped down, his left foot smashing onto my right. My body pitched forward and down, my bare knees skidding along the polished yellow wood of the court. I managed to hold onto the ball as I went down, grunting at the burning pain in my knees.

"Watch it, Gary Coleman," Aldo sneered, a crooked half smile on his long, narrow face. He snatched the ball out of my hands.

I had no idea who Gary Coleman was, but I knew an insult when I heard one. That, plus the sight of my abraded and bleeding knees, set off a bomb-burst of anger in my head.

Aldo turned, lumbering back toward the Shirts' goal, left hand jabbing out to fend off one of my teammates, the right already going out to lob off his famous hook shot.

I got to my feet. Everything in my brain was so laser-focused on Aldo, I don't think I was even breathing at that moment. I sprinted forward, the big ox's freckled back looming ahead of me like a wall. I shot out my left hand. My intent was to grab him by the shoulder, spin him around, and slam my fist into his hump of a nose. His shoulder was slick with sweat, and my hand slipped. The momentum caused my fingernails to rake along his back.

Aldo bellowed like a wounded bull.

I jumped back, raising my fists, ready to fight. But Aldo collapsed, the ball spurting out of his hands and bounding across the floor. He lay on his side, body twisting like a snake dropped on a scorching blacktop road, clutching at his back with his left hand. "Ow! *Owww!*"

Coach Wilson, who'd been sitting on the bleachers going over plays for the basketball team, shot to his feet. "What the hell...?" He ran onto the court, where several guys surrounded Aldo and me in a wide circle.

"Get out of the way," Coach snapped as he pushed his way through the wall of sweating, staring boys.

Aldo rolled over, his body contorted into an arch balanced on his shoulders and feet, keeping his back off the floor. His eyes, wide and glazed with agony, glared into mine. "What the hell did you do to me?" he screamed.

I sneered down at him. "Somebody call this fool's mama to come change his diaper. Jeez. I barely touched him. What's he crying about?"

Coach Wilson knelt down and coaxed Aldo into sitting up. Aldo grimaced and mewled with every move. "Let me have a look," Coach said, gently pushing Aldo's head toward his knees. He took a peep at the redhead's back.

And his mouth dropped open.

"It hurts," whined Aldo, tears pulsing from his tightly squeezed eyes.

"Let's get you to the nurse," the coach said, composure coming back to his face. "She may have to take you to the emergency room. The rest of you boys run laps around the gym. I'll be back before the bell."

The coach helped Aldo to stand. Aldo didn't look at me or anyone else. His whole face was clenched, and every breath he exhaled came out in a long, miserable moan. Coop and a couple of other guys standing behind Aldo muttered startled curses as they caught sight of what Coach had seen.

I rolled my eyes. What the hell was the big fucking deal?

I found out when Coach Wilson and Aldo turned to head out of the gym. From Aldo's right shoulder, five welts stretched across his back, curving down to the left and stopping just above his waist. The wounds were long, thick, hideous blisters, the surrounding skin bright red. It looked as if he had been lashed with some incredibly hot whip.

The breath caught in my throat. I couldn't believe what I was seeing.

All I'd done was *scratch* him.

Looking back over his shoulder, Coach scowled at me. It was the kind of scowl a cop would give a mass murderer who'd just bombed a day-care center. "You're done, Myron. Leave the gym. Right now!"

"But... shouldn't I change first—"

"No. Get your ass to the office and wait there for me."

That's when I realized I was in trouble.

CHAPTER
THREE

"WHAT did you do to Aldo?"

The principal of Killebrew High, Mr. Ellis, wasn't a particularly big man. He was maybe five foot nine, a hundred and sixty pounds, and he was about the same age as my forty-five-year-old dad. He wore these little rectangular, wire-framed glasses and had less hair on his face than I did. But everybody at the school—from teachers to students to cafeteria workers to janitors—respected him. Despite his size, he seemed to be made of steel.

I sat across from him in his office, still in my cut-off sweatpants and T-shirt from PE. I'd been there for over an hour. I rolled my eyes and slumped in the chair, letting my head fall back. We were both frustrated, both pissed. Mr. Ellis had asked that same question three times already, and I'd given him the same answer each time.

"Sit up!" Mr. Ellis barked, his voice as severe as the black suit he wore.

I sat up, but I kept my eyes off him, staring instead at the framed college degrees—there were three of them—on the wall over his left shoulder. I couldn't stand the anger in his eyes. He had no reason to be so upset with me. I was afraid that if I looked into his angry eyes, I'd lose it and jump over the desk at him.

That impulse to jump over the desk at him was strong.

"Now answer me." Mr. Ellis sat rigid in his chair, hands pressed flat against his desktop, probably to keep himself from grabbing me by the neck. "And don't give me that bull about scratching him."

"But… that's… what… happened," I said slowly, pronouncing each word distinctly as if speaking to a creature that had never heard human language.

"That was no scratch on that boy's back. The nurse said those were second-degree burns. The boy was going into shock by the time he got to her office. His blood pressure was through the roof. If she hadn't taken him to the hospital, who knows what would have happened." The principal stopped, and I looked directly at him. His eyebrows went up expectantly.

I bolted forward, out of the chair. Fortunately, some part of my brain was still rational enough to make me stop myself short. I wound up leaning over the desk, eyes blazing, fists balled against my thighs. "*I just scratched him!*"

Mr. Ellis's eyes blazed right back, bright with indignation. After a few moments, his glare intimidated me into sitting down again.

The principal's desk was bare except for a brass lamp, an old-fashioned corded telephone, a pen, and a short stack of papers. In tightly measured motions, Mr. Ellis picked up the pen and signed every paper in the stack. Then he put down the pen, picked up the top page, and slid it across the desktop to me.

"Effective today," he said coolly, "you are suspended. For one month."

"A *month*—?"

"Quiet!"

I chewed down on my lower lip. It was the only way to keep myself from cursing him out. Or taking a bite out of his neck.

I really wanted to do that, take a bite out of him.

Mr. Ellis continued. "You should hope that will be the worst punishment you get in this. The only reason you're not being expelled and carted out of here by the police is because I have no proof you used a weapon to hurt Aldo. But his parents could still press charges against you. Once they actually see what you did to their son, I don't doubt that they will."

Oh, how wonderful. The principal wanted to see me in jail.

The thought made my head pound. *You want a reason to have me arrested? I'll give you a reason to have me arrested! I'll flip this whole damn desk over on your stupid ass—*

I stopped myself, because it wasn't spite that I saw on Mr. Ellis's face. Beneath the anger, there was disappointment and sadness in his eyes. Before I could speculate about what was going on in his head, he opened one of the desk drawers and produced a laptop. When he flipped the computer open, my school file popped up on the screen. My parents' names were listed, along with their work and cell phone numbers.

"Is that it?" I asked, surprised at the hostility that still tinged my voice. "Do I just go home now?"

"No, you wait here," Mr. Ellis said as he picked up the phone and began to dial. "I can't let you leave on your own. As long as school is in session, one of your parents will have to come here and pick you up."

I watched as he finished dialing and held the receiver to his ear, waiting. After several seconds, he abruptly disconnected the call and began dialing another number from the list on the laptop's screen. A contemptuous smile crept around the corners of my mouth.

Mom and Dad had taken the day off from their jobs. They'd driven up to this cabin that a friend of Mom's owned on a little lake in the woods, somewhere on the backside of Fayette County. It was something they did whenever they wanted a bit of uninterrupted "happy together" time. Naturally, they weren't inclined to take calls during their getaway. All Mr. Ellis would get in calling their jobs and their cells was voice mail. I could have told him that and saved him some time. I could have also given him the number to the cabin, which my parents had told me to use only in an emergency. Getting myself kicked out of school certainly qualified.

But I just sat there, my little smile turning into a sneer, and said nothing.

I hadn't eaten lunch.

I was *starving*.

Mr. Ellis watched me, his eyes suddenly wary.

MR. ELLIS'S office was at the end of a short corridor that led down from the main office, where three secretaries and the appointed student assistants conducted the school's business. I sat on a wooden bench in that corridor for three hours.

Mr. Ellis left several messages on my parents' voice mail systems about my suspension. Of course, there was no return call and no one showed up to collect me, so I was banished from his office. Coach brought my clothes and backpack from the gym. The principal offered to let me change in his private bathroom, but I just sneered and turned away. I sat there in my dirty PE duds and stank.

Oddly, most of the time I sat in that hall, my thoughts were on the dark-haired, copper-skinned dude from this morning. When I closed my eyes, it was almost as if I could see him, standing in the elegantly furnished main office of McQuarran and Sons, the only funeral home in town, talking to a woman seated behind a desk who must have been the receptionist. I could smell him too, a hot, piquant scent that reminded me of the spices my mom used when she baked pies and cakes at Christmas.

It felt as if I'd known him forever. His was a face I'd loved, even though at the moment, I could not get a clear vision of that face in my head. I knew the feel of his hand on my ass. I knew the taste of his lips on mine, the sweet pain of his teeth on my neck and down my back. I knew that he liked to hold me in his lap, my bare chest to his, his hands tight around my waist, his dick stuffed way up my ass as he did his hard, nasty grind beneath me. But how could that be? I'd never seen him before this morning. I didn't even know his fucking name. And none of my sexual fantasies, when I spotted him this morning, had anything to do with me sitting on his cock. How could I be seeing him now, crying bitterly next to Mr. McQuarran as they sat side by side on one of the pews in the funeral home's chapel, knowing that I was the reason for his pain?

Other, more pleasant "memories" came to me. There went the two of us dancing under a starry night sky on a beach of black sand, eyes closed, arms around each other's waists, the side of my face pressed to his shoulder. His strong body was firm and warm, and the beat of his heart was the music to which we swayed. The ocean serenaded us too, an aria as powerful as a thousand ancient voices and as gentle as the flitting of the fireflies that wafted around us, their soft, intermittent glow an irresistible call to passion. Our house was on that beach, not far away. We were safe there, so very safe.

And there he was smiling at me over a table in a restaurant half a mile up in the sun-soaked blue sky, the city spread out around and below us like building blocks on some huge plate. His face was lined, and his black hair, cut short, was streaked with silver. He broke into a laugh at some joke I'd told a hundred times over the years, and his now pale-green eyes twinkled at me with such delight it made him look like a kid again.

And there were the two of us, shouting at each other, eyes bright with anger. He said something that hurt me so deeply it stunned me to silence. I turned, ready to walk away from the pain. He grabbed my hand at once and pulled me to him. The rage was gone, his face filled now with limitless regret and endless love as he tenderly stroked the back of my head with his free hand. He was sorry, he didn't mean it, please don't go. And I forgave him. How could I do otherwise? He was my soul. I *lived* for him.

Those sensations stayed with me for almost two hours as I sat in that school corridor, wringing at my heart, making me long to reunite with a guy who didn't even know I was alive, a guy whose presence was dark and frightening and outrageously sexy because of it. Somehow, he was a grim danger to me, but I couldn't shake him from my mind, even when I banged my head back against the wall hard enough to give myself a headache. He was a part of me, as I was a part of him.

I had to find him again. As deadly as he was to me, I had to be with him.

The sensations vanished on their own at the start of seventh period. That was when Bette came into the office to begin her stint. She saw me on that lousy bench and froze, frowning with surprise. My dick was hard from all the faded weird visions and sensations I'd just had, and although the erection was hidden beneath the bundle of clothes in my lap, I still felt embarrassment burn up my cheeks beneath Bette's gaze. I flipped her one, she grinned and flipped me back, and then she went to help some dude who'd come in to get a copy of his transcript.

Just as the final bell rang, Mr. Ellis stepped out of his office. "You can go now, Myron," he said.

I rolled my eyes at him, disgusted, and got up. My erection had shriveled, and my butt was numb. My fiery disposition had also cooled considerably in those three hours. I felt churlish and tired. I grabbed my backpack off the floor beside the bench.

Mr. Ellis stepped in front of me. His black suit was crisp, not a line out of place, not a wrinkle to be seen. In the past, it amazed me how he could look as neat at the end of the day as he did at the beginning. Now it was just one more thing to hate about him. "I have to say, I'm really surprised at your behavior today," he said quietly, his voice dripping disappointment. "You were always a good kid before, respectful and obedient. You never gave your teachers any real trouble. I don't understand where all this anger and aggression is suddenly coming from."

He paused, obviously waiting for an explanation. I saw the hopeful expectation in his face, the concern, and it was enough to make me want to spit in his eye. Or punch him dead in the face. But I hefted the backpack onto my shoulder instead and walked up the corridor into the main office without looking back.

Ordinarily, I would meet up with Garrett after the final period, but I went through the office into the hall and out the school's side entrance, shoving my way through the crowd of kids spilling from the classrooms. I wanted to get the hell away from school. I wanted to get home and lock myself in my room before I went running off, as every bit of my soul demanded, to find that tall, long-haired, salacious menace in the blue jeans and yellow T-shirt.

Heading down Macon at a rapid pace, I heard someone running behind me. "Hey, wait," Bette called out. She caught up to me, huffing. "For God's sake, Ron, slow down. Let me catch my breath."

I didn't slow down or spare her a glance. "This is why you need to leave those damn cigs alone."

Bette's backpack whipped around and hit me in the head, knocking me over.

"Ooh. My bad." Her remorse almost seemed genuine.

I lay on my side, the dark-green grass of somebody's well-tended lawn tickling my bare limbs. At least I hadn't gone down on my already raw knees. The wounds began to sting again. I sat up, wincing. "You know, I'm not in the best of moods right now," I warned, using my backpack to prop up my knees.

"As if I give a shit." Bette plopped down across from me, crossing her legs under her. "So why'd you get sent to Ellis's office?"

I told her about PE class and my suspension.

"Wow. How did you burn that guy like—?"

"Don't ask me, I don't know!"

"Okay, okay. Don't bite my freakin' head off, all right? But do you actually think his folks will be able to put you in jail for—"

"Bette, I really don't want to talk about Aldo *fucking* Farmer right now."

"Good. Let's talk about Coach Frieda." Bette eagerly scooted closer, as if she were about to unload some nasty little secret. Then her face puckered. "Jeez, please! You are rank. Ever hear of deodorant? Soap? *Water?*"

I raised my right hand, exposing my armpit. "Kiss it."

She popped me in the pit with her fist. I jerked away, lowering my arm with a grunting laugh.

Bette stopped smiling, her face suddenly serious. "A few minutes before the bell rang, that police detective called for Mr. Ellis again. I listened in after I put the call through. You remember the straw I told you about, the straw they found inside Coach Frieda's house?"

"Yeah. What about it?"

"The police traced it. They took the straw to some lab and found out it came from wheat. Well, there's only one farm in this part of the county that grows wheat. And that's the Wexlar place."

"That's, like, two miles away from where you live."

"Kinda scary, huh? And get this. The police went out to Wexlar's farm, got a sample of straw, and confirmed it. The straw in the coach's house came from Wexlar." She grinned nervously. "Let's go out there and take a look around."

That sounded like a dumb idea, even to me. I frowned at Bette. "What in the world for?"

"Mr. Wexlar has a bunch of people who work the farm for him. One of them could've grabbed Coach Frieda."

"Even if one of them did, how would we prove it?"

"That's the whole point in looking around. Maybe we'll find something that tells us what happened to the coach. Come on, I don't want to go by myself."

I poked out my lips in a thoughtful sort of way. It appeared Bette had provided a much-needed distraction. My urge to find the guy I'd seen this morning was gone, at least for the time being. "Okay. When do you want to do this?"

"Today. After I take care of a few things I promised my mom I'd do."

"Nope. That won't work." I grabbed her wrist and looked at her watch. "In about forty-five minutes, my folks are gonna turn their phones back on, and they're gonna get those messages Mr. Ellis left about me. Then they're gonna ground me long-distance, and when they get home, they're gonna kill me. So, if you want me to go with you, it better be now."

"No problem. Come on." Bette scrambled to her feet. Then, in a gallant gesture, she reached down, grabbed my wrist, and hauled me up. "I just have to pick up Robbie from his aftercare and drop him off. His mom's car is down. Then you and I can go."

Bette and I took off, hurrying back toward school, where her car waited in the student parking lot.

CHAPTER
FOUR

TWENTY minutes later, we were riding down busy, tree-lined Baxter Boulevard in Bette's red-and-black Mustang.

I wanted to shoot myself in the ears.

Robbie Doss was strapped into the backseat. He was this cute, blond six-year-old Bette babysat on weekends while his mom worked a second job. Robbie was a talker.

That, by the way, was the understatement of all understatements.

Bette called him the mini-commentator. The kid gave you a rundown on everything that happened in his life. What he ate for breakfast. When he ate it. How he ate it. The way his mom cursed when she burned her lip sipping hot coffee. The way his mom cursed at her boyfriend for leaving the toilet seat up. The explosion of laughter that hit when a kid in his classroom lost control of his bladder and had an accident before he could make it to the restroom.

You couldn't shut him up. Bette tried to quiet him today with a piece of candy. Big mistake. Once the sugar rush hit, Robbie's mouth went into overdrive. He was sitting behind me describing, in rapid, run-on, singsong sentences, every freaking color of the crayons in his "art box." It was like having someone slap you repeatedly across the face with a fly swatter.

Forget shooting myself in the ears. I wanted to take my whole head off and pitch it out the window to get it away from this kid.

"Does he ever breathe?" I gasped at Bette.

She crossed her eyes at me and grinned. "I need a cigarette. No, I need a whole *bunch* of cigarettes."

Behind us, the cloud of chatter went on and on, filling the car.

I couldn't take it anymore. I turned. "Rob... yo, Rob... Robbie... *Robbie!*"

The boy paused midsentence—midword, actually. His little mouth was frozen open. His big, bright eyes blinked twice. "Yes, Myron?"

"Shut up."

He looked shocked for a second, and then terribly crushed. His little mouth pursed. His lower lip trembled. Tears sparkled in his eyes.

Man. That was absolutely vile on my part. I'd savaged the feelings of a poor, innocent six-year-old.

Oh, well....

Bette was appalled. "Myron! How could you say that to him?"

Shame kept me from answering her. But a big surge of relief swelled from the top of my head down. It was exactly the way you'd feel if there was a nail stuck up your nose and somebody finally pulled it out.

Bette threw a half glance at the whimpering Robbie. "That's okay, baby. Myron didn't mean it. He wants to hear your story as much as I do. You can finish telling it."

Robbie brightened immediately and picked up exactly where he'd left off. "I put the red crayon inside my mouth and then I put the bright blue crayon inside my mouth too because I wanted to make the taste of strawberries and blueberries together only it didn't come out that way because the crayons don't taste the way they look and I never knew that before because I always thought that crayons were flavors orange tastes like orange yellow tastes like lemon purple tastes like grape red tastes like cherry or strawberry but they don't taste like anything except those little wax bottles that look like soda pop but they aren't and they just have this little bit of juice in them...."

I leaned forward, braced my hands against the sides of my head, and squeezed, slowly banging my forehead against the dashboard.

"Stop that," Bette hissed. She nudged me in the back with her elbow. "Sit up. Be a man."

"Can't," I whined. "The voice hurts my head."

"Oh, just ignore the voice. That's what I do."

I gave it a shot. I reached down and unzipped my backpack. I'd always thought being suspended from school meant you were suspended from class work as well. Not! Mr. Ellis had collected a list of assignments from my teachers for the next four weeks, which I was to complete and turn in during the course of my eviction. This seemed like a good time to get started. But as I began rummaging through the pack for the list, Bette broke in.

"Wait, Robbie, stop." She glanced into the rearview mirror, looking at the kid. "What did you just say?"

In a matter-of-fact tone, the kid replied, "I said, the scarecrow went walking across our backyard again last night."

Bette and I exchanged looks. I frowned, the kind of expression that said *what the hell?* Robbie might run off at the mouth, but he had never made things up before.

I turned and looked back at Robbie. "You saw a scarecrow last night."

"Yes."

"Walking across your backyard."

"Yes."

"What did it look like?"

"A scarecrow."

Bette stifled a laugh.

"Robbie," I said, "you made that up, didn't you? You didn't really see a scarecrow walking in your yard."

"Yes, I did, Myron."

"Okay, I think I'd better pull over," said Bette.

She parked at the curb in front of a music store, under the shade of a big, rustling elm tree. Between the two of us, it took about a million questions, first to pull the story from Robbie, then to get the chronology straight. We wound up with this: Last night, Robbie woke up, went to the bathroom, and then got some water in the kitchen. While he drank his water, he sat on a chair in the dark, looking out the kitchen window. And he saw a scarecrow walk "floppy doppy" through his backyard wearing denim overalls, a green shirt, and a baseball cap. It was half carrying, half dragging a green plastic garbage bag that bulged with some very lumpy contents. The neighbor's three Doberman pinschers—which, Bette remembered, were very alert and aggressive—didn't so much as growl when the thing passed their fence. In fact, they seemed to run away from it, hiding somewhere in their yard and whining loudly enough that Robbie could hear them through the walls. Once the scarecrow made it past the neighbor's fence, it was beyond Robbie's visual range, and that was the last he saw of it.

That was the second time Robbie had seen this thing. The first time, also late in the night when the restless kid had been unable to sleep, it moved past the Doss's yard heading south, empty-handed and walking at a stumbling but rapid clip. The dogs had wanted no part of it then, either. That sighting had been last Thursday.

Bette seemed to find the date of the first sighting significant. "Thursday was the last time anyone saw Coach Frieda. And there was all that straw in her kitchen."

"Oh, come on, Bette," I groaned. "Don't say it."

She didn't answer. Her expression was intense. I could almost hear her brain whirring like a motor.

So I said it for her. "You think the coach was carried off by a scarecrow. A 'floppy doppy' *scarecrow.*"

She looked at me, irritated, and said nothing.

This time, Robbie answered for her. "Anything is possible," he said cheerily, kicking the back of my seat with his little feet.

BETTE and I didn't talk again until after we had dropped Little Sir Talks-a-Lot off at his house. Bette started to ask his mom if she had seen anything strange in her backyard last night, but I stopped her by grabbing her hand and announcing that we really had to go. Not only were we pressed for time, but I was afraid she'd wind up letting Robbie's mom know that he'd been up and about when he should have been in bed. I figured there were enough kids in trouble with their parents already.

We climbed back in the Mustang and Bette fired up the engine, which coughed to life reluctantly. It was fifteen years old, the first car her dad ever bought, and he passed it on to her as a Sweet Sixteen birthday present. (He'd promised her a car, but that was all he could afford after he lost his job.) The Mustang was originally black, but some nut sideswiped her passenger door with his truck in a hit-and-run. Bette went to the junkyard looking for a replacement door, and the only one she could find that would fit was red. She put it on the car herself.

"You're really taking this talk about a walking scarecrow seriously?" I asked as she picked up Highway 54, which would take us toward her house—and the Wexlar farm.

"Robbie saw something, I don't doubt that."

"Maybe he did, but he's just a little kid. He probably doesn't understand what he saw. I'll bet you anything it was just some bum—"

"Yeah," Bette cut in, "and that bum could've had something to do with Coach Frieda's disappearance."

She had a point, but it all seemed too tenuous to me. I thought it would be best if we just told the police what Robbie saw and let the detectives figure out whether it had any bearing on their case. Her face was set, however, and I knew she was determined to at least snoop around the Wexlar place, so I kept my opinion to myself.

My cell phone sang. I shifted my weight onto one side to fish the phone out of my hip pocket. I looked at the screen and saw the number of the incoming call. "Damn."

Bette kept her eyes on the road. "What's wrong?"

"It's my dad."

She gave a mock shiver. "Uh-oh."

The phone sang again. I swear, the tone sounded hostile. "Man, I am so dead."

Bette snorted.

I kept staring indecisively at the tiny screen, debating with myself whether I should answer the call. Ultimately, there was no choice. My parents had ordered me to keep the cell phone with me, and turned on, at all times when I was away from home, except when I was in class. That was one of the conditions they had imposed years ago when they got me the phone. They would be just that much more upset if I didn't answer. And not answering would only postpone the inevitable.

"Go ahead," said Bette. She nudged my shoulder with her fist. "Get this part over with."

Sighing, I thumbed the "talk" button. "Hello?"

"Suspended, Myron?" My father's voice buzzed hotly through the phone. "You got yourself suspended? Fighting in the gym? You were fighting in the gym?"

"Dad, it wasn't really like that—"

"Save it! Where are you now?"

"With Bette. We're in her car on—"

"I want you to take yourself home, you hear me? I want you to call me from our landline in thirty minutes so I'll know you're there. And you keep yourself there until your mom and I get home. We'll talk about this then."

"Uh… can we make it forty-five minutes for me to get home? If you give me that extra fifteen minutes, I can—"

"Boy, are you trying to *negotiate* with me?"

"No."

"I didn't think so. If you're not home in thirty minutes… well, let me put it this way. Be home in thirty minutes, dammit!" The line went dead.

I tossed the cell phone into my backpack, threw back my head, and blew out a long, frustrated breath.

"Sounds like that went well," Bette observed.

"Yeah. I have to be home in half an hour."

"You know, you don't have to do anything your parents tell you. You're eighteen now. Legally, that makes you an adult."

"Yeah. And legally, my parents don't have to give me room and board anymore. So if it comes down to asserting my rights and getting booted out into the streets or doing what I'm told and having a warm bed to sleep in, I'm going for the warm bed."

"Wimp!" Bette laughed. She reached over and patted my knee reassuringly. "Don't worry. I'll have you home with time to spare." With that, she gunned the engine and we hurtled down the highway toward the Wexlar place.

CHAPTER

FIVE

THE farm was huge, at least to a townie like me. It had a circumference of several miles, a fact I discovered by checking Bette's odometer after we turned off the highway and traversed the dirt road that circled the place. We'd almost made it back to the highway before we spotted the graveled lane that led up to the Wexlar house.

The sprawling land was as flat as a cookie sheet, covered with seemingly impenetrable masses of corn and cotton plants bristling stiffly in the warm autumn breeze. If there was wheat growing here, it must have been awesomely shy. Several buildings dotted the landscape to the west, the largest being a barn painted navy blue. The doors to three of the smaller structures were open, displaying tractors, tools, and stacks of what looked like bagged seed or fertilizer.

The lane curved to the east, where the family home stood. The house was small and simple, a lemon-yellow clapboard job with white shutters, the colors bright in the afternoon sun. I'd expected a man with such a large operation to have more impressive digs. There were people in the distance, men and women bent over among the cotton plants, hacking at weeds with hoes or yanking them up, roots and all, by hand, and stuffing the offending flora into long, burlap sacks.

"Jeez," I muttered, "don't they have machines to do that now?"

Bette looked at the workers with longing in her eyes, the way she got when she was dying for a smoke. I knew she wanted to slip up to them, all smiles and innocent intentions, to siphon whatever information she could about events at the farm over the past week.

Because of my deadline, she'd have to settle for talking with just one person today.

She turned to me again and frowned. "Your face looks funny."

"What's that supposed to mean? You making a joke?"

"No. Your face looks darker or something, like you've been out in the sun too much. But knowing you, it's probably just dirt."

"Yeah, I knew there was a joke in there somewhere."

A man stood in the bed of a green, late-model pickup as we reached the end of the lane. He was sweeping debris onto the ground with an old push broom. He was tall, skinny, and wearing olive-colored jeans and a white T-shirt that hung loosely on his gangling frame. His long arms were corded with muscles that knotted and relaxed as he worked. He was at least seventy years old, a white man whose skin was ruddy and wrinkled from a lifetime of striving under the sun.

We exchanged waves with him, and Bette parked off to the side of the lane. We got out of the car. The man put his broom aside, leaning it against the cab of the truck.

"Well, hi there, young people," he said in a thick, loud voice, squinting down at us in the glare, a smile spreading across his face. "What can I do for you?"

"Are you Mr. Wexlar?" Bette asked.

He nodded. "That I am."

"Mr. Wexlar, my name is Bette, and this is my friend, Myron." Bette extended her hand. The old man leaned down to give it a shake. "We go to Killebrew High. I don't know if you've heard, but a teacher there went missing last week—Frieda Blevins."

The smile dropped off the old man's face as if it had been erased. "Oh, I heard of it, all right," he said, his face clouding with something that was not quite anger. "Your police detectives made sure of that. They come out here with the sheriff, going through my fields and my barn, taking straw, making out like the lady's chained up in my kitchen or something."

"Do you know Miss Blevins?" I asked.

"Hell, no. How would I? I can't even remember the last time I went into Killebrew. I usually go to Millington for supplies, groceries and such."

"Then, do you have any idea," said Bette, "how straw from your farm wound up in her house?"

Mr. Wexlar snorted out a dry laugh. "I could no more tell you that than I could tell you how to build a rocket and fly it to Neptune. That's the same thing I told those detectives. And before you ask, no, I don't know if any of the people who work the farm for me were acquainted with this woman."

"Do you mind if we ask some of them?" Bette asked.

Slowly, Mr. Wexlar leaned back against the truck's cab, crossing one foot in front of the other. He folded his arms across his chest, annoyance working its way into his eyes. "Just what the hell is this? You show up here, still wet behind the ears, taking me through the same questions the cops already asked me. I got no time for your school projects and games."

"It's nothing like that, sir. I promise. Coach Frieda is my favorite teacher. Everybody at my school likes her. We just want to find her, get her back home." Damn. Bette was really pouring it on. She never used "sir" with any of the male teachers at Killebrew. Or her own dad.

Mr. Wexlar uncrossed his arms and shoved his hands deep into the back pockets of his pants. A grudging smile edged his mouth. "Well. There's not much I can tell you. Don't know the lady, don't know anybody who knows the lady, and don't know how my straw got in her house. That's about it."

"The police say it was wheat straw they found in the coach's house," I said, "but I don't see any wheat around here."

"That's because I grow winter wheat. I'm just getting ready to sow this year's crop." He gestured at an empty field beyond the house. Some dark-haired, bare-chested guy in tattered jeans was plowing the soil there on a tractor. Of course, the sight of a rugged young dude riding farm equipment sent a charge straight down between my legs. I had to slip a hand into my pocket and squeeze to keep from getting a hard-on. There was something on the guy's right shoulder, probably a tattoo, but from this distance it just looked like a big, dark blotch. "That's my grandson, Pike, by the way. He helps me out quite a bit."

"And after you harvest the wheat, you're left with straw," I guessed.

"Yep. But even the straw is useful. I bundle most of it up and sell it to this company in Kansas that makes biofuel. Some of it I give to a dairy farmer in Tipton County for cow chow. And I sometimes keep a bit for making scarecrows."

Bette and I exchanged looks; hers was smug, and mine was annoyed.

"Uh-oh," Mr. Wexlar said. "Now what?"

"You have any scarecrows on your farm this year?" asked Bette.

"I use 'em every year. Have to keep the birds from taking my seed after I sow. Scarecrows don't work so well by themselves sometimes, but you pair 'em up with some automatic noise guns and it sends the birds flying."

Bette shot me another quick look, and then she turned back to Mr. Wexlar. "Can I ask you a strange question?"

"Kiddo, this conversation went way past strange the second it started."

"Right." Bette smiled. She took a deep breath and exhaled through her nostrils in a gust. "Okay, here goes. Have any of your scarecrows gone missing in the past week or so?"

Mr. Wexlar looked surprised. "I had one disappear out of a little pumpkin patch right there behind my house. Went to bed last Wednesday night, it was there. Woke up Thursday morning, it was gone. I figured it was kids playing some prank." He shifted his head suspiciously. "You telling me this has something to do with your missing teacher?'

"No. Well... I don't know. I'm just asking." Bette paused, and I could tell she was working her brain around to another question. I raised my left arm in her face, pointing with my right hand at the spot on my wrist where a watch would be if I had one. She pushed my arms away and said, "We have to go, Mr. Wexlar. My friend here has this appointment he can't afford to miss. Thanks for talking with us."

"Well. You're welcome, young lady. I sure hope this teacher of yours shows up." He pushed off from the cab, standing upright, and grabbed his broom again. "If I get any more folk out here full of questions, I just might go missing myself."

We headed for the car. Bette, peeved at the way I'd cut her off, punched me in the back. She was only horsing around, but the blow still hurt like hell. She's got a couple of inches on me and about fifteen pounds. I groaned and stumbled forward, hands reaching back to clutch at the pain.

Laughing, groaning, I turned to call Bette a few choice names ("Hulk" came immediately to mind), and I saw Mr. Wexlar. The laugh stuck in my throat. He was staring at me with the strangest look in his eyes, part pity and part concern. My mom looked at people that way when they'd gotten terrible news—the death of a parent, the arrest of a son—and it always gave me an awful feeling of foreboding. I stumbled again, this time over my own feet, and almost fell.

"Good luck to you, now," Mr. Wexlar called down to me.

BETTE dropped me off with only a few minutes to spare. My house was on Chelsea, in a wide cul-de-sac where the street dead-ended. The houses on either side were silent, the shades drawn against the lengthening shadows of early evening, the driveways empty. I shut the door of Bette's car and gave her a wave as she circled the cul-de-sac and went roaring back up the street.

When I was a kid, I thought evil things lived in quiet, empty spaces. I wouldn't go into a room by myself, even with my parents in another part of the house, believing that some horror would jump out just for the sheer pleasure of watching me fall dead of fright in a puddle of my own pee. I outgrew the fear in my teens, but I still hated coming home to an empty house.

Today, the emptiness of the house didn't bother me. I felt strangely jazzed, like a toddler hyped up on too much sugar. I bounced down the hall and tossed my backpack onto my bed, and then I kicked off my sneaks and left them in the floor. The scrapes on my knees were dirty and black with dried blood. They should be cleaned, disinfected. I smelled awful, even to myself, but my mind was racing with other things that needed doing more than catching a shower. My stomach was demanding food. The deadline my dad set was looming large. I decided to get the phone call out of the way. After that, I could chill, at least until my parents got home.

I went to the kitchen, grabbed the receiver from the phone mounted next to the fridge, and dialed my mom's cell. Dad usually did the long-distance driving, and that meant Mom was in the better position to field the call. And I'd guessed right: Mom answered after the first ring.

"Myron?" Her voice had that anxious, disappointed edge it got every time I did something stupid. The rush of wind and traffic was loud in the background. The folks were driving home with the top down, one last dip in the waters of freedom before they got back to the real world.

"Yeah, it's me, Mom. Check your caller ID. I am home."

"So I see. Good. Are you okay? Did you get hurt in the fight?"

"It wasn't a fight. And yeah, I'm okay."

My dad's voice broke in. "Tell him to make sure he stays at the house. He is not to leave there for any reason."

Even if the place catches fire and burns to the ground? Shit.

"Hon—" Mom began.

"I heard, I heard. I'm here to stay."

"And make sure you eat the dinner I left for you. Don't sit there and load up on junk."

My mom. Fretting over the condemned's last meal. "Sure thing, Mom."

"We'll be home around seven thirty. And we'll be ready to talk."

Wonderful. I said goodbye and hung up the phone.

I opened the fridge and grabbed the bowl of tuna salad Mom made for me before leaving this morning. It was one of my favorite dishes. I picked up a soda, got a fork, sat down at the table, and scooped a big gob of tuna into my mouth.

And I almost gagged. The stuff was freezing, darn near flavorless. It looked like Mom's tuna salad, it seemed to have all the things she usually put in it, but it went down my throat like wet paper. It just wasn't... fresh.

Damn. I was *starving*.

I shoved the bowl away and went back to the fridge. There was a case of protein shakes on the bottom shelf. Dad was on a weight-loss kick, and he drank the shakes in the morning for breakfast. Lame. There was a cold-hardened block of lasagna in a plastic bowl, left over from Sunday dinner. Putrid. There was a pack of ground turkey next to the lasagna. Now, that had possibilities. But no, Mom was going to use the turkey in some recipe—probably her white chili. More importantly, she was expecting me to eat tuna salad. She'd be upset if I didn't.

I flopped back into my chair at the table and forced myself to swallow about a third of the tuna salad, washing it down with the soda. There. Not as much as I would ordinarily eat, but enough to make Mom happy. I felt disgusted with myself. After returning the bowl to the fridge, I went down the hall to the bathroom, peeled off my PE duds, and climbed into the shower.

I stayed there a long time. The hot water amped me up again with a bursting feeling that made me want to move—run, leap, fight. I kept flexing my knees and elbows as I washed, trying to work off the energy. My thighs and arms, skinny just a few hours ago in PE, were thicker now, muscles pronouncing themselves as I moved. When I got out of the shower, I looked at myself in the mirror. The scrapes on my knees were just thin red lines now, and they no longer hurt. A fine coating of hair, slicked down with water, covered my chest, belly, groin, and legs. Where'd that come from? My little dick wasn't so little anymore. In fact, it was hanging out over my balls, half hard, a delightful eight inches by my estimate. Fully erect, it would probably be another inch or so longer. My shoulders and chest were broader, my neck thicker. Nothing spectacular, but it looked as if I'd been lifting weights for a couple of months. All my life, I'd been the smallest kid among my friends, the smallest and the weakest. Now I was strong.

My face still looked dirty, smudged. With all that scrubbing, how the hell did I manage to miss this? I leaned forward, putting my face closer to the mirror, and rubbed at the black splotches. They wouldn't come off.

And then I saw. It wasn't dirt. My skin was getting black. Not just a darker shade of good old African-American brown but *black*, like the space between stars.

Strangely, none of the sudden changes freaked me out. They felt… right. They felt good. Very good.

Puberty. Gotta love it.

I WAS careful to shove my dirty PE stuff in the hamper, clean out the shower, and hang up the wet towels. There was no sense in giving my parents any more reasons to rip me apart.

Naked, I charged down the hall to my room. I had to move. There was so much energy in my body, and with my dick sticking straight out, as big and hard as a police officer's heavy-duty flashlight, it was obvious that the largest portion of that energy was sexual. For almost eighteen years, there'd been zilch in the sex department for me, no attraction to or desire for anyone, male or female. It had worried my parents as much as it did me, to the point that they were on the verge of getting me testosterone injections, hoping to jump-start my system. Without a doubt, everything was fully turned on in me now. I wanted another guy's hot, hard body under me, on top of me. I wanted to go pounding away at him. And I wanted something to eat, something hot and fresh, a suitable meal.

I snatched up a softball and fake-dribbled it across the floor, around my bed and dresser, twisting and pivoting to keep the ball away from imaginary opponents. I did jump shots that, in my mind, sailed through far-away nets without touching a thing. Then I let myself fall on my back across the bed. *Wind down, come on, Myron, wind it down.* But adrenaline continued to course through my body, making my limbs tingle, and I kept moving, moving, moving. An observer would have thought I was having a seizure. I laughed, exhilarated.

I grabbed my still hard dick with my right hand, stroking it, pulling at it. *God,* how I wanted to shove every inch of my stick deep into some guy's ass. Memory of that dude from this morning, with the long black hair and tall, muscular body, swept across my mind. Gone was any sense of familiarity with him, leaving just the image of him walking down the street in the bright morning sunlight. The way those jeans had fit around his fine, round butt made me groan now with passion. I'd never had sex, never read or watched porn, but I knew exactly what I wanted to do with that buff dude. I wanted to rush out and find him, bring him back here, tear the clothes off his body, and throw him down on my bed. Then I'd be on him, sliding one hand under to grab his ass, squeezing it hard enough to leave angry bruises, hard enough to make him moan. And I'd bite him, his neck, his shoulders, his nipples. I'd bite him and make him squirm, make him beg me to stop, make him beg me for more.

Then I'd flip him over, shoving his face down against the mattress, rolling that nice ass of his into view. I'd slide my dick right into that ass, all the way to the bottom, skewering him. And I'd ride him, pounding him hard, making him squeal with every thrust....

"Shit!" I hissed between my teeth, curling my head and shoulders up and forward off the bed as the explosive burst hit me. My insides seemed to flex like some powerful pump, again and again, and cum went everywhere, splashing my face, chest, stomach, thighs, and the bed. A long, strangled growl squeezed from my throat at the incredible pleasure. This felt so good, so perfect, and I never wanted it to stop. I wanted to fuck that fine bronze-skinned guy forever.

The orgasm died away, and I heaved out a satisfied sigh. But my dick stayed hard, a stubborn thing, demanding more. I laughed, the sound loud and rolling, my body squirming with sexual heat. I wanted to run, wanted to hunt....

Mom and Dad would be home in little more than an hour. Something in the back of my head told me they shouldn't find me like this, bare and hysterical, no matter how appropriate it felt for me. I wrapped my arms around my chest and hugged myself tightly. Gradually, I willed myself to stillness. The elation passed and my erection faded, leaving me awash in shame. I got up, cleaned myself and wiped the splatters off my sheets with a wet towel. After pulling on a pair of boxers and a T-shirt, I climbed back into bed.

My whole body suddenly ached. I curled into a ball and, within minutes, fell asleep.

A SOUND pierced the murk of sleep. It was annoying and familiar. Where had I heard that drone before?

My cell phone. I sat up, only half awake. The room was dark and the house was quiet. I patted the bed, feeling for the phone. Where was it?

The backpack. I slid off the bed, reached down, and unzipped the pack. I plucked out the phone, flipped it open, put it to my ear. "Hello?"

"Myron...." Bette's voice was hushed and full of panic. She breathed heavily, rapidly. "I couldn't get my mom... Myron—!"

And then she was gone.

CHAPTER

SIX

I POUNDED on the door with my fist. Footsteps approached quickly, and the door opened, light flooding out to erase the darkness on the porch, where I stood.

"Myron, hi." The annoyance in Mrs. Herron's eyes eased quickly when she recognized me. She frowned. "Why is your skin so dark?"

"Where's Bette?" I snapped, ignoring her question.

"I was just about to ask you the same thing." Her brow knotted with worry. "She left me a message that she had to do research after school for some kind of project. I left for my date with Walter at five, figuring she'd be here when I got back. I came in a few minutes ago, and there's no sign that she's been here."

Walter. Bette said he was some doofus her mom started seeing three years after divorcing her dad. Bette also said her mom sometimes turned off her cell phone or "forgot" to take it with her when she was out with the doofus. Dumb. Such a dumb, stupid, unforgiveable thing to do when your daughter's safety was at stake.

Those thoughts flashed through my head in about two seconds, and a second after that, I was furious.

Mrs. Herron stepped back from the door, suddenly shocked. "Myron? Why are you looking at me that way?"

This foolish woman was a waste of my time. I spun on my heels, jumped off the porch, and climbed back onto my bike. The bike had been leaning untouched against a wall in the garage for nearly two years because I thought I'd outgrown it. Only kids rode bikes. Mom's car was parked in the garage, but I didn't have the key and I had no experience at hot wiring. I needed speed, and I'd grabbed the bike without hesitation.

I'd started my search for Bette at the closest, most obvious place. Now that I knew she wasn't home, I headed for the second closest place where she might be. I pedaled down Harper, easily outpacing cars driven by people on their way home or running errands. I could distinctly feel the heat of the car engines as I passed, and even the heat of the towering lamps lining the street. A man hurrying across the street ahead of me looked red in the darkness. So did the people riding in the cars. Crickets were chirping, the sound sharper and more crisp than I'd ever heard it before. I could tell which of the homes I rode by had dogs fenced in the backyard; I smelled them. Not just their waste, but the hot, dusty scent of their furry bodies.

I whipped off Harper onto Moorsdale Drive and, seconds later, skidded to a stop in front of Coach Frieda's house. My heart started pounding.

Bette's car was parked in the driveway, behind Coach Frieda's blue sports coupe.

I dropped the bike and ran across the yard. "Bette!" There was no answer. The hood of her car had a faint and fading red glow. The interior was dark. I went to the driver's door, and when I stepped forward to reach for the handle, I heard something crunch loudly underfoot. Lifting my foot, I saw the smashed remains of a green cell phone.

Bette's phone.

Anxious, I snatched open the door of the car. Bette wasn't there. I scanned the interior. Her backpack was on the backseat, along with an empty potato chip bag and a wadded cigarette pack. The rearview mirror had been knocked askew, angled toward the passenger window. And both front bucket seats, as well as the floorboard, were covered with straw.

I moved back from the car. Looking down, I saw now that there was straw on the ground near the door. I'd been standing in the stuff. It had a faint moldy odor that made me think of dank, open graves. I looked toward the coach's house. There was still yellow crime-scene tape across the front door. I ran to the door and tried the knob. Locked. I looked through the front window and saw the vague outline of furniture in the darkness of the living room. There was the chair where the coach had been watching television. The set had been turned off and the plate of food had been tossed, but otherwise nothing appeared to have been touched. The feeling I got from the place was one of coldness and dust. No one had been inside the house for days.

Someone had to have seen Bette get taken away. A neighbor, maybe. I started for the house next door, and then stopped. The straw. I could still smell its dead scent. Maybe I could follow it. Or, even better, maybe I could pick up Bette's scent. I returned to her car and closed my eyes. And there it was, her smell, one of ash mixed with sweat, spearmint gum, a flowery deodorant, and a hot, acidic odor that I quickly realized came from fear.

I got back on my bike and rode it around the side of the coach's house. There was a gate to the wood fence that surrounded the backyard. The gate stood open. Entering the yard, I spotted a few more bits of straw. A big green garbage bin on wheels stood near the back door, reeking of rotting food. At the rear of the yard, where the fence bordered the alley, a couple of boards that had been yanked out lay on the grass.

I pushed my bike through the hole in the fence and slipped after it. The alley was paved with asphalt and was wide enough to accommodate the mechanical arms of the big trucks that emptied the garbage bins. The smells here rose up in one big, noxious swirl, but I could somehow make out the individual sources: roaches, mice, rancid potatoes, motor oil, cats, dogs, dried cheese, rotting cabbage, and birds. The smell of Bette was there as well, and it led me on.

My parents were home by now. They were fuming, no doubt, at finding me gone. And I didn't have my cell phone with me. I didn't even have on shoes. I'd just grabbed a pair of jeans from the closet, slipped them on and headed out into the deepening night. My folks would think I'd gone insane, openly defying them. But I couldn't worry about that now. I had to find Bette.

Ahead, the alley opened out onto a street. Before I reached that point, the scent trail veered off to the right, through a fenceless yard.

This one had lots of trees with families of smelly squirrels nestled in the tops. Past the house, the yard led to another street, across which lay a wooded area. I plunged through the trees, the bike's tires bouncing over the uneven terrain. The air filled with skittering sounds as foraging rodents raced for cover.

Suddenly, I lost Bette's scent. I hit the brakes, the bike skidding to a halt. I laid the bike down and walked back, taking deep breaths, trying to reacquire the trail. There was damp earth, mingled with the odor of wet leaves and pine needles, but no Bette.

Wait. There she was again. I could sense the trail, leading back the way I'd come. The trail disappeared entirely in an oddly circular clearing among the trees. It was as if she had lifted off from that spot and flown away. I looked up, eyes searching the red and yellow canopy of thinning leaves shifting against the starry blue-black of the clear night sky. "Bette?"

A new scent came to me on the wind, sharp and sour. It was the stench of raw emotion, fear mingled with anger. A thrill swelled through me, and I began to move toward the source before I was even aware I wanted to do so. At the edge of the clearing, the ground sloped downward. About forty feet away, someone huddled behind a tree, the person's exposed arm and foot glowing orange-red in the darkness. The reek of fear grew stronger, bringing a snarling grin to my face. I slipped silently among the trees, excitement rising as I closed in.

My quarry did not move. I was barely six feet away when I realized the fear smell was not coming from this person. No, there was a familiar, sweet scent on the air now, and I froze for a moment, trying to associate a name with it. And that left me unprepared for what came next.

To my right and slightly behind me, a yell erupted, combined with a flash of motion. I never saw what hit me. There was no pain, just a complete and instant plunge into blackness.

I CAME awake in a surge, a panicky cry rattling in my throat. The memory of the ambush rose instantly, and it spurred my body into full strike-back mode. My range of motion was limited, however, in that I was wrapped from neck to ankles in chains. I lay in the dark on the warm concrete floor of a tool shed, one that was only slightly larger than those plastic portable johns you see at construction sites and outdoor concerts. There were pegs on the walls for hanging implements, but they were empty, the tools removed, presumably, to keep me from using them either to escape or defend myself.

Although I was helpless, the situation made me furious, not afraid. I was angry that someone had jumped me, and even angrier that I'd been stupid enough to let them do it. I'd sensed the person coming seconds before he struck, plenty of time for me to have ducked. Instead, I'd just stood there, sniffing the air, holding my fat head up like the target it was.

The chains made standing (and just about any other action) impossible, so I stopped struggling and started thinking. In that moment, the walloping throb in my head asserted itself, making me wish my lights had stayed out. The side of my head, above the right ear, felt badly swollen. Damn. What had the sucker hit me with? And just who was the fool who clocked me?

It made sense that my attacker and the one who'd lured me out of the clearing were the same people who took Bette. And probably Coach Frieda too. Bette must have gone snooping around the coach's house after she dropped me off. Maybe she surprised the kidnappers, who'd come back to the house. But what would have made them risk going back to Coach Frieda's place?

I had come chasing after Bette, gotten too close, and they'd taken me too. Which brought up a personally more disturbing question: What were they going to do with me? I hadn't gotten a clear look at either one of them, so it wasn't as if I could point them out to the cops. Of course, they didn't necessarily know that. And just the fact that I'd been tracking them was reason enough to get me murdered.

So why wasn't I dead?

I had no idea how long my lights had been off, but surely once I was unconscious, there had been ample opportunity for them to take me out. Those woods I entered were dense, but they bordered a residential street. The lowlifes might have been concerned someone would see them doing me in. Maybe they tossed me into this shed until the time and place were right.

There's an old black-and-white movie version of *Frankenstein* that has this scene where an angry mob uses torches to burn down an old mill where the monster is hiding. It's a weird scene because it makes you afraid... for the monster. That scene came back to me now as I picked up the unmistakable aroma of gasoline and burning tobacco. It was faint at first, and then grew stronger with the rustle of feet crushing fallen leaves as three people approached the shed. A cigarette might not have the fearsome impact of a blazing torch, but together with an accelerant, it would be just as effective in melting this shed into the dirt.

And that was exactly what the trio outside had in mind, their intentions confirmed by the liberal splashing of gas over the roof and sides of the shed.

The idea that they were actually planning to roast me sent rage throbbing in my head so violently that I think I blacked out again. There were flashes of activity afterward, but they had a distant, dream-like quality about them, and I couldn't be sure what was real. I clawed at the chains with my fingers, and the links snapped like strings cut with a knife. In my head, some deep, malicious voice sneered, *fucking fake chains.* Then I was on my feet and started clawing away again, this time at the molded resin walls and ceiling of the tiny shed. The plastic came away in gooey, almost liquid strings that seemed to stick like hot tar to the concrete floor. Within seconds, a substantial hole had opened in an upper corner of the shed.

The people outside gave startled shouts, and one of them backed away. That fear smell rose again, sharper than before. Someone, some horrible, inhuman thing, howled in the night. I reached up, grabbed the soft, hot edge of the ragged opening, and hauled myself in one swift motion onto the roof.

"Throw it! Throw it!" someone screamed.

I heard the thin hiss of the cigarette as it flew through the air. I crouched and leaped from the roof seconds before the cig made contact. It bounced, burning embers scattering as it rolled along the slope of the roof, and the gasoline went up in an explosive gust.

Behind me, the night flickered with harsh yellow light, and confused, frightened voices cursed and yelled. Footsteps pounded after me as ugly black smoke filled the air. I could have turned and made my kidnappers regret their foolish actions, but the thrill of being on the move again was too great.

Somehow, I hurtled from treetop to treetop. I went deeper into the woods, never touching the ground, wild, ecstatic howls of laughter bursting from my lungs. Soon, I could no longer hear the sounds of the people who wanted to kill me, nor smell their sweaty hides or the fumes from the liquefying plastic of the shed. Now I sensed other things—animals, birds. I heard their alarmed grunts and scuffles, sniffed out their hides and their fear. My presence agitated them, sent them scattering in blind, delicious panic.

Excellent.

The night was endless blue, the moon a white shining face that lit the way, and I was electric with desire. From the trees, I plunged downward, seeking, screeching.

CHAPTER
SEVEN

GARRETT pulled back the curtain and flinched. He fumbled with the lock and got the window open. "Myron? What're you doing out there?"

"Let me in, man."

He looked back over his shoulder. The door to his darkened room stood half open. He hurried over to shut it, then came back and lifted the screen out of the window frame. It was still night, but I had no idea what time it was. Garrett's eyes flicked over the street behind me. "Hurry...."

On my knees behind the prickly, manicured shrubs that edged the front of the Chess house, I reached up and grabbed the windowsill. My body shook so violently that I could barely manage to pull myself upright. Garrett hooked his hands under my arms and hauled me into the room.

I stumbled over to the bed and dropped clumsily to the floor, my back against the footboard. I wrapped my arms around my knees in an effort to stop the shakes. Garrett switched on the lamp atop his nightstand, turned to me, and stepped back, stunned.

"Stay right there...," he gasped, and he went for the door.

"Where're you going?" I said.

"To get my dad."

That struck me as an incredibly wrong thing to do. "No, stop!" I hissed, reaching out desperately.

Garrett's eyes flashed with astonishment. "Man, you're *hurt*."

"No, no. I'm okay. I just need to rest for a minute. Just let me rest."

Garrett made no further move, and a few moments later, I relaxed a bit, slumping against the bed. Conflicting sensations were at war within my body. My skin seemed stretched and tight and sticky. My arms and legs were so heavy I didn't think I could move them again, but my head felt light and loose. I thought my brain was floating around the room. I closed my eyes; that made the floating stop. My stomach felt pleasantly full, and there was this lush sensation in my chest, but my throat and mouth felt thick, filthy, and foul.

I moaned and lay down on the floor.

With my head on the floor, it felt safe to open my eyes again. Garrett was standing in the same spot. When we were in fifth grade, he shinnied up the pole in front of the school one morning. He wanted to touch the flag, and he did, but once he got up there, he couldn't come back down. I remember the look on his face, this sick fear, the kind where it seems that your apprehension is going to make you throw up all over the place at any moment. He had that look on his face now.

"What happened to you?" he asked.

The question confused me. I frowned at him.

"Your mom called here earlier, looking for you. She was pissed off because you left the house." Garrett shifted uncomfortably from side to side. "Myron? Who beat you up?"

I shook my head.

"Was it Aldo?" He frowned doubtfully. "Were you in a... wreck or something?"

There was pain, in my head and my limbs. Everything ached, and my body was wasted. I tried to find the memories, but I couldn't even recall how I'd gotten to Garrett's house. I shook my head again.

Garret raised his hands warily. "Look. Don't freak out or anything, but I'm gonna get my dad."

"No."

"I think you need a doctor, man."

"No."

Frustration burned through the fear in Garrett's face. "Look, Ron, this is worrying me, okay? You're all torn up. You need help."

I scowled at him. "Don't say anything to your dad."

"You got blood on the window, on the carpet, on my bed. My dad's gonna see that. I have to tell him *something*."

I looked. Blood smeared the frame of the window and the wall beneath. Dark red footprints stained the floor. My feet were bare and dirty and cut and still bleeding.

An overwhelming wave of shame swept through me. I looked back at Garrett. "Don't tell anybody. Please."

For a second, it looked as if Garrett would cry. I hadn't seen him cry since his mom died when he was ten. I wanted to apologize to him, but his feet finally came unglued and he crossed over to the bed.

"Come on," he said, pulling me to my feet. My short time on the floor seemed to have weakened me even more, and he pretty much carried me. In the hall, he stopped us, looking down to the opposite end. The door to his dad's room was closed, but I could still hear the loud rumble of Mr. Chess's snore.

"Be quiet," said Garrett, and the two of us crossed the hall to the bathroom. He flipped the light switch. He got me to the sink, and I leaned against the basin for support while he turned to the linen closet for towels.

I stared at myself in the mirror. Dirt, twigs, and leaves were matted in my hair. Blood was pasted to my face, neck, and chest, and it soaked my blue jeans, which were ripped all over. Sticks, leaves, and tufts of fur were stuck in the blood. There were claw marks and bites across my torso, but they weren't bad enough to account for all the gore. I opened my mouth and saw bits of raw meat stuck in my teeth.

Oh.

"Whoa!" Garrett caught me in his arms. "Myron! Myron, you okay?" He was trying to keep his voice low, but alarm made it loud. He dragged me to the toilet, flipped the lid, and sat me down there.

"What happened?" I asked.

"You passed out. You dropped like a rock and almost hit your head on the sink."

He stared at me as if he thought my eyes were going to melt and dribble down my face.

"I'm okay," I whispered. I stood up slowly and paused. The room didn't flip, which seemed to be a good sign. "You got some dental floss?"

Using the floss Garrett handed me, I cleaned my teeth thoroughly, blanking my mind to what I was doing. I followed that with a thorough mouthwash rinse. Garrett kept his hand pressed to my back the entire time, as if to steady me.

Finally, he reached over and turned on the shower. He scooped up the towels he'd dropped on the floor and put them on the rack next to the tub. "You need help getting in?" he asked nervously.

"No. I can make it."

I walked carefully to the bathtub and started fumbling with the button on my jeans. Garrett turned away and stared at the door. Whether that was for my comfort or his, I didn't know or care. He had to stay in the bathroom in case his dad woke up and heard the shower.

The water ran red down the drain forever, it seemed. When it finally cleared, I soaped a washcloth and scrubbed myself from head to toe.

Even when I was clean, I didn't feel clean.

After about fifteen minutes, I shut off the water and stepped carefully out of the tub. The wounds on my chest and stomach didn't look so bad now. Just pale and dull. There were a few claw marks on my thighs. The cuts on my feet had stopped bleeding. My skin, I noticed, was its usual light brown. I dried off, and then wrapped the towel around my waist.

Garrett turned. He looked me over. "Guess you weren't hurt as bad as it looked," he whispered. "Side of your head's swollen. You got knocked a good one."

Using a bath towel, he wrapped up my torn, bloody jeans and underwear. He opened the door and peered out. "Come on."

We returned to his room, where he shoved the towel with my ruined clothes under the bed. He got a pair of his jeans and a T-shirt and handed them to me with a pair of his boxers.

I handed the boxers back to him. "I'm not wearing your drawers."

He tossed them aside and waited until I had dressed. "Now, you gonna tell me what happened to you?" he asked.

I sat down on the floor. I remembered going into the woods looking for Bette, and I remembered being hit in the head. After that, there were only the flashes of movement and emotion, none of which made sense to me now. I considered briefly telling him that Bette had been kidnapped, but I was afraid that revelation would make him call his dad *and* the cops. That was more than I even wanted to think about, let alone deal with.

"Just let me sleep for a minute," I said. "Then maybe I can talk." I crawled into the space between Garrett's bed and the wall, where Mr. Chess wouldn't see me if he happened to look in.

I was asleep within seconds.

THE dude was gorgeous. He had green eyes and copper skin and black hair. We were both naked, our dicks hard. His body was beautiful. I could feel the heat from him, throbbing like a heartbeat. We stood face to face in the dark, which was the perfect place for us to be.

His stare was icy. I wanted to touch him, touch his face and his arms. I wanted to kiss him and feel his body pressed up to mine. His skin looked so smooth, so sweet. His bare arms were lean and muscular. But his eyes worried me.

I tried to speak, but my voice wouldn't cooperate. I tried to turn away, but his eyes wouldn't let me. Very slowly, he reached out toward me. It looked as if he was raising a gun to my heart.

A hand shook my shoulder. The touch was gentle, and my heart pounded suddenly because I thought it was him. But when I opened my eyes, Garrett was looking down at me.

My friend's expression was serious. "Hey."

I was on my back beside the bed. My throat was dry and my neck hurt, but the rest of my body felt better. Faint gray light was filtering through the curtains. I coughed softly. "What time is it?"

Garrett raised a finger to his lips, motioning for me to be quiet. "Your dad just called," he whispered. "I talked to him. The man's so worried about you, he's hysterical."

I sat up. It was only then that I realized my dick, as in my dream, was hard, bulging down the left leg of my loaner jeans. Mention of my dad made my cock wither instantly. "You didn't tell him where I am—"

He shook his head. "No. But my dad got to the phone before I could. He's up now, making coffee. He's gonna go over to drive your dad around to look for you." His face was so serious. It was a cop's face, a judge's face. "Ron, come on. You have to tell me what's up. What happened to you last night?"

"I don't know, man." But there was a terrible feeling in the back of my mind, an aching certainty that I'd done something... bad. Really bad.

"Why are you so afraid to go home? Did you get into some more trouble last night? You do something stupid? I mean, you've got this guilty look all over you."

"Garrett, I don't know. I don't remember much about last night." He looked skeptical, so I added, "I *don't*."

He shook his head. "You don't know how hard it was for me to get on that phone with your dad and lie to him. I did it because I thought that's what you wanted. Your dad called the police when you didn't come back home. You know that?" His face became pained. "You're scared and you want to hide, I get that. But your mom and dad... I can't do this to them, man. I can't let them go on worrying about you. You have to go home."

It was an edict. But more than that, I knew Garrett was right. "Yeah, I know." I got to my feet. The legs of Garrett's jeans came down well past my feet. I rolled them up into country-boy cuffs just above my ankles. He gave me an old pair of his sneaks. I sat down on the bed and pulled them on. They were too big, but it beat walking home on my sore bare feet. "Your dad's in the kitchen?"

Garrett nodded.

"I think I'll sneak out the front."

"Hold on." He got a pair of pants from his closet. "First, I'm gonna tell my dad that you're here. That way he won't go making a trip over to your house for nothing, and he can call your folks to let them know you're all right. Then I'm gonna walk you home."

That was an insult. "I don't need a damn escort," I hissed at him. "I know where I live."

"Sorry, Ron, but I get this feeling that you'll take off again." He started pulling on his pants.

I swept past him and out of his room.

"Myron! Stop!"

Behind me, I heard Garrett's stumbling footsteps. I went plunging up the hall and into the living room, anger tingling in my head. By the time I shoved my way outside, Mr. Chess's voice rose up, confused and shocked. "Myron? What—"

I ran. I twisted my fist into the waist of the jeans to keep them up. I looked back over my shoulder a couple of times, but no one was following me. When there were two blocks between me and the Chess house, I slowed to a walk. Despite what Garrett thought, I *was* going home. There was still some instinct telling me that was not the wisest course of action for me, and I knew it had nothing to do with any fear of my parents' wrath or the very real possibility that I might be arrested for hurting Aldo. Going home was wrong, but I wanted to be there. Besides, I didn't know where else to go.

The sky was brightening in the east. The street lights were still on, though, and a gray darkness hung in the air like smoke. Cricket song filled the quiet with a drone that reminded me of the hum of my family's refrigerator, when it was the only sound I could hear after the lights were out and everybody was in bed.

I rounded the corner onto my street. There was my house, down in the cul-de-sac. It was the only house with all the windows lit up. I sighed and kept walking.

Ahead, in the shadows between street lamps, something moved. I stopped. The hair on the back of my neck rose. Something in me snarled. There was another movement in the darkness, and a guy became visible, standing just beyond the edge of the light pooling on the ground below one of the lampposts. He was dressed in black now, but I recognized him. It was the dude Garrett and I had seen on the way to school yesterday.

The dude I'd just dreamed about.

I walked up to him and met his icy green eyes. He towered over me, taller even than Garrett.

"Come with me," he said.

He was beautiful. And he was terrible. I wanted to run. I wanted him in my arms. I wanted him in a way so profound it took my breath away.

My instincts told me to *run*!

He reached out and the passenger door of a car parked at the curb slowly opened. Unable to take my eyes from his, I got into the car. He strode around the front of the car, his long black hair flowing out behind him like a cape. He raised his hand over the hood and the engine started like a cat purring. The driver's door opened, and he slid behind the wheel.

Once the doors of the car closed, he wouldn't look at me. He took the wheel in one hand, put the car in gear with the other, and backed up into a driveway. Then he pulled out of the driveway, heading away.

Away from my home.

CHAPTER
EIGHT

WE DROVE a long way.

He did not look at me or talk. His eyes stayed on the road.

I wanted to look at him. I wanted to hear him talk. He could have said anything, recited the alphabet, counted to a hundred, cursed me to my face. I just wanted to hear his voice.

But I didn't look at him, or ask him to speak. I couldn't. I couldn't move at all. I sat in the passenger seat of his car and stared straight ahead. It was as if I was paralyzed, and that was scary as hell.

He was scarier still.

The sun came up, bright and full in the clear sky. We went north on Highway 80, into the hills, into Nehemiah Forest. Mr. Chess had brought Garrett and me up here to camp out for a week, years ago, when I was eleven. I remembered being nervous because Mr. Chess said black bears lived among the trees and warned us not to leave food lying around where it would draw them in. I was glad we came, though, because it was about four months after Mrs. Chess died, and Garrett hadn't talked much or laughed in all that time. But in these woods, he came alive. We hiked. We climbed trees. We swam in a stream. We caught fish and cleaned them and cooked them over a fire. And Garrett laughed.

Other vehicles passed the bronze-skinned guy's car, and sometimes I could see the occupants looking back at us. I wanted to wave my arms, let them know I was afraid, get myself some help. But I knew my body was useless, and I didn't even try.

The sun went higher. There was no clock on the dashboard, not that I could see, but I could tell by the sun what time it was. If I were home, and if I hadn't gotten suspended, I'd be sitting in homeroom now, probably trying to finish up some homework. My parents. Jeez. They must be climbing the walls by now.

The dude turned off the highway onto a dirt road. The car yawed back and forth as it rolled over uneven ground, heading down into the bottoms. The trees grew large and thick here, nurtured by the rich, muddy waters of the Wapanocca River. Because little sunlight got through, the area was cool and dark and damp.

The road ended at a circular clearing that was much like the one I'd seen in the woods last night. The guy stopped the car at the edge of the circle and turned off the engine. He waved a hand at the door and it opened for him. He got out, leaving the key in the ignition.

My door opened suddenly, and that seemed to lift a weight off my body. I could move again. I turned and saw the dude standing on the other side of the car with his back to me.

"Get out," he said.

I obeyed. I shut the door and stood there, keeping the car between us, studying him. He wore black jeans and black sneakers and a black muscle T-shirt. His arms looked strong and warm, the biceps bulging like cantaloupes. His legs were long and muscular beneath his jeans. Desire made me whimper.

Without looking at me, he said, "Over here."

I went to him, shaking.

He seemed more human now than he had in the darkness. His face sported thick black eyebrows but was otherwise hairless, the nose sort of snubbed, the lips full. He looked Native American, or maybe Mexican. No, he was Native American, definitely. I knew that, somehow. His hair was tucked behind his ears. He wore no jewelry, not even a watch. His ears were not pierced. He stared down at me.

I couldn't stop shaking. "Why'd you bring me here?"

He nodded toward the center of the clearing. "Go. Out there."

"Not until you tell me why you brought me here."

He hooked his thumbs in his front pockets. "If I put you down there myself, it's going to hurt you."

It wasn't a threat. There wasn't even any anger in his voice, but his words chilled me anyway.

I walked down into the circle. The jeans sagged, and I tugged them up at the waist with both hands. I stopped in the center of the clearing, looking up at him. "Will you tell me now why I'm here?"

"No." He began to walk slowly along the edge of the clearing.

"Why not?"

"Because I don't want to."

"Will you tell me your name?"

"No."

"But... why not?"

"Telling you my name would be pointless." He stopped at a towering pine tree and started carving something into the trunk with a pen knife.

Terror began to swell in my chest like pain. Whatever he was about to do, it would be bad. I could feel that all the way down to my feet. The fear made me rattle off like Robbie. "My name is Myron. Myron Mitchell. I go to Killebrew High, down there in Killebrew. Twelfth grade. I got kicked out of school yesterday for a month. Over some bull. I've never been kicked out of school before. Do you live around here somewhere? Bartlett? I'll bet you're from Bartlett. You go to school there?"

He finished with the carving in the pine. Then he doubled back, retracing his steps. He kept going until he reached a poplar tree that stood directly across the circle from the pine.

It could not be good that he was so careful to stay out of the circle himself.

"I want to go home," I wailed loudly. I sounded like a five-year-old, but I didn't give a damn.

He started carving something into the poplar tree.

"Please. Please take me home."

The guy turned away from me abruptly, and his hair fell in a shiny black cascade over his shoulder, hiding his face. After a moment, he said sharply, "Stop talking."

I watched him. He went back to work on the carving. When he was done, he stepped back to evaluate his work. I could see that the symbols in the pine and the poplar trees matched. They looked sort of like a stylized number three turned on its back and encased in a circle. When I spoke next, my voice was hushed. "Are you going to kill me?"

He didn't answer. He went back to the spot in front of his car. I saw now that it was a dark-blue two-door BMW convertible sports coupe. He kept his eyes off me, but they were weighted with a sorrow that seemed to drag his entire face down.

"Tell me what you're doing," I said.

He closed his eyes and began to speak, but he was not answering me. His voice was so low I couldn't even hear it.

"Wait! Stop, please!"

His mouth kept working. And while there was no sound beyond the slight rustle of a breeze through the trees, I could sense a subtle shift in the ground beneath me.

Something was coming up. Something incredibly evil, something *hungry.*

"Please, I'm begging you. At least tell me why. I don't understand. Who... did I do something to hurt you? Did I hurt somebody you know? Why are you doing this? Oh, God, man, please tell me!"

He stopped speaking.

Whatever had been rising up beneath me reluctantly settled down again. I sank to my knees, suddenly too weak to stand.

He opened his eyes and sighed. "Knowing will only make this harder for you." He spoke without making eye contact. Then, out of the blue, he looked right at me, curiosity in his face. "Tell me something. Why haven't you tried to run?"

"Because the circle won't let me go," I answered immediately. And then I was surprised that I knew that, and that the thought of running had never occurred to me.

His face filled with admiration. "You're... intuitive. Are you a practitioner?"

"Of what?"

His face fell. "I guess not." He hooked his thumbs in the pockets of his jeans and stared flatly at me. "Myron Mitchell, you are a monster."

I didn't know quite what to do with that declaration. "Okay. If you say so."

The dude frowned. "You must realize I mean that literally, after the things you've done over the past twenty-four hours."

I sat down hard. Now I was the one who looked away. The ground here was loose soil, covered with dead leaves and sticks. I began brushing my hands back and forth through the debris. "I don't know what you're talking about. I don't remember—"

"You don't *want* to remember. Some time ago, someone laid a curse on your family line. It passes down from generation to generation, manifesting in certain individuals and turning them into monsters. Predators. Killing machines. You are afflicted in this manner."

"No. No, I'm not." Then I remembered the red lumps of flesh in my teeth. "Oh, God. I killed...."

"Yes. Last night. You hunted, and you killed, and you fed. Fortunately, you were in the woods when the transformation took you. You attacked a wolf pack. I got there afterward. There were eleven of them. You tore them all apart."

I remembered. I remembered seeing the wolves running below me, the heat of their bodies making them red in the night. A ghastly, hollow screech—my wild laughter—set the beasts to whimpering as they ran. The back of the biggest wolf seemed to rise up to meet me as I plummeted down on him. The impact broke his neck. And I took his loose neck in my mouth, biting through fur, muscle, and bone in a single snap. I plunged after the rest of the pack with the gaping, bleeding head in my mouth.

I took a young female next, my hand swiping her left flank. There was smoke, an agonized howl, and the creature's left hind leg flew off into the darkness. The force of the blow sent the wolf spinning into a tree with a horrible crunch.

There had been three cubs running with the female. They hunkered down on the forest floor when their dam was struck, frightened yowls coming from their throats. I flung the wolf head from me and attacked the cubs. My jaws smashed together on the first one, and the furry little body burst like a water balloon in my mouth.

I ate the cubs, even as I plummeted through the woods after the rest of the pack.

I laughed that horrible, screeching laugh as I tore into the others, slashing, ripping. Some of them fought me for their lives, clawing at me, biting.

It did not save them. And I got drunk on their pain, their blood, their flesh.

I remembered it all, sitting in that magic circle before the most beautiful guy I'd ever seen. The guy who was going to kill me for what I'd done. I drew up my knees and buried my face against them.

"That's the way the curse works," the dude continued. "It gives you inhuman speed, strength, stamina, and agility. Heightened senses. Unhinged emotions. It takes your reason. You stalk, kill, and eat whatever crosses your path. And then it lets you revert to normal so that you torment yourself with the memories of what you've done."

I lifted my head enough to look at him. "What can I do? How can I stop this?"

"The transformations will take you at random. You can't stop them or control what you do once you're in the predator mode. You are part of the reason I came to your town. You can't stop yourself, but I can stop you."

"So... you *are* going to kill me." My voice broke.

He shook his head. "No. I couldn't kill you even if I wanted that. The curse makes you immortal, for the most part. That's another way it is intended to maximize your suffering."

"Then, if you aren't gonna kill me…."

He pointed at the trees bearing the symbols. "I wrote the name of a demon there and there. That allows me to summon the fiend through the circle. Once it comes, it will take you and feed on your immortality. Forever."

CHAPTER
NINE

I SCREAMED. I couldn't help it.

I screamed because I knew, in some deep part of my soul, that everything the guy had said was true. I screamed because I was a killing monster. I screamed because he had the power to bring up some primal, horrific thing that would make me its own and take me away from everyone and everything I knew.

The guy waited until the howling died in my throat, fading to hoarse croaks and then stopping completely. He asked, "Are you ready?"

If I hadn't been a trapped, trembling mass of terror, I would have thrown myself at him. "Don't do this to me," I begged. "Please don't."

"I take no pleasure in feeding you to a demon. But there is no other option. If you transform at home—and sooner or later, you will— you'll kill and eat your parents without a second thought. You'll do the same to your neighbors, your friends. You will carry the memory of that horror with you throughout a very long and unnatural life. Surely you don't want that to happen."

I balled my fists into my eyes. "No...."

"Then, you understand." He took his thumbs from his pockets and bowed his head again.

"Wait!"

The dude sighed, forcefully this time, and did not open his eyes. "I am not going to let you stall forever."

"This isn't right." I could feel anger boiling over my fear. "It's not like I... sold my soul to the devil or something in exchange for being this monster. I didn't ask for any of this. Why am I gonna have to suffer for something I had no choice in? It's not fair."

"I agree that you are the victim here," he replied, looking at me again. There was a flicker of sadness and something else—desire?—quickly replaced by a firm, grim stare. "But, as they say, life is not fair. Every one of us carries a burden that is not ours by choice. In a just world, someone would track down the person who laid the curse, force its removal, and punish the practitioner. But this is not about justice for you, Myron Mitchell. I have to focus on the safety of the people you would hunt, and they are just as innocent in all this as you are."

I gasped, my mind locked on something he'd said. "This curse can be lifted?"

"Any curse can be lifted by the one who set it."

"Then why can't I go after the fool who put this curse on me and—"

The guy turned, clearly frustrated, and moved back to his car. He sat on the hood and folded his arms across his chest. "This is why I didn't want to have this conversation with you. It is wasting time and giving you hope where there really is none."

"But you just said—"

"There are too many variables involved in tracking down the practitioner. First of all, you're under a legacy curse, and the one who laid it may have died years, even centuries ago. Second, if he is dead, you'd have to find his descendants—assuming there *are* any. And even if he left descendants and you do find them, there is no guarantee they will be practitioners themselves. Or have the necessary skills to undo their ancestor's curse if they are practitioners. Third, and most important, you will continue to transform all the while you're looking for the practitioner. People will die. I can't let you put lives at risk on the small chance that you might be able to get the curse lifted."

"But I can fight the transformation. I can keep it in check. I know I can."

"Myron, you can't." His eyes became gentle, almost pleading. He gestured at the demonic name carved on the trees. "This is the only way."

My throat grew flush with tears. I tried to swallow them back, to save a little of my dignity, and it felt as if I was going to choke. I took a deep breath to steel myself. "Can I just do one thing before this demon takes me to... wherever it's gonna take me?"

The guy let his head fall wearily forward on his neck. "Myron—"

"Please, just hear me out. A friend of mine got kidnapped yesterday. That's why I was in those woods last night. I was trying to find her." I could see the refusal already building in the tall dude's face, and that made me want to scream again. I paused to get control of myself. "Her name is Bette," I said after I'd calmed a bit. "She's a good person. Her dad's divorced and out of job right now, so she's just about the only thing that keeps him going. I have to find her."

The guy didn't say anything. He just stared at me. His eyes went cold, and I felt a strong impulse to sit down, shut up, and hide my face.

But Bette was in trouble. She needed help, and I forced myself to buck up. Straightening my shoulders, I locked gazes with the dark-haired dude. "Twenty-four hours. A day. That's all I'm asking. A chance to find my friend and bring her home."

"No," the guy said flatly.

Desperation made my voice tremble. "I'm not making this up just to stall things. My friend really is in trouble—"

"I know that. Her disappearance is part of a larger situation I'm looking into. You'll have to trust me to find her."

I sneered at him, looking him up and down with disdain. "Hell, I don't know you. I don't know if I can trust you. You just want to get rid of me, and once I'm out of the picture, you could go riding off in your fancy-ass Beemer and leave Bette to get killed. It has to be me. I have to find her."

"If I were stupid enough to give you the time you want, I can guess what will happen if you don't find your friend in a day. You'll ask for another extension, and another, on and on until—"

"No, I won't. If I don't find her in a day, you can bring me back here and send me off to hell. I won't fight it or ask for anything else. I promise."

"And what if you transform in that time?"

That stopped me flat for a second. Then I cocked my head shrewdly to one side. "You controlled me when I was in your car, didn't you? I couldn't move the whole drive up here. You did that."

"Yes, I did."

"Then you could control me when I turn into this monster—"

"No, I can't. When you become the predator, you are too strong for me to control in any significant way. A circle of power, like the one you're standing in, can contain the predator, but it takes time to set up, and you will hardly hold still for that. I can protect myself, but if you transform in a crowd, I will not be able to defend everyone there. Someone, probably several people, will die."

I cursed, frustrated. "Can't you keep me from changing in the first place? Stop the change before I get to the monster stage?"

Reluctantly, the guy said, "Yes."

My mouth dropped open. The shock of his response went so deep it actually made me choke on my own spit. I coughed harshly. "What? What did you say?"

"I have, in the past, arrested the transformation in some afflicted like you. Temporarily, at least, to allow me time to have a demon take them."

"That's it, then." Through the despair, a spark of hope began to build in my chest. "You can fix me up so I don't change, I'll go find Bette, and maybe…." The look on the guy's face stopped me. The hope drained out of my body like water from a tub. I didn't ask what the look was about. I didn't think I could stand to hear it.

"I would have to be near you when the transformation starts," the guy explained, sighing. "If I don't catch it early enough, you will still be a danger to those around you. And once you walk out of that circle, I will be accountable for anything you do." He scowled. "That is not a responsibility I want to take on."

I closed my eyes and sat down on the ground again. I hoped that Bette would be okay. And Coach Frieda. And my parents. I hoped Garrett would have a good, long life.

I wondered what it would be like when the demon took me.

There was another sigh from the dude, followed by the sound of the wind rustling through leaves. I raised my head and saw leaves tumbling over the ground as if in a strong breeze, but only along the edge of the circle. Once the leaves settled, I felt an oppressive pressure, one that I hadn't been fully aware of until now, vanish from the air around me.

I looked at the guy. He was staring at me in a way that made my dick jump in my loose jeans.

"You have twenty-four hours," he said. "Let's go."

CHAPTER
TEN

"ARE you cold?"

The question both surprised and puzzled me. The temperature inside the BMW, per the digital thermometer glowing on the dashboard, was a very comfortable seventy-two degrees. The dude hadn't spoken since we left the clearing nearly half an hour ago. His face had been as unreadable as a freshly washed pane of glass.

I shook my head. "Why do you ask?"

"Well, you're shaking." He nodded at my clasped hands, which I now noticed were shivering between my quaking knees. "Either you're cold or you're afraid."

"No, I'm okay." I forced my lips into a smile, hoping it would hide my nervousness. After the bouncing drive back along the dirt road, we'd turned north on Highway 80. This was taking us further from Killebrew, but I felt it would be pressing my luck to point that out. Besides, anywhere away from that demon-summoning circle was fine with me.

The area we were traveling through was mostly wooded hills, and there was little traffic. My feet felt stiff. I leaned forward, reaching down to massage them through Garrett's dingy sneaks. "Is it okay if I take my shoes off?"

The dude gave me an oblique glance. "Do your feet smell?"

"Probably."

His lip curled slightly. Then, reluctantly, he nodded.

I pulled the sneaks off and stretched out my bare feet. My toes seemed to have gotten longer, and the cuts were gone, leaving only a few thin, fading scars. "Hey...." I touched the side of my head. It was neither swollen nor painful. Amazed, I yanked up my shirt.

The guy jerked away from me. "What in *hell* are you doing?" He averted his eyes from my body.

"My chest, my stomach...." I ran my hand over my torso, amazed to find only a lattice of thin, dark lines—which were also fading—where wounds had been last night. "I got pretty torn up when I went after those wolves. All those cuts and bites, they're healed up, just like that. I can't believe it."

"You can't hunt if you're hurt," the guy said in a bored way that made me feel stupid.

I let the shirt drop and turned to him. "So I'm a bloodthirsty monster. Who are you?"

"My name is Anoki," he replied.

"And you're a... what? Wizard?"

Anoki rolled his eyes. "Oh, great gods of the hunt. Here we go with the Harry Potter stuff."

"Hey. You're a guy. You were making magic-type stuff happen. That's a wizard."

He lifted his fingers slowly, one by one, before curling them back around the steering wheel. He inhaled and blew out the breath quickly. His face became relaxed, indulgent. "I don't make magic, not the way you're thinking. I'm a thaumaturgist. More specifically, I'm a necromancer."

I looked up as if watching something fly fast, high, and wide over my head. Then I turned back to Anoki and shrugged helplessly.

"It's simple," he said, with just a hint of impatience in his voice. "I have a talent for communing with spirits. Ghosts and demons, primarily. There are other kinds of spiritual entities out there, but some of them are both unpredictable and a great deal more powerful than ghosts and demons. They are best left alone."

"So, the spirits you call make the magic?"

"In a manner of speaking. If I want to manipulate a living person, I can have a spirit possess him or her to do my will. And spirits move things around for me. If I need to get through a locked door, they open it for me. If I need a brick wall torn apart, they break it down for me."

"They're, like, your slaves?"

"Hardly. All spirits are willful. Those that act freely on your behalf do so only when they get something they want in return. Others have to be forced into acting for you, and once you force them, they are forever your enemy."

"Even so, that's gotta be sweet, having a ghost do the heavy lifting for you." I thought about Dad making me mow the lawn, prune trees, and trim the hedges, about Mom making me wash dishes and move furniture. That brought a pain to the back of my throat, and I pushed the thoughts out of my head.

"There's nothing 'sweet' about it," Anoki replied. "There's always the danger that a spirit will attach itself to you."

"Attach itself to you? What does that mean?"

An odd look twisted Anoki's face for a moment. "I think you've heard enough about that topic." He shifted in his seat so that he was sitting even taller. "You haven't asked me where we're going."

"I did wonder about that. You mind telling me?"

"Not at all. We're going to Covington."

My hands were shaking so badly I could feel the vibrations all the way up in my biceps. There was something vague in the air. Just what it was, I couldn't figure, but it made me want to open the door and throw myself out of the moving car. I shoved my hands under my thighs as I said, "Can I ask you why we're going to Covington?"

"We're going to wait there until nightfall. The Killebrew police are looking for you."

"I know. My friend Garrett told me that. But how'd you know?"

Anoki reached down and pressed a button to the right of the ignition. A small screen mounted above the radio and CD/DVD player (none of which I'd noticed until now) flashed on, displaying a page from the Killebrew police station intranet. My junior-year headshot— the most recent picture of me my parents had—floated midscreen. Stamped above the picture, in bold capital letters, was the word "missing." Listed below was my name, birth date, height, weight, address, school, parent's names, telephone numbers, the date I went missing, and a little factoid that surprised me.

"I'm the eighth person to come up missing in Killebrew?" I asked, my eyes staring at the screen.

"Yes. Over the past three years, seven teenagers—not counting you—have disappeared in Killebrew. It's been in the news—"

"Yeah, I don't watch much news. Or read newspapers."

"I might have guessed." Anoki shook his head in a hopeless way. "Here. I have the whole roster pulled up." He punched another button on the dashboard, and seven smaller headshots replaced my picture on the screen, arranged in a grid.

I recognized Bette, of course, but the others—three guys, three girls—were unknown to me. "Somebody kidnapped all these kids?"

"There were signs of a struggle in Bette Herron's car. Aside from that, the police have no witnesses and no evidence of foul play with the missing. Most of them have been written off as runaways."

"But you don't think they're runaways."

"I *know* they aren't." Anger flashed over Anoki's face. "There's a necromancer at work in Killebrew. He is tied to the disappearances."

"And you know that how?"

"Because I'm a necromancer too. We can sense each other's handiwork."

This was getting a little too spooky for me. I turned my attention back to the pictures on the screen. I squinted at something I saw on the shoulders of one girl and two of the guys. "Hey, is there any way to enlarge these three pictures?" I asked, pointing.

Anoki waved a hand over the dashboard. I leaned sideways, as if to get a better look at the screen, but I really just wanted to press up against Anoki's big, muscular shoulder. In addition to his exotic good looks, he was mysterious, with an air of menace that had my dick and balls practically tingling. He scared the hell out of me, and that somehow made him all the more alluring. I leaned against him.

Instantly, a shiver ran the length of my spine, and I had to clench my thighs together to keep from pissing my jeans. I jerked away, and the sensation vanished.

Anoki froze for a moment, and the hand he held over the dashboard trembled slightly. He exhaled slowly, seemingly getting control of himself. He started to turn his head toward me, but some strange emotion flickered over his face and he stopped himself. "Don't do that again," he said quietly to me. Then he waved his hand again.

The display on the screen shifted, and the three shots I'd indicated arranged themselves side by side. In the now larger shots, I could see that the girl wore a pink sundress, one guy wore a gray wifebeater, and the other wore a polo shirt with the sleeves cut out.

"I've seen this before," I said, pointing to the wide black mark that stood out on the bare shoulders of the three kids like some massive, ugly bruise.

Anoki's eyes sharpened. He glanced at the pictures on the screen and then shot a quick look at me before turning back to the road. "Where?"

"On this guy, at this farm Bette and I went to yesterday. We went to talk with the owner to see if he knew anything about a missing teacher from our school. The owner's grandson was there, and he had a mark like that."

"You're going to take me to talk to this guy," Anoki said, his breath quickening with excitement.

"Yeah, okay. But what's the deal about those blotches?"

"They're like a cattle brand. Some necromancers use them to mark their property." He flipped on his turn signal and eased the car to the right, taking the Covington exit. "Put your shoes on. We'll be stopping in about ten minutes."

I bent down and began slipping my feet back into the sneaks. "I thought you were all anxious to talk to that guy at the farm."

"I am. But I want to get you another pair of pants first. The ones you're wearing are too big, and I can't stand to see any more of your butt."

Ah, damn. I'd been hoping someday a sexy dude would tell me I had a cute butt. Humiliated, I reached back and tugged my shirt down over the gaping waist of my borrowed jeans.

Anoki pulled into the parking lot of Covington's Hollow Trace Mall, a sprawling complex of gray-and-white brick buildings, interconnected like giant Lego blocks in the middle of a field on the town's southwestern outskirts. He parked in a space about fifty miles from the mall entrance and forty miles from the nearest car.

He gestured with his right hand and the door of the glove compartment popped open. Inside, I saw the owner's manual and the car registration resting atop a mound of cash. There were some loose fives, tens, twenties, and ones, but most of it was in tightly wrapped stacks of Benjamins. Begging my pardon, Anoki reached between my knees and grabbed a fistful of cash, sending another violent shudder clanging down my back. The moment he withdrew his hand, the compartment door snapped shut with a ravenous bang.

There had to be somewhere in the neighborhood of twenty thousand dollars in that glove compartment.

The compartment wasn't locked.

We got out of the car, and Anoki didn't bother to lock the doors.

I did not say one word to him about any of this, mostly because I was afraid of him. On the other hand, I was convinced that anyone stupid enough to try breaking and entering his car would live to regret it.

Or maybe not. Live, that is.

"Come on," Anoki said, tucking his hair behind his ears with his thumbs. He pulled a pair of glossy black shades from the collar of his shirt and put them on.

I followed him into the men's department of Sears, where I found tan jeans and a yellow jersey in my size. When I turned to head for the cash registers, Anoki stepped in front of me, saying, "Aren't you going to try those on?"

Coming from anyone else, that would have annoyed me. While part of me loved having this gorgeous guy in my face, the proximity made me so uncomfortable I wanted to run away screaming. I backed up a few steps and said, "Don't have to. I've been wearing the same size for over a year."

"Suit yourself," he said skeptically. He turned, motioning for me to follow. We stopped at a display of men's underwear. "What size?"

"Small," I replied, my face getting hot. *The good thing is, when this is all over, I'll be in hell.*

He swept his hand decisively over the racks, as if he knew exactly what he wanted. He plucked a pair of black-and-white striped boxers free and tossed them to me. "Now you need a pair of shoes."

By the time we'd finished, he'd bought me jeans, the jersey, boxers, athletic socks, black Nikes, a baseball cap, shades, a sports watch, and a leather wallet. ("All men should have a wallet," he'd said when I told him I'd never owned one.) I went into the men's room to get dressed.

When I walked out, I was stunned. The jersey was snug, the boxers were pinching in places best not described, and the cuffs of the jeans rode above my ankles. (But the sneaks fit perfectly: I always bought them one size too big.) "I don't get it. This is the size I've been wearing forever." I looked sheepishly at Anoki. "Guess I should have tried this stuff on, huh?"

To his credit, he did not make me feel like an idiot, although there was a bit of amusement in his eyes. "I have the receipts. We can exchange whatever you like." He nodded, and for just a second, it almost seemed there was something… tender in the way he looked at me. Then he shook his head, and a scowl dropped over his face like a curtain.

CHAPTER
ELEVEN

WE EXCHANGED the jeans and jersey for a larger size, and Anoki bought me a larger pair of boxers. When I was finally dressed, Anoki said he had something to take care of, told me he'd be back as soon as he could, and walked away. I was left sitting on a metal bench outside the mall's food court.

Yes, it was the perfect opportunity for me to sneak away.

But I never even considered escaping. Without Anoki to keep me in check, I would eventually turn back into that murderous creature I had become last night. I didn't want to kill anyone, especially not the people I loved, and if preventing that meant I'd have to cuddle up with a demon for the rest of my life, I was willing to pay the price.

And if you're thinking Anoki was stupidly trusting to leave me that way, you'll be glad to know that he was neither stupid nor trusting. About fifteen minutes after he took off, I had to go to the bathroom. The moment I stood up, chills started running up and down my body. As I walked toward the restrooms, the chills intensified, making me shiver. When I got about thirty feet from the bench, my knees locked. It felt as if two steel bands had snapped suddenly and tightly around them. Momentum sent me swaying forward, spinning my arms for balance, and I fell flat on my face.

A middle-aged woman sitting alone at a table, eating a burrito, frowned at me distastefully, apparently taking me for drunk. I tried to get up, but my knees wouldn't bend. "Hey," I said, reaching out a hand to the woman, "can you help me here?"

She sniffed, grabbed her burrito, purse, and shopping bags, and took herself to another table on the opposite side of the food court.

Several shoppers passed by me over the next few minutes. They all looked down at me. Some shook their heads while others scowled. None of them stopped to help.

If I hadn't been so scared about my suddenly uncooperative body, I would have cursed. After a few minutes of floundering on the floor, I discovered that my difficulty lay in the fact that I was facing away from the bench. The moment I worked myself around to where I could see the bench, my knees loosened up and I was able to stand. As I walked back toward the bench, the chills began to fade. When I sat down again, all was right with my body.

Except that I still had to go to the bathroom.

By the time Anoki came back, nearly an hour later, I was rocking back and forth on that bench, knees bouncing like crazy, both hands clenched at my crotch.

"You seem uncomfortable," he remarked calmly.

There were tears in my eyes. "Can I go to the bathroom now? *Please.*"

"Oh. Of course." He bowed slightly, gesturing toward the restrooms.

I took off, moving at a pretty fast clip despite being bent at the waist and having my hands between my legs.

When I came back, Anoki was sitting at a table, sipping bottled water. There was another bottle on the table, which he offered to me.

"Thanks," I said, grabbing the bottle as I sat across from him.

"Would you like something to eat?"

That made me think of what I'd eaten last night, and a swell of nausea hit me. "No," I said, fighting back a gag.

"You should put on your shades and your cap," Anoki said, still wearing his own shades. "The Killebrew police sent your description to the surrounding towns. The police here will be on the lookout for you."

I tucked the navy Tennessee Titans cap on my head, pulled the brim down low on my forehead, and slipped on the glasses. "Where'd you go?" I asked, leaning toward him, inhaling his smell. I liked the way he smelled, a cinnamon sort of scent that made me think of the holiday season.

"To meet with a contact I have in the Covington Police Department. A seventeen-year-old boy was found dead here this past Friday. It hasn't been made public yet, but he is one of the missing from Killebrew."

A sudden shiver went through me. The anxiety that came from being around Anoki was kicking into gear again. "How'd he die? Was he murdered?"

"The autopsy revealed a massive heart attack. He also had high levels of alcohol and illegal drugs in his body."

"So this dude just ran off and got high?"

Anoki lowered his voice even more. "He was no runaway. My contact was able to get me in to view the body. The Killebrew necromancer traded that boy off to a spirit, which used him as a physical vessel. I sensed the residue of the possession immediately. Some ghosts want to experience certain things again from their past lives. In this instance, the ghost was one used to what some call 'hard living'. It turned out to be more than the boy's body could handle."

"Do the cops know when he died?"

"The coroner estimated the time of death between one o'clock and four o'clock Thursday morning."

With the bottle halfway to my mouth, I froze.

"What is it?" Anoki asked.

"There's all this weird stuff that started happening last Thursday. A teacher from my school disappeared. Frieda Blevins. A scarecrow got stolen from that farm I told you about earlier. And a little kid saw something that looked like a scarecrow walking past his backyard. Could this necromancer you're after be behind all that?"

"Yes. A spirit can inhabit an inanimate object as well as a living body. The necromancer could very well be working with a spirit that is using a scarecrow as a vessel. And while he seems to have a preference for teens, there's no reason the necromancer could not use an adult in his otherworldly dealings." He paused as if weighing options in his head. "The chances of your being sighted would be lesser after dark, but we can't afford to wait that long. We'll stop at this farm you mentioned so I can talk to the guy you saw there. Then we have to get back to Killebrew."

WE PARKED just off the dirt road that circled the Wexlar farm, beneath the low-hanging, balding branches of a peach tree.

I was baffled. "How do you know the dude is gonna come out here?"

"He will," Anoki said coolly.

Silence fell between us. The windows were down, and a cool breeze blew lazily through the car. The drone of insects filled the sunny afternoon air, along with the rush of traffic on the highway. The Beemer had a state-of-the-art sound system, but Anoki hadn't so much as turned on the radio in the time I'd been riding with him. He didn't seem to mind the quiet, but I was as anxious as ever and needed a distraction.

"Back at the mall," I said, eager to get up a conversation, "how'd you keep me on that bench?"

"I left a spirit with you," Anoki replied matter-of-factly. "If you tried to move beyond its range of influence, it would encourage you to turn back."

"Yeah, it was really good at that. Thanks."

"And if you'd begun to change, it would have held you long enough for me to get back and stop the progression."

"By the way, how will I know when I start to change?"

He put his head to one side and gave an annoyed sigh. "Sometimes you ask the most pointless questions."

"Sorry." I didn't know what else to say.

"You transformed less than a day ago. Did it never occur to you to use that experience as a guide?"

I thought about it. "I started feeling very, very pissed before it happened. And hungry. For raw meat."

"There's your answer. If you start feeling that way again, just let me know."

Another memory came to me. I raised my hands, curving the fingers over to look at the nails, which were badly in need of trimming and sported black bands of dirt underneath. "I think I burned things with my fingernails."

"You did. The curse endows you with Devil's Fire."

"What's that?"

"A form of energy shed by certain higher entities. It burns through physical forms and debilitates spiritual beings. It is all but impossible to control, but there are a small number of thaumaturgists who have a talent for manipulating Devil's Fire. The one who cursed you is—or was—obviously so talented."

"Yeah. I've been thinking about the whole curse thing, and I can't come up with a single relative of mine who turned into a freaking monster. If this was passed down from generation to generation like you said—"

"The curse doesn't afflict someone in every generation. It manifests randomly down the family line. Is there no parent or grandparent, no aunt or uncle, who was accused of murder, or who disappeared suddenly?"

"My mom's mother. She took off when Mom was only a year old. Grandpa says she just ran off one night and no one ever heard from her again. Could she have been a monster like me?"

"Some of the cursed, once they realize what they are doing, will leave their homes to avoid harming their families. Or a necromancer imprisons them with a demon. One way or the other, they eventually disappear."

So. The grandmother I knew only from pictures could be, at this very moment, serving as some evil spirit's lunch. Again and again. Forever.

There were only so many of these cheery thoughts that I could take. Time to move on. "You live around here?"

"No."

I waited, but Anoki didn't exactly seem inclined to elaborate. I decided to try a different tack. "Are you in school? Like, college or something?"

"No."

Wow, Anoki. Don't talk me to death here. "What about your friends? What're they like?"

He turned away, looking out the window. "I have none."

"What's that supposed to mean? Everybody has friends. In the neighborhood where you grew up, there had to be somebody you played with in the sandbox. Somebody who came over for your birthday parties. Some dude you hung out with, maybe went to movies with him or—"

"Myron. You are irritating me. And you really shouldn't do that."

No doubt about it. *That* was a threat.

I began to itch all over.

I shut up.

CHAPTER
TWELVE

IT WAS another fifteen minutes before Pike Wexlar showed.

He came around the bend, where the road disappeared behind the green wall of cornstalks that bordered the edge of the farm. Barefoot, wearing blue jeans and a red T-shirt with "I Believe" spread across the chest, he walked in slow but fluid motions, arms barely swinging. When he reached the spot where the peach tree stood, he made a crisp turn off the road and stopped right in front of the Beemer. His face was spotted here and there with red pimples, but it was kind of cute. Instantly, I wondered what he looked like naked.

Both doors swung open, and Anoki and I climbed out. Pike's blank eyes suddenly blinked, and he seemed to come back to himself. He looked around, surprise quickly giving way to confusion in his eyes.

"How the hell did I get out here?" he asked. Then he saw Anoki. "Hey. I dreamed about you. I wanted to talk to you."

"I'm here," Anoki said. "We can talk now."

Pike was tall and lean and muscular, like his grandfather. He was maybe nineteen or twenty. The skin on his neck and arms was well on its way to being sunburned. His dark-brown hair, curling down to his shoulders, was bleached in streaks, but I couldn't tell whether that was from the sun or chemicals. He was sexy, and I could see myself bending him over and pounding the hell out of his farm-boy ass. The bulging Adam's apple in his neck bobbed up and down as he swallowed nervously. "What do you want to talk about?" he asked.

Anoki held out a sheet of paper with pictures of the seven missing kids on it. "Do you know, or have you seen, any of the people here?"

Pike studied the pictures closely. "This one," he said, pointing at Bette's photo. "She was here yesterday, talking to my gramps."

"Did you see her at any time before yesterday?"

"No. But this guy, I remember him." He pointed to another of the pictures on the sheet, one that showed a blond dude with a zit-covered face and a scraggly goatee. "He was at a couple of the soccer games I came down for at Killebrew High. He used to cheer really loud for this particular girl on the team that he must've liked."

"Did you attend Killebrew High?" Anoki asked.

"No. I went to school in Millington. I graduated two years ago."

"Then why would you go to Killebrew High's soccer games?"

Pike swallowed hard, looking as if he were about to choke on his Adam's apple. "So I could see Frieda."

Huh? I looked at Anoki and raised my hand, seeking permission to step in. When he nodded at me, I said, "Uh… Pike, you were… like, *dating* Frieda Blevins?"

Anoki sighed.

"Yeah," Pike answered, looking very afraid. "But she didn't want anybody to know, so please don't tell anybody. I'm fourteen years younger than she is, and she didn't want folks gossiping about her."

Coach Frieda was pretty, but she had to be close to my parents' age. Picturing her cuddling with Pike was just plain gross. I shook myself, trying to get that image out of my head. "How long have you been dating her?"

"Almost a year."

Anoki stepped in again. "When did you last have contact with this Frieda Blevins?"

"Last Thursday," said Pike. "She called me after school to make sure I received the plane ticket she'd bought for me. She was taking me to Miami for the weekend, so we could have some real time together. But then… something happened to her, before we could go."

Anoki moved closer, getting right up in Pike's face. The two of them were roughly the same height, but the look on Anoki's face was so dark it scared me. It also set my crotch to tingling. The hot, creepy bastard really turned me on. Pike shuddered violently and shrank back, a stifled scream escaping his throat in one quick yip.

"Did you harm Frieda Blevins?" Anoki growled.

"No! No, I love her! I wouldn't hurt her for nothing in the world!" Pike's eyes were wide and frantic, silently begging Anoki to believe him. "It scared me when the news came out that she'd disappeared. I've been so worried about her. I just want her back."

The dude convinced me, and apparently Anoki as well. Anoki stepped back. Pike exhaled loudly, the breath coming out in a grunt of relief and sorrow. His nose suddenly ran. He wiped it on the back of his hand.

I could see the dark blotch on Pike's right shoulder, peeking out below the sleeve on his right arm. As Anoki didn't seem to have anything else to say at the moment, I asked, "How'd you get that?"

"How'd I get what?"

I nodded at his arm. "That mark. On your shoulder."

Pike lifted the sleeve, baring the mark in all its repulsive glory. He looked right at the blotch, and then gave me a scowl that insinuated I'd been smoking meth or something. "What're you talking about, dude?"

"Who else do you know in Killebrew?" Anoki interrupted.

"Just Frieda," Pike replied. "I mean, there are a few kids that I met when I came down for the games, but Frieda's the only person I really know there."

"How did you meet her?"

"At the farmers' market in the Shelby County Ag Center. My gramma raises mums and sells 'em at the Ag Center in the fall. Frieda walked by when I was manning Gramma's booth, and we just took this instant liking to each other."

Anoki slowly turned away from Pike, facing toward the Wexlar house, the roof of which bulged over the rustling green wall of cornstalks. With a slight scowl, he whispered something in a soft but authoritative tone. A gust tunneled narrowly into the corn directly ahead of him, the long leaves lifting briefly into the air like the arms of spectators waving at a football game as the wind headed toward the house.

"That's all we need for now," Anoki said abruptly, his back to Pike. Anoki turned and climbed back into his car. I hurried after him and slid into the passenger seat. The engine came to life and we drove off, leaving a bewildered Pike standing in the shade of the dying peach tree.

"WHY'D you cut me off before he told us about the mark?"

It had taken me almost twenty minutes to work up the nerve to ask the question. I immediately shifted away from Anoki, bracing my back against the car door for the answer, which I expected to come with plenty of temper.

He seemed to be lost in thought. "Pike doesn't know that he has been marked," he said vaguely.

"Yeah, he does. He looked right at it. You saw him."

"He couldn't see the mark. It's only visible to necromancers and spirits."

"But I'm neither. How is it that I could see it?"

"That, I'm not sure of."

"Anyway, that's all beside the point," I said, shaking my head. "The police found straw in Coach Frieda's house, and I saw the same straw in my friend Bette's car after she was taken. The straw comes from the Wexlar farm. Pike could be the one behind both disappearances."

"So could any number of people who work the farm."

"Yeah, but Pike actually knows Coach Frieda. The night she disappeared, all her doors and windows were locked from the inside. That means that whoever took her was somebody she knew, somebody she would have let into her house. Then, once they were inside, they grabbed her."

"And once they did, they took her out of the house. Right?"

"Yeah."

"Then, if the abductor took her out of the house, how is it that the doors and windows remained locked from the inside?"

Okay. He had me stumped there.

Anoki swept his hair back from his face with one hand, keeping the other on the steering wheel, ignoring the stupefied look on my face. "I mostly wanted to meet with this Pike Wexlar to see if he had ever been possessed," he said. "I detected no foreign spiritual residue within him, so he hasn't been traded off yet. The spirit that brought him out to us has returned him to his grandfather's home and will hold him there until tomorrow morning. That should keep him safe and give me time to find the necromancer who marked him."

"How do you plan to do that?"

"It would help if I knew where the necromancer has made his circle of power. He will need one to summon and bind the spirits until he completes his transactions with them."

"And what would the circle look like? I mean, beyond just the obvious."

"He could draw it in the dirt with a stick, or with chalk on any smooth surface. If he wants a truly powerful circle, however, he will carve it out of the woods, much like the one I placed you in earlier."

"I saw a circle like that last night, when I was looking for Bette. Her scent led me to these woods not very far from Coach Frieda's house, and the scent disappeared in the circle there."

Anoki's face went completely still for an instant.

"What's wrong?' I asked anxiously.

He shook his head. "I searched those woods myself last night but never found a circle. The necromancer must have warded it to deflect other thaumaturgists from the site. Do you think you can take me to it?"

"I don't know. I sort of followed my nose to it, so I wasn't really paying any attention to what I saw along the way. And once I reached the circle, I got jumped by these two people who knocked me out and carried me off. When I came to, I was tied up in a shed in another part of the woods. I don't think I'd know how to get back to the circle."

"You will find it today the same way you did last night."

"But… I was going predator then. I had, like, this super sense of smell. And I don't have that now."

"You will when I induce you."

"Induce me to what?"

"Becoming the predator."

I gasped. "You can do that?"

"Yes. Don't worry. I will stop the progression before you fully transform. With the heightened senses, you should be able to find your friend's scent again and take me to the circle. Or perhaps you'll even detect the scent of the Killebrew necromancer himself."

"But I don't know who that is."

"It's very likely he was one of the people who attacked you last night. What do you remember about them?"

"There was this sweet odor from one of them," I said, the memory so fresh I could almost smell the scent now. "It was like rotten fruit or something, and it was stronger than any other scent from them. I think I've smelled it before… there was something familiar about it."

"After I induce you, you'll see if you can find that scent again. Maybe you can lead us directly to the necromancer."

After we left the Wexlar farm, Anoki took Nebler Road back into Killebrew. Nebler ran along the western border of the town and was lined with factories and warehouses. I suggested that route to him, figuring it was less likely I'd be spotted there, since few townies besides the industrial workers used the road. We were coming to the end of the industrial district, where the two-lane road changed over to four lanes and ran down to Memphis. There was a little diner there that catered primarily to the workers. I looked over at the diner as we passed.

And I shrank down in the car as if someone had taken a shot at me.

"What is it?" said Anoki.

"My dad…," I whispered. I pointed, keeping my eyes shut so that I wouldn't see him again. But the sight was etched into my mind.

Dad was tall and twenty pounds overweight, but he looked wasted somehow, standing in the diner's parking lot in his wrinkled khakis and pale-blue dress shirt. He was hammering a flyer onto one of the lampposts. Even though I didn't get a good look at the flyer, I knew the gray square it bore was a photograph of me. He had been awake all night, trying to find me; his eyes were red, sunken, and tired. He was broken.

I had broken him.

If I had been home last night when I became that monster, my mom and dad would be dead now. Just the thought of what I would have done to them made me weak. But I knew they were devastated because they didn't know where I was or what had happened to me.

I wanted to go to Dad. I wanted to hug him, tell him that I loved him and that I was okay. I wanted so very badly for him to know how sorry I was that I'd hurt him, and Mom.

And I knew that would never happen, that I would never talk to him again.

"Shit," I muttered softly, fighting back tears.

"Myron," Anoki said very softly. "Ah, Myron. I am so sorry."

He reached toward my face.

I needed his comfort. But he stopped himself before he could touch me. Slowly, he pulled his hand back.

If I was going to make it through the next twenty-four hours, I couldn't let myself feel anything. I wiped my tearing eyes and slumped in the seat, staring down at my lap as I tried to blank my mind. My emotions slowly but steadily shut down like an appliance with the plug pulled.

"I know this is hard for you to believe now," said Anoki, his voice seeming to float from everywhere and nowhere, "but everything is going to be all right."

Yeah, it will, I thought. *Once I'm in hell.*

CHAPTER
THIRTEEN

ANOKI got a room in a small motel just outside Killebrew. The room was in the back, facing away from the street. He unlocked the door and held it open for me. The tears had stopped and I felt dead inside. I went straight to the bed and lay down, too tired to even wash my streaked face.

I woke up without memory of having fallen asleep. The room was dark except for the red-glowing numbers on the bedside clock radio, which read 7:07 p.m. "Anoki?" There was no response. I was alone.

I switched on the lights, went into the adjoining bath, and made use of the facilities. That included a long, hot soak in the bathtub, during which I made every effort not to think about my parents. The bath refreshed me. The weariness was suddenly gone, replaced with a warm vitality that hummed through my body.

I all but leaped out of the tub. While toweling off afterward, I felt a little tingle of fear go up my spine. I froze. For a moment, I couldn't pinpoint the source of my sudden apprehension. Then the reason became clear, and the burn of fear flared even brighter.

I was getting hungry.

Naked, I crossed the room and opened the door. The Beemer was nowhere in sight.

Great. Just great.

I stood in the doorway, staring out over the motel parking lot. A light burned over the door of each unit, casting the only illumination in the area aside from the cool moonlight above. Thin gray clouds scuttled across the black sky. Four cars and a pickup were parked along the white concrete walkway that separated the lot from the building.

A dog barked, one of those little yappy kinds, and I could pinpoint the sound to the unit at the very end on my left. I smelled the flea powder the little bugger wore. The unit immediately to my right was unoccupied, but I could hear water dripping in the bathtub there. The man in the room beyond that was snoring while music wafted softly from the television. I could hear his heartbeat.

I wanted to chew on his heart.

Damn! Where the hell was Anoki? His paramount purpose in life, at least where I was concerned, was to make sure I didn't hurt anyone. How could he do that if he wasn't around? I started grinding my teeth as I felt anger rise on a wave of alarm. There were nine people in the units on either side of me. I could hear them, smell them. Every time I breathed in their scents, something in me blossomed further, wanting to tear through the flimsy doors they lounged behind and get at them.

I wanted to hear them scream. I wanted to see them run. I wanted them to fight me, as pitifully futile as that would be for them. How glorious it would be if they ran and fought before I tore them apart and bit into—

No! No. I couldn't let that happen. *Fight this. You can fight this.* I crouched down in the doorway, clamping my arms over my head in an effort to block the sensations. The pulse of their hearts hammered away at me still. Their warm, salty aromas pulled at me. With every passing second, I could feel inhibitions within my head snapping apart like taut cords chopped with an axe.

I had to get away from the motel. I had to get myself as far away from other people as possible, while I still had the chance. I would run. There was a line of trees on the other side of the parking lot, and a field beyond that. Maybe there were enough animals in the field to keep the predator occupied. Maybe there were woods out there where I could lose myself.

I stood upright and bolted from the room. Just as suddenly, some invisible force seized my right forearm like a giant fist and yanked me off my feet, snatching me back through the door. I hit the floor with a bone-crushing thud and slid across the carpet until my head and shoulders slammed against the wall.

For a moment, I couldn't quite figure out what had happened. The blow temporarily scrambled my brain, but when my head cleared itself seconds later, I thought: spirit. Anoki had left another spirit with me, one that was not going to let me leave the motel.

Or so the fool spirit thought.

I snarled and was on my feet in a flash. I crouched, muscles coiling powerfully, and then leaped. There was, I swear, a massive sucking sound, and a great gust swept inward as all the air in the room made a mad dash toward the back wall. The door snapped shut with such force the walls rattled, sending pictures sliding to the floor. A second later, I hit the door headfirst.

I bounced off and landed on my ass. And I promptly got to my feet. Hah. Didn't so much as ring my bell that time. I was even more impressed when I saw that I had left a crack as wide as my forearm running the length of the metal door, the middle of which now bowed outward from the blow I'd struck. Cool. One more run and I was going through that sucker, ghost or no ghost.

I backed up and charged, shoulder down, a growl rumbling in my chest.

About five feet from the door, it felt as if I'd plunged bodily into a mass of putty. My forward motion stopped cold, the kinetic energy apparently absorbed into whatever invisible thing had encased me. I twisted, writhing like a wild animal caught in a snare. The more I thrashed, the more mired I became until I could barely move at all.

Furious, I screamed, and the sound reverberated as if I were under water. That caught my interest, and despite the insane urge to use the inhuman power swelling through my body, I actually took a moment to study my present circumstance. Slowly, I realized that I could see the thing that held me. It was faint in the room's incandescent light, but it was definitely there, a thin, green haze that slowly billowed and shifted around me, like smoke caught in a draft. The haze brightened momentarily, going almost white, and I got a sensation of surprise. Then the thing vanished from my sight altogether.

It held me no less firmly, and that sent my rage blasting upward again. My body was growing stronger and faster by the minute, as was the urge to hunt. The invisible mass around me was beginning to give. I managed to take a step toward the door. Then another. I raised my hand, slowly but steadily, reaching for the doorknob.

In what seemed to be an act of desperation, the spirit lifted me in an abrupt sweeping motion and slammed me down on the bed. The pressure it exerted to hold me there was intense enough to crush the bed's metal frame to the floor. I grinned like a maniac. Soon I would be the predator. Then I would tear through this ghostly force like it was paper.

The door opened and Anoki stepped into the room.

The grin died slowly on my face. He now wore stylishly faded blue jeans and a blue-and-gray Dallas Cowboys jersey. His startling good looks were still there, but beneath them I could see something as awful and inhuman as the creature that was rapidly growing within me. It was gone from Anoki in an instant, shutting itself away from my vision. He crossed the room without seeming to move and leaned over the bed, staring down at me.

"That's far enough, Myron Mitchell." He only mouthed the words, I realized, but they seemed to ring in my head as if he had spoken aloud.

His heartbeat was steady and strong and close, too much for me to resist. I lunged at him, but my head only rose a few inches off the mattress before the invisible spiritual goo stopped me. He repeated the words again and again, and they were anesthetizing. I was soothed to the point that I sighed with deep pleasure. Things took on a dreamlike quality. The ghostly pressure on my body abruptly rolled away. I lay on the bed, feeling more relaxed than ever before.

I smiled up at him, patting the mattress at my side. "Want to join me?"

He stared back at me without speaking. There was a lifetime of familiarity in his gaze, as puzzling to me as it was hellishly sexy. The pain-filled look on his face was awful, and I wished I'd kept my mouth shut. His eyes shimmered, full of anxiety and rage and a sudden, blazing lust that made him look crazed. With obvious reluctance, his gaze drifted slowly down my body, and when it settled on my bare crotch, he flinched and stepped back. He squeezed his eyes shut, shaking his head. When he opened his eyes again, his gaze found mine, and his anger had grown into trembling rage.

"Why do you tempt me like this?" he snarled. "Why do you keep showing me your body? Do you not see how dangerous, how impossible this is for us both?"

Anoki's words didn't register with me at the time. I was too mellow and too caught up in how ruggedly attractive his face and body were. I could only think how much I wanted to peel off his clothes and pull him down beside me. In a dramatic flourish of frustration, he grabbed the edge of the bed's comforter and flung it over me, covering my nakedness.

He moved back from the bed and paced frantically across the room. My eyes locked on his ass, loving the way his buttocks flexed in his jeans as he stalked back and forth. The cinnamon smell of him was stronger than ever; it filled my nostrils with every breath. The rustle of his clothes as he moved was acute, adding to my excitement. Something about him, something in him, moved me profoundly. It was more than just his hot body and handsome looks that stirred me. This guy, this beautiful, frightening guy, was mine. He had always been mine, in a way that went way beyond the physical. Beneath the comforter, my dick got hard, bulging up over my belly. I wanted to fuck Anoki. I wanted to throw him facedown on the bed and fuck him hard.

Anoki clenched and unclenched his fists repeatedly at his sides, signs of an inner struggle I could only guess at. About a minute later, he stopped pacing and turned, staring at me again. One corner of his mouth curled up in a snarl, and he muttered something silently. That horrible thing in him surfaced briefly, a vague, grayish cloud of malevolence that drifted quickly away from him before fading once more from my sight.

His face filled with lustful determination, Anoki swept forward, snatching off his shirt as he came to the bed. He opened his jeans and shoved them down. His arms, shoulders, chest, abdomen, and thighs rippled with finely honed muscle, a sculpture of masculine perfection, his skin smooth and brass-colored. His cock stood out from a curly black pubic patch: long, thick, and heavily veined, as dark and angry as his soul. He kicked off his shoes, stepped out of his jeans, and yanked the comforter off me. Once again, he looked down at my dick. This time, he reached out and wrapped his hand around it. He squeezed firmly, sending a spasm of pleasure shooting into my groin that made me moan.

He looked up at me again. Rage and urgent desire seemed to shine like searing rays from his eyes. "Damn you," he growled. Grabbing me by the shoulders, he flipped me onto my stomach as if I were weightless. His hands cupped my buttocks, massaging them roughly. His touch excited me all the more. Pain and bliss mingled delightfully in me.

I was so relaxed that everything seemed to flow in slow motion. After what seemed a very long time, Anoki stopped squeezing my ass and moved away from the bed. I just lay there with my chin propped on the mattress and a lazy smile on my face, staring at the headboard. My dick pulsed eagerly beneath me.

I heard feet skimming over the carpet, and suddenly Anoki was back. He climbed onto the bed, planting his knees on the mattress outside mine. There was the squelch of a plastic bottle being squeezed, followed by a squirting sound, and the smell of aloe and mineral oil filled the air richly. Anoki's long fingers, slick with silky lotion, slipped between my ass cheeks.

Wait a minute. I wanted Anoki, but not that way. I turned my head and started to roll my butt away from him, just as one of his fingers slid into me.

I sucked in a breath. The finger entered in one smooth, quick, easy motion. There was no discomfort, just a feeling of pressure that was wonderful and decadent. My ass clenched, tightly and involuntarily, as if to trap the invading digit.

The finger slid in and out, twisting, probing. That went on for a minute, maybe two. Time became an elusive, inconsequential concept. I closed my eyes, pleasure humming low in my throat. Just as my ass muscles relaxed, he pulled his finger out of me. The desire to kiss

Anoki, to touch his body, was suddenly overwhelming. I started to push myself up, eager to turn over and face him.

Anoki slammed his hand between my shoulder blades, pressing my face back down into the mattress. Just as quickly, the fat knob of his cock pushed between my butt cheeks. Something in my brain balked at that. My fantasies so far had mostly been about my screwing another guy, not about me taking anything as big as Anoki's hard piece up my rump. I was going to tell Anoki to wait a second, to give me a moment to psych myself up for this. Before I could even open my mouth, Anoki, in a single lunge, shoved his dick up into my ass.

Eyes bulging, I yelped, not so much from pain as from surprise. I could feel how outrageously deep he plowed into me, grinding my pelvis into the mattress. I could feel the pulse of his heart in every vein on the shaft of his cock, could feel the bulbous head of it burrowing through me. The sensation thrilled and scared me. His dick seemed endless, and I began to grab at the sheets, trying to pull myself away from it.

Anoki draped his big body over me like a blanket as he slid his hands along my arms to grasp my hands tightly. His long hair draped over the side of my head and my shoulder, the scent of it spicy, like cinnamon and cloves. He covered my body completely with his, trapping me, making it impossible to escape him. But it also made me feel protected, secure. He moved his hips slowly and surely, sliding his dick back and forth in me.

A weight settled suddenly on the bed, making the mattress sag as its springs creaked in protest. Anoki froze above me. Something cold and ancient and dreadful surrounded us. An arm, the skin as dark as my own, planted itself to the left of my head, bracing the weight of its owner. The scents of Anoki's body and my own, the hiss of our breathing, the beating of our hearts, filled my senses, but the newcomer's body had no scent or pulse that I could detect. I turned my head, trying to see who had joined us, only to discover that Anoki's arm and shoulder blocked any further view. Jealousy burst like an explosion in my head.

I felt the muscles in Anoki's body tense sharply. He grunted, then gave a gasp of pain. "Easy, *easy*," he hissed. "I am flesh and blood, remember?"

Pressed from above, Anoki crushed his hips down, shoving his dick deep into me again. Helplessly, I snarled as he pounded into me, his thrusts driven by the force atop us both. Our thrashing might have lasted a minute, an hour, a lifetime. I remember raking my fingers at the mattress, ripping it apart as Anoki's cock spurted hotly inside me. I remember Anoki screaming something in a language as old as the being that held us on the bed, followed by a disembodied, orgasmic, inhuman cry that shook the walls of the room.

Then the presence above us was gone. Slowly and carefully, Anoki pulled his dick out of me. He got up as I rolled over onto my back. He stepped away from the bed, gesturing for me to sit up. I did, swinging my feet over to the floor.

Anoki anxiously studied my face for a moment. "How do you feel?" His own brow was sweaty, strands of his black hair wet and clinging there.

"Like I could tear that door off the wall, chew it up, and spit out bullets." I didn't mention that I no longer felt afraid of him. Cautious, maybe, the way one rogue lion might be around another, but not afraid.

"Are you angry?" Anoki asked sharply.

"Nope." It surprised me to realize this was true, despite the fact that my dick remained hard because, unlike Anoki, I hadn't gotten a climax out of all the action. My senses continued to hum, picking up motion, sounds, and smells from outside the room. Anoki's dick hung half erect, dripping strings of cum barely two feet away from my face. That made my own cock ache even more for release. A growl rumbled through my stomach. "I am hungry, though."

"Hunger we can deal with. The important thing at this point is to keep your emotions, especially anger, under control."

My toes felt cramped. I glanced down as I wriggled them. The skin on my feet was as black as if it had been painted. My toenails, just as black as my skin, had grown into one-inch curved claws. I raised my arms and saw the same blackness there. My fingernails had also curved into dark, inch-long scythes.

I got up to go into the bathroom. I wanted to see my face.

"We should go," Anoki said, peeking between the slats of the blind at the window. He dashed into the bathroom, treating me to the sight of his flexing bare butt. Damn, he had such a beautiful ass, and I wanted nothing more at that moment than to ram my dick into him. I stumbled into the bathroom after him, my legs unsteady. He was hastily washing himself at the sink. I pressed against him, too short for my crotch to quite reach his butt. Instead, my erect cock thudded into the juncture between his thighs.

He shoved me away. "There is no time," he snapped. He tossed a wet towel to me. "Here. Clean yourself." He rushed from the bathroom.

I snarled, feeling horny, hungry, and dissatisfied. After cleaning myself up, I went back into the bedroom where Anoki was hurriedly slipping into his clothes.

His hair was pulled back and tied in a long ponytail. When he spoke, his voice was even, but there was an unmistakable tone of urgency to it. "I'm afraid our antics here disturbed some of our neighbors. One of my spirits informed me that someone called the police. We are not going to be here when they arrive. Get dressed, Myron."

I grabbed my clothes and got into them quickly. Once I was dressed, Anoki pulled the door open, pausing long enough to look at the ragged split in the metal. "I'll have to wire money back to the owner to cover the damages," he said. "Come on. And don't run. Just walk at a steady pace."

I snagged my sneaks, cap, and shades and followed him out the door. As I hurried along the walkway, I could hear the other motel guests moving around in their rooms, obviously disturbed by the sounds of my earlier struggle with the spirit and my sexual escapade with Anoki and whatever the thing was that had joined us. The guests were trying to open their doors, to peer out the window and see what the hell was going on, but I could sense the vague, ghostly force that kept the doors shut, kept the blinds from opening. Some of the guests banged on their doors in frustration. The sounds of their breathing, their heartbeats, made my stomach hanker all the more.

"Where's the car?" I asked uneasily. The sooner we got away from there, the better.

In response, Anoki waved his hand, and I heard the Beemer's engine purr to life. When we rounded the corner of the building, the car was there with its doors open. We slid in. As soon as the doors were shut and I'd fastened my seat belt, I flipped down the sun visor and looked in the mirror mounted on the back.

A demon stared out at me.

I'd never seen a real demon before, but the image in the mirror would have worked just fine as a dictionary illustration of one. My small, triangular, curved, and wickedly serrated teeth, and even the whites of my wide, almond-shaped eyes, were deep black. They were set in a face of such absolute pitch black it all but blended into the darkness within the car. My cheekbones were high and angular, my nostrils slanted and flared, my ears Spock-like, and my tongue tapered to a point so sharp I was willing to bet it could pierce flesh.

I touched my face with my fingers and exhaled softly and slowly. "Wow."

Beside me, Anoki waved his hand, and the visor quickly folded itself back into place. "Admire your beauty later," he said.

He drove calmly out of the parking lot, turning onto Nebler Road and heading back toward Killebrew. We'd gone barely half a mile when the flickering strobes of a Shelby County sheriff's car appeared ahead, approaching from the opposite direction. I looked over my shoulder as the white-and-green car passed us, siren screaming, and then turned into the motel parking lot.

CHAPTER
FOURTEEN

"WE LEFT just in time." I ran my fingers over my face again and realized that my skin was as hard and cold as ice. I looked at Anoki, irritated. "I thought you were gonna gum things up before I switched completely over."

"I did," said Anoki. "You progressed a bit further than I would have preferred, but you are well shy of the full transformation."

"Yeah? Well, maybe you could've stopped things right were you wanted 'em if you hadn't run off and left me trapped back there with that damn spirit babysitter."

Anoki shot me a level gaze. "Myron, remember. You have to remain calm."

"Right. Okay." I inhaled deeply and then blew out the breath through my mouth.

"Uncontrolled emotion," Anoki continued, "speeds up the transformation. For the moment, I have lulled your predator soul to sleep, so to speak, but I need your help to keep it there. That 'damn spirit babysitter' triggered the process. As for my leaving you, that was to help the process along. The anxiety of finding me gone pushed the transformation into overdrive."

"Well, thanks a lot." The anger kept humming within me. "You owe me twenty bucks."

Anoki frowned at me, confused. "What?"

"According to my friend Bette, that's the going rate for a hooker in these parts."

"Myron, what are you talking about?"

"You had your fun back there in bed, got your rocks off. But you didn't even kiss me. All I got out of it is a sore asshole." I was finally a man, legally and physically, and in a few hours I'd be checking out of this world without ever knowing what it was like to put my dick inside another guy. It hardly seemed fair. And damn it, I *hated* that fucking ghost-thing for taking a part of Anoki that was *mine*.

Pain and regret filled Anoki's face. "I'm sorry," he said. "I didn't mean for any of that to happen. I was very attracted to you from the moment I first saw you seven months ago—"

"You've been watching me for seven months?"

"Yes. You must have just hit puberty then, which is substantially delayed in the afflicted. Puberty activates the curse, and that is what brought you to my attention. When I came for you this morning, you were wearing those loose jeans with no underwear, and you kept giving me glimpses of your butt. Every glimpse made me want you desperately more. You are a very beautiful soul, Myron Mitchell. And when I saw you naked on the bed back there, it was more than I could resist. I had to have you. But I shouldn't have taken you, not under those circumstances. When I am that aroused, I am neither gentle nor considerate. Worse, taking you may have cost us both dearly."

"Yeah, that's another thing. You didn't use a condom." The talks my parents had with me about sex, and Coach Frieda's lectures in health and hygiene class, came back to me frightfully. "How could you do what you did to me without putting on a condom? I mean, considering what's going to happen to me after my twenty-four hours are up, I guess it doesn't really matter as far as I'm concerned, but you—"

"Myron, you're a virgin—or at least you were until twenty minutes ago. And the curse protects you from anything that would inhibit your ability to hunt and kill, including disease. Plus I have certain protections of my own. Sexually transmitted pathogens are the least of our worries in this. The point is that I shouldn't have had sex with you. I'm sorry that it left you feeling used. You deserve more than that. I apologize, and I promise you I will never touch you sexually again."

"You won't?"

"*Never* again."

"Well… you didn't really make my butt all that sore."

Anoki's attention was fully focused on his driving now. "No?"

"No. Actually, I kind of… sort of liked what you did to me."

"It is strange. I have known of you only seven months now, and I've only had a few hours of direct contact with you. But, in so many ways, you seem to be the… complement to my soul I have always needed. Stranger still, it feels as if you have been missing from my life for so very long a time." He paused, his gaze through the windshield becoming distant. For a moment, a smile tugged at the corners of his mouth, and suddenly I wanted to take his hand. But before I could move, he shook his head and the contented smile was gone. "Nevertheless," he continued, frowning now, "what I did back at the motel placed us both at risk. It was foolish of me, and it shouldn't have happened."

Three times now Anoki had mentioned the danger in our having sex, and he clearly wasn't referring to any of the complications the average person frets over. I realized the cold, ancient thing in him was a spirit of some kind, one that had probably taken up residence in his body. Somehow, it had made itself a separate physical form while Anoki was screwing me. "What was that thing back there in bed with us? I saw its arm, which looked human, but I know it wasn't a man."

A grimace flickered over Anoki's face. "That's enough for you to know on that subject."

"Please. Tell me what it is. If it's a danger to me, I think I have a right to know."

He nodded reluctantly. "I suppose you're right. Remember my telling you that a necromancer runs the risk of having one or more spirits attach themselves to him?"

"Yeah. Is that what happened to you?"

He nodded. "What attached itself to me is a demiurge, an unformed essence as old as the world, something that shapes and molds things. Demiurges are extremely powerful but lack initiative and imagination, and so seek direction from other beings. This demiurge—

or my shade, as I call it—is one that has formed a deep emotional bond. It is, for lack of a better phrase, in love with me, and so jealous that it will not even let me make a friend. Anyone who gets closer to me than it likes is made to feel uncomfortable in the extreme—numb, cold, sick, terrified—until they have no choice but to back off."

"So that's what made me feel so creepy when I tried to flirt with you?"

"Yes."

"But… if it's so jealous it wouldn't even let me flirt, how were you able to have sex with me?"

For the first time since I'd known him, Anoki looked embarrassed. "I struck a bargain with it. My shade has wanted physical intimacy with me for years, and I always resisted that. I wanted you so badly, however, that I offered to let the demiurge mate with me if it allowed me to mate with you."

"It wasn't just a spirit in bed with us, though," I protested, feeling like I was missing something here. "There was another guy there. I felt his weight. I saw part of him."

"My shade is capable of manifesting a physical body for itself. Remember, it is a shaper of things. It doesn't have to possess another's body, the way ghosts and demons occasionally do."

Part of me thought this was all so much crap. But there I was, a half-demonic killing machine who could see spiritual forces at work. Who was I to question the existence of a lovesick supernatural so-and-so that could make manly bodies at will? "Okay, but it got what it wanted, right? It screwed you while you screwed me. Where's the danger to you and me in that?"

"The danger is in its perceiving that I feel more for you than I do for it. If it feels that I am rejecting it in favor of you, it will torment us both in ways you cannot begin to imagine. It has had several masters over the eons, some of whom were quite creative when it comes to evil acts. And it remembers everything it is commanded to do."

Neither of us had anything more to say after that uplifting thought. I could detect no part of Anoki's "shade" around him at the moment. The thing must have hidden itself from my senses again. Or maybe it had gone off somewhere. But just where the hell would something like that go?

Anoki turned off Nebler onto a narrow street that led through a field of scrub and spindly wildflowers. The field gave way to a wide stand of trees, beyond which lay a new residential subdivision that had recently begun construction. Three lots had been graded, each sporting the wooden skeleton of a house. There were no people about, but there were plenty of rabbits, raccoons, and squirrels, plus a few deer and a pair of foxes. Anoki pulled off the road and parked in the dark under the trees, and then turned me loose.

Slipping behind a tree, I shucked my clothes. I went after the animals that I figured would put up the most fight, meaning the foxes and a couple of the raccoons. That lessened the guilt over what I did to them. I'll spare you the bloody details.

When I was done eating, I uncapped the subdivision's recently installed fire hydrant and showered off the gore. (Hunting can be messy.) If I had time to become human again before my morning appointment with the demon, I'd undoubtedly be sickened at the thought of my meal, but for now I was pleasantly full, and that made me feel even more relaxed.

After I was dressed, I climbed back into the car. Anoki drove into Killebrew. I wanted neither to see nor be seen, so I pulled my cap low on my head, slipped on the shades, and kept my eyes on the dashboard.

"Who is that?"

I had fallen asleep again but remained in my semi-transformed state. I raised my head and saw that we were in front of Coach Frieda's house. Bette's car was gone, but the coach's car was still in the driveway. The porch light was off, and in the darkness, some guy was standing on the steps, spraying water over the front of the house with a garden hose. Judging from the streams of water running down the sidewalk, he had already soaked the lawn and the shrubs. I took off the shades for an unobstructed look. His body glowed red under my inhuman vision, and his scent came to me clearly, even over the acrid smell of the chlorine in the water.

"His name is LaVelle. He goes to my school. Why the hell is he washing everything down?" I hissed at Anoki.

"To erase scents and any other traces that might lead us to the necromancer," Anoki replied. "It seems someone was expecting you."

CHAPTER
FIFTEEN

LAVELLE began to walk along the porch, directing the water back over the yard again. When he turned, a cold, dark spot appeared in the neon warmth of his body, at the base of his neck, just above his chest.

"He's marked," I gasped.

"So I see. He could already be possessed. I would have to get closer to be certain." Anoki unbuckled his seat belt and, as if taking its cue, the engine abruptly shut off. "Do you sense anyone else? In the house or in the yard?"

I sniffed once, my mind parsing the scents that came to me. "It's just LaVelle, nobody else."

"Wait here. I'll call if I need you." He got out of the car and crossed the wet walkway to the porch.

LaVelle followed Anoki's approach. He shut off the water and dropped the hose. He moved toward the steps, as if to meet Anoki, but I could hear the sudden spike in his heartbeat, and my bet was that he was going to make a run for it. I grabbed the door handle, ready to jump out and stop him.

When he reached the edge of the porch, LaVelle turned his lips up in a little smile. He probably thought he had Anoki faked out and was going to make a clean getaway. Anoki had longer legs, but LaVelle was pretty fast. Still, Anoki, as it turned out, had some fast moves of his own. Just as LaVelle was about to jump off the porch, Anoki blocked him.

LaVelle's eyes got big, his smile froze, and he half stumbled as he reached out, grabbing the porch rail to steady himself. "Hey, what's up." He somehow put a good bit of cockiness into the greeting, but the fear coming off his body was as pungent as hot tar.

Anoki mounted the steps and got right up on LaVelle, using his height and implacable eyes for maximum intimidation. "This isn't your property," he snapped, biting the end off each word. "What are you doing here?"

"Just... watering the grass. That's all."

"Why? Who asked you to do this?"

"A friend of mine."

Suddenly and sharply, Anoki brought his face down to LaVelle's level, forcing him to back up. "Give me this friend's name."

LaVelle might have been more afraid of the person who sent him than he was of Anoki. Or maybe he'd finally begun to wonder whether Anoki had any more right to be on the premises than he did. Whatever the reason, his backbone seemed to grow in at that moment, and he defiantly clamped his lips shut.

"The name," Anoki demanded. "I want it."

"Wh-why should I tell you anything?" LaVelle actually put something that sounded like scorn in his shaky voice. "Just who the fuck are you, anyway?"

Anoki's face went calm except for the cold glitter of anger in his eyes. "I am someone you would be wise not to defy."

LaVelle's gulp was so loud I'd have caught it even without the supernatural hearing.

Anoki waited, but LaVelle didn't give up the information. "There is more at stake here than you realize," Anoki said finally. "There are lives in danger, including your own."

LaVelle gave a soft snort. "Yeah, right."

Anoki raised his hand. It was an unhurried, casual gesture, the kind you'd make to wave off a bothersome bug.

With a loud, startled gasp, LaVelle slammed instantly to his knees.

Anoki folded his arms across his chest. "Little boy, there are forces in this world that are far beyond your understanding. That makes them no less real or deadly. Someone involved with those forces has laid a claim on you, and will trade your body off to be used in ways that will most likely kill you. That someone may be the very person who sent you here tonight to 'water the grass'. For your own sake, tell me who that is."

LaVelle had always struck me as the kind of guy who was good at talking the talk but not much else. Over the years, he'd gotten out of a lot of butt-kickings by convincing bigger guys that he was someone who'd reach down their throats, yank out their livers, and fry up the fresh organs with onions. Same thing with playing defense in basketball. He was very good at taunting opponents into making stupid mistakes. Kneeling on that porch before Anoki, he was stinking of fright, but you could see the calculation in his face as he tried to work out a getaway. He was sneaky, all right.

Sneaky enough to creep up on me in the woods and knock me unconscious.

Damn. It made sense. The fear I'd perceived in those woods was the same I smelled on LaVelle now. LaVelle had taken me down when the necromancer Anoki was after had lured me into that circle—the same necromancer who'd sent LaVelle here to wash away anything that might enable me to follow them again.

I opened the car door.

Anoki heard the sound of the door and shot me a warning look. He motioned for me to get back in the car. I had my eyes on LaVelle. One way or another, I was going to make my friend tell us who the necromancer was. If, in the process, I got a chance to pay him back for the sucker punch to my head... well, it would only be in the interest of rooting out the bad guy and finding Bette.

LaVelle looked at me, and his eyes went blank with disbelief. I started to grin, but in that same moment, I picked up a moldy, dead odor and a faint rustling noise. LaVelle opened his mouth to scream, just as I realized that he was not looking at me at all. I spun around.

Something swept past me in a flash. In the instant it took me to turn back, the thing was scrabbling up onto the porch. It moved bonelessly, its arms flouncing about with loose aimlessness, its legs horribly bowed, giving it a monstrously crablike appearance. It was dressed in old, ragged denim overalls and a tattered green shirt. Beneath a black baseball cap, there was only a bulging mass of dirty brown straw. My paranormal vision showed me more. There was a gray-blue aura pulsating wildly through and around the thing, an unmistakable intelligence that inhabited the inhuman form and directed its movements. The spirit was furious, and it was clearly after LaVelle.

A hoarse squeak issued from LaVelle's gaping mouth, and he backed distraughtly against the wall of the house. Anoki raised his hands, but before whatever spirit he called upon could act, the scarecrow flicked one of its arms in his direction. The dirty blue life force lashed him, and Anoki slid swiftly backward across the porch on his feet, as if shoved by some powerful gust. The scarecrow's left arm whipped around LaVelle's neck like a hungry boa.

I'm ashamed to say that I watched all this frozen in stunned, open-mouthed silence, my brain unwilling to accept what I was seeing. This was no human dressed up in straw and old clothes, as I'd suspected after hearing Robbie describe what he saw. The thing leaped over the porch railing onto the lawn, then leaped up and over the house, taking the gagging, desperately struggling LaVelle with it.

I might have stood there on Coach Frieda's wet lawn for the rest of the night if Anoki hadn't screamed at me. "Get that boy back!"

Galvanized, I raced around the house into the backyard and vaulted the wooden fence, just in time to see the scarecrow running down the alley in long, loping strides. It managed to keep LaVelle's head elevated, but the poor dude's legs and feet were bouncing along the ground in a rough-and-tumble manner that sent sympathetic phantom pains up my own limbs. LaVelle was choking. Clutching at the snakelike arm, he gave short, terrified gasps as he fought to breathe.

I went after them, my legs churning up more speed than a car could muster in the alley, keeping pace but unable to close the distance. For something so "floppy doppy," that damned scarecrow was *fast*. And smart. It cut across somebody else's lawn, carefully sticking to the shadows. When it reached the street, it took a flying leap up and over.

I hurtled over the street, coming down on all fours. I began to lope like some sleek, powerful panther and found myself flying over the dewy ground at a blistering pace. The scarecrow dragged LaVelle into the woods, disappearing among the trees. Smart move, but useless. I could still hear both the thing's rustling movements and LaVelle's pained, frightful grunts, as well as smell the scarecrow's death odor. The red glow of LaVelle's body and the grayish smolder of the spirit itself were as clear as beacons in the dark. There was no way the scarecrow was going to lose me in these woods.

Suddenly, I knew where the thing was going. The circle. It was taking LaVelle to that circle where Bette's trail abruptly and completely vanished last night. My heart began to rage. Every instinct told me that if the thing reached that circle, LaVelle would be lost.

My four-limbed gait had me gaining on them. The scarecrow apparently sensed the rapid narrowing of the gap between us. Its faceless head spun completely around on its neck, and it hissed at me, an eerie, grating sound, like fingernails scraping a chalkboard. Tendrils of its gray, ghostly substance shot upward, slicing at the treetops, and severed limbs crashed down in its wake. The action bought it precious seconds, forcing me to break stride and weave about to avoid getting struck by the falling branches.

I cleared the last of the timber and poured on the speed to make up the lost ground. But the thing wasn't done. Its essence reached out and stirred up everything on the ground—leaves, sticks, dirt, rocks, broken branches—whipping them into a howling, blinding cloud. I plunged into the mass before I could stop. Every part of my body was assailed, blasted with flying debris, some of it large and heavy and painful. Groping around, I found a tree trunk. I dug in with my claws and climbed up until I could see again.

We were closer to the circle than I'd realized. It was visible through the treetops, a darkened bare patch some thirty feet across, barely a quarter mile ahead. The glowing forms of LaVelle and the scarecrow were almost there, moving fast.

Damn.

I began to leap from tree to tree, passing over the still-whirling storm of debris below, moving fast but not as fast as I could have on the ground. "Stop!" I screamed in helpless frustration. I threw myself down, knowing that I was nowhere near close enough, even as the scarecrow bounded upward. The thing came down in the center of the circle, hauling the now screaming LaVelle after it.

They plunged into the ground, vanishing from even my supernatural sight.

There had to be a conduit of some kind, one that would undoubtedly close within seconds. I had to get there before that happened. I hit the lower branch of a tree and pushed off with my legs, going into a high arc and then dropping down into the circle.

I met hard, unyielding earth.

"LaVelle!" I was *not* going to lose another friend to that thing, even one who had tried to crack my head open just the night before. I clawed at the ground, sending huge chunks of dirt flying through the air. If it took the rest of my life, I would dig down and find my friends, and then I would tear that marauding spirit apart with my bare hands. Or maybe with my teeth.

I heard Anoki's footsteps, softly crackling among the dry leaves, but I ignored him. My work was more important.

"Myron."

"Get outta here, Anoki."

"Look at me."

I had no intention of stopping. The compulsion to turn rose in me suddenly, however, and in the next moment, I was standing upright, looking back at him.

He stood at the edge of the circle, arms at his side, surrounded by what could only be described as an aura of serenity. "Myron," he said quietly, "listen to me carefully. Come out of the circle."

Some part of me, swiftly dimming but still present enough to assert itself, wanted to roar at him and go back to my work. I opened my mouth, and then I hesitated.

"This could all have been a ploy to trap you," Anoki said, his gaze steady, his voice soothing. "If the necromancer is here, he can close the circle and it will hold you. You must come out of there now."

I reached out toward the ground. "LaVelle...."

"You won't find your friend by digging. The opening the spirit made there would take them elsewhere, into another part of the world, or perhaps the ether itself, but not underground." He reached out with both hands, opening his arms. This time, there was no mistaking the tenderness in his once-fearsome green eyes. "Come to me."

It was an invitation I couldn't refuse. I climbed out of the car-sized hole I'd gouged in the ground and walked toward him. As I drew near, I encountered a wall of incredible cold, the kind that must exist between the stars. It made me want to curl up and simply die. I gasped and stumbled to a halt. Anoki frowned and lowered his arms, then gave a shake of his head so slight that someone with mere human vision would never have caught it.

The cold faded slowly, almost grudgingly. Once it was fully gone, I sat down awkwardly on the ground, draping my hands over my knees. My lungs seemed to have been without air for about a hundred years. I gasped heavily, trying to catch my breath.

Anoki didn't move closer or try to touch me. "Just rest. You'll feel better in a moment."

I wanted to ask him what the hell had just happened, but something in his eyes stopped me. It was that deep, pervading sadness again. Granted, Anoki hadn't exactly given me his life story, but from what I could see, he had it all. Great looks. Fantastic body. Intelligence. Money. Power. What reason could a person like that possibly have to carry such terrible misery in his heart?

"That spirit may have gotten away with your friend," said Anoki, "but we now have the means of putting everything right. I have the necromancer's circle. With it, I can call up the spirit he last invoked here."

That caught my attention. I looked up at him. "You can bring that scarecrow back?"

"If it was the last thing summoned here, I can. But, Myron, above all, let me do the talking. Do not engage the entity in conversation."

No problem. I didn't want to talk to it. I just wanted a chance to rip it into bite-sized pieces.

Anoki stepped past me, moving closer to the circle. He raised one hand and a wind whipped around the perimeter of the circle. With my curse-enhanced vision, I could see strands of pale, vaporous energy rise from the circumference to form a hazy dome over the circle. He shifted to his right, placing himself squarely between me and the circle, and then bowed his head and began to speak. His whispers were in that weird language he'd used briefly when we were having sex, the words so old they made me shiver.

For several long minutes, nothing happened. Then the ground within the circle stirred like a living thing in torment, and suddenly something was standing there.

CHAPTER
SIXTEEN

IT LOOKED like somebody's kid brother. The thing appeared to be a
boy who was maybe twelve, right about five feet, with big gray eyes
and straight black hair that hung in long bangs down to his eyebrows
but was cropped short over the rest of his head. With his bronze skin,
he seemed to be Hispanic, or perhaps Native American, like Anoki. He
was slender and wore green fatigues, big, black scuffed work boots
with the laces undone, and a yellow plaid short-sleeved shirt,
unbuttoned to reveal a white T-shirt.

I knew the body was just a convenient shell, but my senses
couldn't detect sight or scent of the invasive spirit. It didn't help that
Anoki seemed determined to block me from getting a good look. Spirits
preferred to keep their actual forms invisible to human eyes, and this
one—like the shade inhabiting Anoki's body—was going to great
lengths to hide itself from my enhanced vision.

The boy's expression was decidedly surly. "What the hell do you
want?" he spat. "I was just about to get some fool woman run up on a
corrupting-the-morals-of-a-minor charge."

"Information is all I need," Anoki said in the kind of voice that
should have made the boy-thing mind its tone with him.

The boy sniffed disdainfully and cocked an eyebrow at him. "In
exchange for what?"

"I'll pay the standard price—your freedom from the circle."

"Hell no. I want more."

"There will be no negotiation. You give me information on all the topics of my choice, I set you free. Or you keep the information and I trap you forever in the circle. Your choice."

The boy scowled, and all the grass within the circle blackened instantly, as if seared with invisible, scorching heat. "Bitch," he snarled at Anoki through clenched teeth. Then his eyes narrowed even more. "Who is that behind you?"

"That is not your concern."

"Oh, I get it. It's some little flower boy too scared to speak for himself."

I shot to my feet, anger flaring. "What did you call me?"

Anoki turned and shook his head warningly, eyes flaring.

The boy laughed at me, then looked at Anoki. "Why'd you bring *that* thing with you? Devil's Fire ain't got nothin' on me. Neither does fairy dust." He did a little twinkling dance.

I snarled, baring claws and shark teeth. "Let him outta there," I growled as I started to pass Anoki. The tall Native American gestured, and something invisible grabbed me around the waist, holding me back.

"Oh, you want in on this, sucker?" The boy-thing grinned, gray eyes shining.

"I *am* in on this!" I shot back. "And I wanna know what you did the last time you came through this circle."

"Cool. I tell you that—only that—and I go free."

Anoki gave me a look that said, *I am going to choke the life out of you when this is over.* It sobered me enough that I was able to rein in my hot temper and step back.

"Well. This could take a while." The boy leaned over and stretched out as if lying down on a bed, using one hand to prop up his head. His body hovered three feet off the ground. "We might as well relax and be civil now. My name's Benito."

Unable to stop myself, I snorted. "You lying sack of—"

"Okay, okay," the boy said, waving his free hand in a conciliatory gesture. "That was the name this meat bag went by before I moved in.

But it's the name I use for everything now. So, I introduced myself. You gonna play nice and do the same?"

"Yeah." I gestured, first at myself, then at Anoki, saying, "I'm Fuck and he's You."

Anoki sighed wearily.

Benito's eyebrows arched, disappearing entirely beneath his bangs. It was a damned good simulation of shock. "Wow. Who raised you? A couple of goats?"

Anger flashed white hot in my head. I sprang, screeching like a cat. Before I even got halfway to the circle, something grabbed me from behind and slammed me to the ground. The force yanked my body over the forest floor until I found myself looking up into Anoki's face.

He knelt over me, green eyes blazing, but his voice was steady and soothing. "This is probably our only chance to get information from one of the necromancer's direct contacts, and you are ruining it," he said, keeping the volume low so that Benito would not overhear. "Not to mention the fact that, if you keep this up, you will trigger the transformation again and force me to take action neither of us wants. Now, sit here, stay calm, and be quiet."

It was hard to fight back my increasingly brutal impulses, but I knew that if I didn't, I'd lose my reprieve and there would be nothing I could do to help Bette or LaVelle. I nodded my compliance at Anoki, and the ghostly force pinning me to the ground lifted. I sat up, shaking dry leaves out of my clothes, and tried to recover my dignity.

Benito gave me that greedy, amused grin of his. "Okay, then. Now that 'Fuck' has been put in his place, I suppose the adults can talk." He shifted his attention to Anoki, ignoring me completely. "Let's see. My prior appearance here was last night. I'd been in negotiations with the summoner three days running, but I was holding out for a payment that would actually do me some good. And last night, I finally got offered something that made it worth my while to play errand boy again."

"What was the errand the summoner charged you with?" Anoki asked.

"Nothing too big. Just deliver an offering."

"What was the offering?"

Benito rolled his eyes. "A human soul. Duh. Same as always." He stuck a finger in his ear and began rooting around, looking bored. "I'd done it three times before but, come on, it's no fun. If you're gonna call me up, at least give me something interesting to do. That's why I held out for a bigger price last night."

"And what was the price you were to be paid?"

"Oh, no, Mr. Broken Heart." Benito smiled, wagging a finger. "That wasn't what you and your little fruit boy there asked for. You wanted to know what I did last night, not what I got paid."

Anoki hooked his thumbs in his front jeans pockets. He shoved down so hard it was a miracle he didn't tear the pockets right off his pants. "To whom did you deliver the offering last night?"

"Well, that's the thing. I never actually made the delivery. The payment fell through at the last minute, so I backed out of the deal." Benito sat up on his unseen, airborne perch, bracing his hands on his knees. "You know, pumpkin, I like you. Even if you are keeping company with a brick-brain. I'm gonna give you a freebie. The price I was supposed to get was a burnt offering all my own. I understand the subject was some sort of immortal halfling, so it wouldn't actually die, but I was really looking forward to the agony while it was being toasted. There's nothing like the taste of hot buttered pain." He smacked his lips sloppily.

"You said the deal fell through. How did that come about?"

"That fool halfling got away before it could be cooked. Naturally, I don't give something for nothing—except to you, dear pumpkin. And since the summoner couldn't pay, I was free to go about my business. Which, as always, was really about pleasing myself. I took off to Madrid and caused a delicious nine-car pileup on the Gran Via. It's truly amazing how stupidly humans react when one punk kid runs into the street. You'd think they would just plow over the little snot and keep going. But nooo, they actually try to stop their cars—"

Anoki raised his hand, stopping the boy-thing. "Was your action in Madrid done on behalf of the summoner?"

"No, honeycomb, that was all for me."

"Please only give me information that is related to last night's summoning. Did you see the soul you were to carry as an offering?"

"Never got that far. Remember the whole deal-fell-through thing?"

"You said that you delivered three prior offerings—"

"I did, and I already know where you're going, so let me shoot you down before you get there. I'm not telling you who I delivered those souls to, because that wasn't part of last night's transaction. Pumpkin."

Something about the way the obnoxious, snotty creep said "pumpkin" and "honeycomb" made my skin crawl. His tone was much too familiar, not to mention nasty, and I had to gnaw on my lip to keep from exploding.

If Benito was dancing on Anoki's nerves, the dude wasn't showing it. Anoki kept his flat, steady gaze on the boy-demon. "What about the soul you were to deliver last night? Which demon was that going to?"

Benito gave a casual shrug. "Geryon."

Anoki froze. Completely. I mean, for about fifteen seconds, he didn't take a breath or even blink. I watched him, anxiety swelling slowly though my gut in a cold wave. He didn't seem afraid himself, just stunned, but that was enough to let me know that things had gotten a hell of a lot more complicated for us.

Suddenly, he drew in a breath. A few strands of his hair had come loose, and he smoothed them back from his face. His eyes became steely as he faced down the grinning boy. "At least tell me whether the prior deliveries were to demons of higher or lower order than Geryon."

Benito screwed up his face and began to chew on his thumb. He twisted his shoulders in tight little movements, his expression beaming big fake doses of innocence, reluctance, and doubt, as if grappling with some monumental dilemma. Finally, he smiled, pulled his thumb away, and said, "Lower," in a growling whisper.

Anoki drew in another breath. Anger glistened on his face now. "Who was the summoner?"

"Cookie, there is no way you get *that* for free." Benito hopped off his invisible seat, his boots clumping loudly when he hit the ground. "That's part of what I know from last night, not what I did. A technicality, but you know how it goes. Now, if you're willing to bargain, maybe I can give you a name. Or two. A fair trade. I get the batty halfling you've got there to make up for the one I missed last night, and you get the information you want. How does that sound? Hmm? Come on, now, this offer won't stay on the table long—"

"I already told you," Anoki said in a tense voice. "I am not bargaining with you, little peon."

"Well. If you're going to be all insulting...." Benito sniffed, offended. "I believe our business here is done. So, if you don't mind, break the circle and I'll be on my way. I'm sensitive, you know, and I need to do something to soothe my hurt feelings. There's this kid out in Denver I got hooked on painkillers. Think I'll go see if I can get him to move on up to some of the real hard stuff, steal his pop's gun and knock over a twenty-four-hour drug store that has a big, armed moose of a security guard. Maybe I can get the kid shot. That'll make me feel better."

Anoki pointed his finger at the boy, and a wind rippled around the edge of the circle. The pale dome of energy evaporated instantly. "Go, before I change my mind and feed you to one of your superiors."

"Thanks, pumpkin. Ta-ta for now." Benito waved at Anoki and then blew a wet, noisy kiss in my direction. He turned and walked off into the woods, heading for the street. It only took a few seconds for the red glow of his host body to be swallowed by the darkness.

CHAPTER
SEVENTEEN

I DIDN'T say a word to Anoki on our trek back to the Beemer or during our drive across town. I was struggling the whole while to restrain my anger. It infuriated me, of course, to know that LaVelle had been willing to torch my butt to get in good with some punk demon wannabe, but a fair amount of my rage was directed at Anoki.

On the east side of town, close to Saint Mary's Hospital, Anoki pulled into a Taco Bell drive-through and ordered himself a taco salad, sans the ground beef, cheese, and sour cream. Suddenly, words started flying bitterly from my mouth. "That's so dumb! Why get a taco salad without the stuff that makes it a damn taco salad? Why not just go to a place that has a frickin' garden salad if that's what you want?"

Anoki didn't even bat an eye at the outburst. Having placed the order, he pulled ahead to the pickup window. The cashier, a plump, smiling woman in her midthirties, announced the total and stuck out her hand for payment. As Anoki dug down in his pocket, the cashier looked at me, shrouded in the darkness of the car's passenger side. She squinted, puzzled.

"What's that your friend's wearing?" the woman asked. "Some kind of costume?"

"You might say that," Anoki replied, forking over the money.

"Hey, that's really neat." The woman squinted at me again. "It looks like he's not all there."

"Trust me, he isn't."

Laughing, the woman slid the window shut.

Now I was mad at the cashier as well. "Is the stupid woman blind or something? What the hell was she talking about?"

"The curse camouflages you in shadows to make it easier for you to stalk prey. The blackness of your skin makes you blend into the darkness, and you become almost invisible." Anoki turned to me. "Now, since your anger obviously has nothing to do with either my dinner or that cashier's vision, let's talk about what's really bothering you."

"Yeah, all right, let's do that. That crazy little demon you called up back there is plain evil. He ran off to hurt people, maybe even kill somebody, all for the fun of it. And you just let him go. Not that I'm trying to get out of anything, but you're gonna chain me up in hell for being a menace to society and—"

"Myron." He looked into my eyes but didn't say anything else for several seconds. In that time, the edge came off my boiling emotions. I found myself settling back in my seat.

"Sorry," I said, giving him a little smile. "I don't know why I was feeling so upset about everything." I laughed. If I got any mellower, I'd melt into a warm, gooey puddle on the Beemer's fine nubuck leather seat.

"I understand your concern, Myron. But you should know that, while Benito is dangerous—as all demons are—he poses no immediate threat to any ordinary person here in town. He is a demon who revels in pain—"

"Is he the one you're gonna feed me to?"

"No. He isn't strong enough to hold you very long. You'd fight him with Devil's Fire, cripple him, and set yourself free."

"But he said Devil's Fire can't touch him."

"He lied. It's what demons do. Benito is a demon of the Seventh Order, the weakest class."

"Well, how do you know he wasn't lying about all that stuff he told you?"

"If I discover that he lied to me, I can summon him back, trap him in a circle, and make him wish he hadn't. He knows that as well as I do."

"Oh. Okay." It was hard to speak. The words seemed to be thickening in my throat. Or maybe my mouth was shrinking. I propped the side of my face against the headrest. "I think I'm drunk."

"You're fine," said Anoki.

"I never drank before. Alcoholic stuff, I mean. Honest."

"I believe you."

"Hey. How old are you? Can I ask that?"

"You just did. I am 119 years old."

"Really?" That struck me as funny for some reason. I giggled. "Wow, that's *old*. I thought you were, like, twenty-one or twenty-two. You're so tall." My eyes traveled from his head to his feet and back again. "Hey. Can I have some of you?"

Anoki's eyebrows slowly went up. "Take a moment," he advised, "then try that question again."

His reaction puzzled me for a second. I replayed my last question in my head. Oh. "I meant some of your height!" I thought about it some more. "Not that I don't want to... you know, fuck you too. I do. Really, really bad. You have a great-looking butt."

Something very close to a smile crept across Anoki's lips. He shook his head, amused. For a moment, he stared at me. "Even wearing the face of Satan," he said, his voice soft and low, "you have the prettiest brown eyes."

My face got hot at that, and I wanted to lean over and kiss him, the impulse so strong it actually hurt. I probably would have worked up the nerve and done it, but the cashier appeared again, leaning out of the pickup window toward Anoki with a large white bag and two bottled waters. "Here you go, sweetheart," she said.

"Thank you." Anoki put the food in the backseat and drove quickly across the parking lot. He parked in a nice, shadowy corner behind the restaurant.

"Here, drink this." He passed one of the bottles to me.

"That's really nice of you. Thanks." I took the bottle and stared at him, smiling in a way that probably hinted at a lack of brain function. "Hey. What if Benito goes after some kid and hurts him, like he said he would?"

"He won't, not tonight." Anoki pulled the lid off the salad and squeezed lemon juice over the greenery. "Right now, the person who's in the biggest danger from Benito is you."

"Me?" That struck me as funny, but for some reason, I couldn't bring out a laugh.

"Yes. You're immortal, but you can still be hurt in certain ways. Benito may not be able to imprison you for long, but in the time he does hold you, he can inflict torture that would kill an ordinary mortal within minutes. That sustained level of pain would put him in heaven. So to speak." He twisted the cap off his bottle of water and took a sip. "Of course, he'd like nothing more than to get you to strike a bargain that forces you to bind yourself to him. You wouldn't be able to use Devil's Fire against him then, and you would be his to torment for as long as he chooses. You're too much of a temptation for him to move on to anyone else now. He's going to come after you."

"Let him. I got something for his evil ass." I raised a fist, intending to shake it defiantly for emphasis. The fist had other ideas, however, and punched a hole in the Beemer's roof.

Ooh. Dumb fist.

Anoki sighed.

I forced myself to look at him. He was motionless. His eyes were fixed, staring straight ahead. He looked as if he had a headache. No, a migraine. A *bad* migraine.

"Hey, sorry," I said in my thick voice. "No worries, though. I can fix this." I reached up.

"Never mind, I'll take care of it," Anoki said quickly. He waved his hand, and the ragged pieces of the damaged roof pulled inward and knitted themselves together. In a downpour, the patch would leak like an open faucet, but at least it was less conspicuous. "That should hold it until I can get it repaired."

"Sorry," I said again. "Damn that Benito…."

"Myron, stop worrying about Benito. When I get the chance, I am going to rip him out of that body he's inhabited, but he is the least of our problems right now."

I sensed that there was a question to be asked here, but I couldn't seem to get my brain into gear. I looked helplessly at Anoki.

He plunged ahead. "There are seven orders of demons. The Seventh Order contains the weakest and least influential—imps, tricksters, what some would call the scum of hell. The First Order contains the fallen angels, the spirits God evicted directly from his presence. Geryon is a demon of the Second Order."

"So, it's a big deal that this necrowhoever you're after wants to send something to Geryon?"

"It is an extremely 'big deal'. The necromancer has been working his way up through the orders, which indicates that the lower demons are unable to give him what he wants. Whatever his goal is, it is apparently something only a very powerful demon can provide."

"So. The necrowhosey is after something really bad, huh?" I slumped further down in my seat and closed my eyes. In that peaceful darkness, someone snored. How rude….

A huge, cold thing grabbed my entire head and pulled me up until I was practically levitating in the car. "What? What?" I yelped, suddenly wide-eyed. I tried to look around for the gorilla that had me in its grip but saw nothing. "Hey, I can't move my head!"

Anoki muttered something angrily beneath his breath. "Pay attention just a bit longer, Myron." The lock on my head vanished, and I dropped down against the backrest again. "Are you with me now?"

"Yeah. Yeah, I'm with you all the way." I felt more alert now than I had a few moments ago, but not by much. "We were talkin' about Gary, right?"

"Geryon. He is a guardian of hell, one of one hundred and forty-four thousand demons who are second in power only to the fallen angels themselves. Among other things, he protects hell's stolen portion of the Unwas."

"Un what?"

"Un*was*. It is the void from which God made the universe, and a source of unlimited power. Satan led a league of rebellious angels in an effort to take the Unwas. They managed to get only a tiny bit of it before they were thrown from God's presence. I suspect this necromancer is after that piece of the Unwas. We can't let him strike a deal with Geryon. It would be disastrous in ways you can't even imagine."

We looked at each other for several seconds without speaking.

I couldn't believe how fucking handsome he was.

Anoki frowned. "Myron? Do you understand?"

"Got it." I gave him a thumbs-up.

That got me an eye roll from Anoki. He turned away and started eating his salad.

I watched him, studying his profile, and a sudden deep sadness settled into my chest like a big bubble. Tears, I knew, were not far behind. Damn. I'd never cried in front of other people, not in third grade when bigger kids bounced me around like a basketball. Not in sixth grade, when Coop accidentally slammed his locker door on my hand and dislocated my thumb. Not even when I sat in the back pew of Southern River Holiness Temple with a crack in my heart as I watched Garrett sob over his mother's casket. Crying made you look weak, and Anoki was the last person on earth I wanted to think of me as weak. So why was I about to break down in front of him for the second time in less than a day?

I made a series of quick, noisy sniffs.

Anoki paused, a forkful of tomato and lettuce halfway to his mouth. "Are you all right?"

"I wish… I wish I had time to get to know you better," I whispered, my voice trembling.

Anoki's face had been open and unguarded, a fact I had not realized until I saw that expressionless veil close over his features. He put the fork down, turning away from me. "Why?"

"You just look so lonely. And... I don't know. I wish I could be your friend."

I hoped that he would turn and look at me, really *look* at me for once, and that maybe he would open up to me, just a little. He blinked a few times and closed his eyes, pinching the bridge of his nose between his thumb and forefinger.

He stayed that way for a very long time.

Then, without opening his eyes, he said, "Myron, you look tired. Why don't you take a nap?"

My lights went out instantly.

CHAPTER
EIGHTEEN

"MYRON. Wake up."

The voice sounded far away. It could wait.

"Myron. Can you hear me?"

No. Go away.

"Myron?"

Five more minutes, okay?

"Wake up. Now!"

My eyes popped open against my will. A tiny bolt of pain went through my head, and I pictured someone driving a spike into my brain with a nail gun. The pain brought an instant clarity that was as sharp as anything. I remembered that I had fallen asleep while Anoki and I were parked at Taco Bell. Now we were outside the emergency entrance of Saint Mary's. It was still dark, and the lot around us was filled with cars. A man stood smoking nervously under a kind of portico designated for ambulance unloading. I don't sleep well in moving cars. The constant vibrations and the hum of the tires over the road keep me so close to the surface of consciousness that I never really get into the deep part of a nap. I must have been dead not to have wakened on the trip from Taco Bell to here.

What the hell did Anoki do to me?

I sat up anxiously. "What's up?"

Anoki sat with his hands folded calmly over the steering wheel. He'd apparently finished his dinner; the bag and bottle were gone. He was staring sharply at the emergency room's automated double doors.

"Pike Wexlar received a telephone call half an hour ago. Afterward, he tried to leave his house. The spirit I placed to keep him there made him violently ill, but he was so determined he crawled out of the house, vomiting the entire way. So I decided to release the spirit and follow him." Anoki pointed. "That's his truck. He went into the emergency room just now."

"Dude probably freaked. Getting sick as a dog will do that to you." I yawned. My bottled water was still in the cup holder. I grabbed it, twisted off the cap, and took a big swig.

"I've been meaning to ask you," said Anoki, "whether you noticed any uncharacteristic behavior among the people at your school. The necromancer has been active for some time. There must be others who have been traded off to spirits and possessed."

"Uncharacteristic how? What do you mean?"

"A teacher who is reckless or unprofessional. A kid who uses out-of-date references. Or who behaves in ways that are too mature. Say, a kid who forgoes things that everyone else enjoys."

"The teachers at my school are all very teacherly, believe me. Unless you want to count Coach Frieda. But then, Pike isn't a student at the school, he's an adult, so technically her fooling around with him is no big deal. As for the kids...." I thought about it. "Well, there's my boy Garrett. He has this whole maturity thing going. I can't tell you how many times he's missed out on doing stuff with me and some of our other friends so he can do something that his dad wants him to do around the house, or study for some test that nobody else is even thinking about."

Anoki shook his head, as if I were the most pathetic creature in a pool of pathetic creatures. "He just sounds like someone with a good sense of responsibility."

"No, that's definitely weird." I took a final swig from the bottle, draining it, and then tossed the empty plastic onto the floor. Anoki flicked a look at me. I snatched up the bottle and placed it back in the cup holder. The skin of my hands was still black, and my fingers ended in claws, so I knew I was still half-demon.

I looked at the clock on the dashboard. It was 11:45 p.m. I'd been asleep for roughly an hour.

An hour out of my one-day life. Gone. Wasted.

I sighed. "You know, Garrett's already got a lot of stuff about his life figured out. He knows he wants to go to the University of Memphis so he'll be close enough to come home and help his dad and his grandma keep up their houses. He's doing his best to keep his GPA over 3.0 so he can qualify for one of those state lottery scholarships and save his dad from paying tuition. He knows he wants to be a certified public accountant. When summer comes, he's gonna get himself a part-time job at a fast-food joint and save up some money so he can get himself a car and buy his own clothes."

"All very practical decisions. Hardly the kinds of things a freewheeling spirit with a physical body in its possession would be plotting."

"I never even thought about stuff like that. I mean, I knew wanted a car when I turned sixteen. My dad said he would get me one but only if I could pay my own insurance and buy my own gas—which is why I don't have a car today. I was hoping I could talk my mom into footing those bills, but I never had any luck with that. And college? That's all my parents have been talking about for the past year. 'Myron, have you checked out any universities online?' 'Myron, you ever talk with your guidance counselor about where you're going after high school?' And I was like, *Jeez*. Just let me be a kid."

Anoki didn't say anything. He kept staring at the emergency room doors.

"I know what you're thinking. I'm already eighteen and only a few months away from graduation. Yeah, it was about time for me to start thinking about college and careers." The idea depressed me. I always thought there'd be plenty of time to figure out such things. What would I have wanted to do with my life? Dad worked as an electrical engineer at an architectural firm in downtown Memphis that designed systems for high-rise buildings. Mom had degrees in computer science and did software programming at some big outfit with offices in Germantown. I inherited my math skills from somebody else entirely, which is to say I had none. Mom and Dad both loved their jobs, but I definitely would not have followed in their footsteps. So what would I have become, if I hadn't become a monster?

"There," Anoki said suddenly, leaning forward.

I snapped out of my funk and gazed through the windshield. Pike strode through the open emergency room doors, followed by another guy who was just as tall but walked kind of hunched down, with the hood of a sweatshirt pulled over his head. His hands were jammed into his pockets, but the green plastic patient identification bracelet was still visible on his right wrist. Even without the unmistakable scent that came to me seconds later, the gait and girth of the second dude would have told me who he was.

Aldo Farmer was sneaking out of the hospital.

The make and model of Pike's truck were a mystery to me, and the thing had to be at least fifty years old, but it was fast. Anoki followed it south on Highway 80, hanging back so far I was afraid we'd lose it. Pike was upset, as evidenced by the frequent bursts of velocity that shot him way over the speed limit before he apparently caught himself and eased off the accelerator. His head and shoulders burned bright red in the dark cab of the truck, and his free hand kept flapping around in Aldo's face. You could tell Aldo was getting royally cursed out, but the big lump just sat there, taking it, his head glowing a cooler yellow.

"Dang, what's that all about?" I wondered aloud. "Get closer, Anoki. Maybe I can hear what Pike's saying."

"There isn't much traffic out here," Anoki replied. "I don't want them to suspect they're being followed."

Just before he crossed the Killebrew border, Pike took the County Line Road exit, the truck winding sharply along the curving ramp. We followed him down County Line past rows of tiny, narrow shotgun houses that probably dated back to the early 1900s. Some had been restored, with small cars parked out front and chairs on the porch. Others were abandoned and crumbling. Pike's right turn signal began to flash. Anoki pulled over, parked at the curb, and turned off his lights.

Pike turned into the driveway of a house at the end of the block. Aldo slid out of the truck, briefly exchanged a few less than pleasant words with Pike, and then slammed the door. As he walked toward the house, Pike backed the truck out of the driveway.

"Uh-oh." Reflexively, I slid down in my seat. "He's coming back this way."

Anoki didn't seem bothered.

"He'll *recognize* us," I hissed, spelling it out for the big, handsome dummy.

"No, he won't."

Pike drove past us as if we weren't there, so close that I could see the scowl on his face. He headed back down County Line toward the highway, his taillights disappearing after he crested a small hill.

"What'd you do?" I asked. "Put a spirit on him?"

"Just long enough to keep him from looking at us," Anoki said. "I can't risk leaving a spirit in him while he's driving. There's a chance the spirit would impair him enough to where he'd have an accident." His door opened. "Come on."

We left the Beemer and walked down to the house Aldo had entered. The front of the place was all of fifteen feet wide, and it was sealed in aluminum siding the color of mustard, with dark-green faux-wood shutters. The wooden porch was covered with grit and dry leaves. The yard was mostly weeds, pocked here and there with big patches of dry brown clay where nothing grew at all.

Not exactly the kind of place that I figured the rich and ritzy Farmer clan would call home.

We moved to the shadowy backyard, which was overgrown with waist-high weeds. A light came on in the back window, and a tall, thick, yellow-glowing silhouette became visible through the thin curtains, moving quickly around the room.

Anoki leaned toward me. "It looks as if he's packing," he whispered. "I want you to get in there and slow him down. I need a few minutes out here to make sure he stays put."

I nodded. "I can do that."

I crept back to the side of the house, stopping at a small, darkened window high off the ground. Grabbing the sill with one hand, I pulled myself up to peer in. Bingo. It was the bathroom. With my free hand, I ran one clawed finger along the edge of the frame, cutting through the window screen with a slight, dry rasping sound. The window's wooden frame was clumped with about a hundred coats of paint, some of it probably as old as the United States, and the stuff had sealed the window shut. Shit. Anybody here ever hear of paint remover?

It couldn't be helped. I pushed at the top of the frame. The window went up with a thick ripping sound. Leaving the window open about an inch, I quickly dropped down, pressing myself against the wall. I heard Aldo's approaching footsteps. He stopped at the bathroom door, no doubt peering in to see where the noise had come from. He stood there for maybe a minute. Even through the dense cloud of odors within the house, I could smell the tingle of apprehension in him. It sent a little thrill rushing through me that I quickly brushed away. Then his footsteps receded.

I stood up, raising my head to peer through the window and make sure the coast was clear. A sudden coldness swelled open behind me. I turned.

Anoki stood there, close, barely a step away. Shit, how had I not heard his approach? He was as delectable as always, tall, lean, hard-bodied perfection, but his skin seemed darker and his green eyes much colder than usual, almost... dead, in a way. Those eyes studied me with all the interest of a scientist looking over some newly discovered bacterium. There was something sensual in that look, and it sent heat rushing down into my groin.

He stepped toward me, leaned down, and nuzzled my neck. He inhaled deeply, drawing in my smell, but without the sound of air whispering into his nostrils. There was no warmth from his skin, just glacial waves of an arcane vitality that brought my nipples and dick to instant erection. The nearness of him filled my entire body with a lust more powerful than anything I had ever felt, and I had to bite my lip to keep from screaming.

Slowly, Anoki pulled away from me and stepped back. His long, black hair flowed to one side behind him, fluttering on the breeze. Looking into my eyes, he held his hands out to either side, an unmistakable invitation. The next move, it seemed, was entirely up to me.

I stared at his cold, impossible beauty. There was a vague notion in my head that he was 119 years old. Shit, that was crazy. And yet, in that moment, he seemed far older than a mere century. I started to say that he picked a hell of a time to get sexy with me, but I was so hard now just the brush of my underwear over the head of my cock was about to make me erupt. And I wanted Anoki now more than I ever had.

I was on him in a heartbeat, pressing my body to his. I put my left arm up, around his neck, clutching him to me. I slid my right hand under his jersey, fingering the ripples of muscle on his belly. He mirrored my moves—left arm around my back, right hand caressing my stomach.

His touch was eerie and electric, singing along my nerves and making my muscles twitch. I squeezed my eyes shut against the sensation, moaning deeply. My desire swelled, and I frantically undid the button of his jeans. I shoved his pants and underwear down to his knees. His long, uncut cock was not hard. Determined to change that, I grabbed his dick in my right hand and began stroking it firmly.

Again, Anoki mirrored my moves, getting my pants down to my ankles. He wrapped his hand around my incredibly hard cock, and I gasped loudly at the sensational spasm his cold, rough palm sent spearing through me. He jacked my dick swiftly, steadily, and the blazing pleasure of that made me weak. I let go of his cock and fell back against the wall of the house, sliding down to the ground. Anoki dropped with me, down on his knees, never missing a stroke.

Fucking hell! How could anything feel so damn good? My eyes and mouth gaped. I sucked in a breath and held it as the pressure built down below. I clamped both hands over my mouth. Anoki pressed his free hand over mine, completely dampening the scream that rose up from the bottom of my chest as I exploded in orgasm. My legs jerked in erratic spasms, my entire body shivering for what seemed like hours. When the bursts from my cock finally died away, I sagged against the ground, so drained I couldn't even keep my eyes open. I felt Anoki let go of my dick, easing it gently down between my legs. I felt him stand up. The coldness in front of me seemed to fold itself up, and then it simply wasn't there anymore. When I forced my eyes open, Anoki was gone.

My emotions went haywire. I felt angry and sad that he was gone, ecstatic at the pleasure he'd just given me, and hungry for more. I wanted that horribly cold touch of his skin on mine again. I wanted him with me, in me, pounding me brutally. I wanted to fill him up with every inch of me and pour out all of my lust in him.

But he was gone, off to do whatever it was he going to do to keep Aldo from leaving this place. And I had a job to do, as well. There was no way I would disappoint Anoki, not after what he had just done to me. I'd do anything to make sure I would have more of him.

I got shakily to my feet, brushing dry leaves and dirt off my bare ass with my hands, and pulled up my jeans, then buttoned them at my waist. For a few moments, I stood there, taking deep breaths, getting my heart rate and breathing back to normal. Then I reached up and slid the window open. Grabbing the sill with both hands, I silently climbed in, carefully making sure no part of my body or clothing scraped against the frame. The bathroom was a lot like mine at home— completely filthy. There was a ring in the tub. The old-timey mirror on the old-timey medicine cabinet was speckled with soap and toothpaste scum. Three wet, dirty towels lay in the sink. A pile of damp bath towels had accumulated in one of the corners, mixed in with some overripe underwear. The toilet seat was up, and the rim of the bowl was covered with yellow stains. The floor around the toilet reeked of piss.

It's a guy thing, I guess. My mom hated to even walk past my bathroom. I can't tell you the number of times she'd looked at me with helpless bewilderment on her face. "I don't understand, Myron. It looks like you put that stuff everywhere but in the toilet. Can't you *aim,* for God's sake?"

To which I'd shrugged. "Sorry. I guess it kinda splashes."

There was a lady from the south side of town, Mrs. Strait, who came in twice a week to help keep up with the housework. Mom wouldn't let her near my bathroom. "We can't afford hazardous-duty pay," she'd said, and then she started making me clean the room myself.

I felt a sudden stirring of kinship with Aldo.

I paused, reaching out with my senses. As I suspected, there was no one in the house except the two of us. From the bathroom door, I looked up the hall into the living room and saw a brand-new wide-screen television perched on a row of plastic milk crates, along with a DVD player and a game console. In front of the entertainment gear, there was a mound of blue and green beanbags. Scattered around on the floor were several video game and DVD cases, dirty dishes, and empty soda cans.

I moved slowly, silently down the hall to the bedroom, keeping my back close to the wall. There was only a stack of mattresses on the floor, piled with comforters. Clothes were thrown everywhere. Aldo was rushing around, snatching up clothes and stuffing them into a big plastic garbage bag. He'd taken off his sweatshirt. He wore one of those hospital gowns that tie in the back. The gown was tucked sloppily into his jeans, and the opening gaped, revealing his bandaged back. His face was dripping sweat and worry.

There was an instant where I wanted to rush him and feel the skin of his throat separate under my claws. That would be so sweet!

I shook the thought away.

Then I stepped into the light where he could see me.

CHAPTER
NINETEEN

ALDO'S back was to me. He went on gathering up his clothes, moving fast but gingerly out of respect for the wounds I'd dealt him. He was muttering something to himself, speaking so rapidly that I couldn't make out what he was saying, even with the super hearing. He shifted suddenly to his left, reaching down for a pair of tan cowboy boots, and he must have caught sight of me in his peripheral vision. His head jerked up, and he looked at me.

The color washed out of his face. His red hair flared out like a tangled cloud around his head. The bulging sack of clothes slipped from his hand as if all the strength had drained from his muscles. For a second, I thought he was going to drop flat on his butt, like a toddler who'd lost his balance.

He made a dash for the window instead. I jumped across the tiny room, getting to the intended exit well ahead of him. Aldo stopped and backed up a few steps, staring at me with shock. He went for the door next. I jumped and blocked him again.

He tried to stop and his feet slid out from under him. He slammed to the floor on his back. His mouth gaped from the pain, but he didn't cry out. I admired him for that. I stood there, waiting to see what he would do next. Then it hit me. I was playing with him, the way a cat does with a mouse. I hunkered down in the doorway, wrapped my arms around my knees, and tried to think nice, calm thoughts.

Grimacing, still obviously hurting, Aldo scuttled back, pushing himself with his elbows and feet. He didn't try to get up, and since I made no further move, he just eyed me warily for a few moments. "What—what kind of demon are you?"

I sighed. "Aldo, it's me. Myron Mitchell."

Aldo sat up slowly, now eyeing me with disbelief. "Myron?'

"Yeah, man."

His right eye twitched. "What happened to you? What *are* you?"

"Hell if I know. None of this was my idea."

"I *knew* there was something about you. You always creeped me out. From the day I met you, you creeped the hell outta me."

"Yeah, well, you did a pretty good job of making my skin crawl from day one too." I looked around at the disheveled, barely furnished room. "So. This is where you live, huh? I kinda thought you crashed in a castle or something, with all the money your folks are supposed to have."

"My parents...." Aldo flinched, arching as another jolt of pain apparently went up his back. "Well, my family situation's a little complicated."

"I'll bet. Why don't you tell me about it?"

"Look, Myron. I've got no idea what's going on with you and I don't think I want to know. Whatever you came here for...."

"I just came to talk. Can't we do that, enemy to enemy?" I grinned. It must not have been a pretty sight, since Aldo flinched again.

"I don't have time." Aldo started climbing to his feet. "I gotta get out of here."

My grin vanished. "Sit down."

The smell of fear coming off Aldo suddenly flared into a wave. He plopped himself back down on the floor.

"Now." I rolled my head like a cat. "Tell me why you sneaked out of the hospital in the middle of the night, and why you're so ready to jet outta your house."

Aldo's face started trembling. "That principal, Mr. Ellis, he... after the nurse sent me to the hospital, Mr. Ellis tried to call my parents. So did the hospital. The phone numbers on my school records are fake.

Now some woman from Children and Family Services is supposed to meet with me tomorrow because no one can find my folks."

I shook my head. What an idiot. I'd thought once or twice about giving the school a fake number for my parents, but had I done so, I would have used the cell phone of a friend who could pose as my dad, to avoid the exact situation Aldo the Idiot had put himself in. "Well, just fess up to your parents and let them talk to Mr. Ellis and the doctors."

"I can't. They can't. They're dead."

Very awkward moment there. I felt a rush of regret for how I'd been treating him. "Hey, sorry, man." After Garrett lost his mom, I spent almost a year worrying about my own parents' lives. I think I would have gone crazy if one of them died. Looking at Aldo now, I could see in his face the kind of pain I know I would have felt if I were in his shoes. "Did that… just happen recently or something?"

"My momma died in 1987. My poppa died two years later, in 1989."

"Wow. Man, I… wait a minute." I blinked, trying to do the math in my head. "You're, like, fifteen or sixteen. That means your parents would have died years before you were even born." I thumped the heel of my hand against my head, feeling like a fool for letting myself get taken in like that. "What're you trying to pull here? You telling me you're some kind of test-tube experiment or something? A frozen embryo?" I rolled my eyes to make it clear I wasn't going to buy into any of those scenarios.

Aldo gave me a suspicious frown. "I thought that you were, maybe, like me."

"Dude, what the hell are you talking about?"

He closed his eyes for a moment and took a breath. "I died in 1984."

THE intelligence I knew as Aldo Farmer was born in the summer of 1970, in Alexandria, Alabama, to Stephen and Ramona Nelson. His parents named him Bertrand Ray. He came along late in their lives, a welcome surprise, and they spoiled him from day one. He loved swimming with his friends through the long, hot summers. It was that love that ultimately did him in. Celebrating his fourteenth birthday with a backyard pool party, he took a running leap across the pool deck, something his parents had warned him against since he was four. He tripped, hit his head on the concrete edge of the pool, tumbled into the water, and drowned before any of his friends could get to him.

"It just about drove my momma crazy," Aldo/Bertrand said, shaking his head sadly. "I hung around my house for years after I died because I just didn't want to move on. Momma sorta folded up like an umbrella. She had this big inheritance from her parents, plus my poppa was making a lot of dough from his law practice, so she never had a job. But she'd been doing all kinds of volunteer work and fundraising, and she stopped doing everything after she lost me."

"She got depressed?" I ventured.

"Oh, yeah, really bad. Poppa took her to doctor after doctor, but nothing they did helped her. She just kept sinking until she died of a heart attack." Aldo/Bertrand sniffed loudly. "Once she was gone, Poppa retired from his job and just sat out in the garden, day after day after day. Heart attack took him too."

"So, you were, like, back with your folks after that? All together in death, or something?"

"No. They both moved on when they died."

"Moved on to what?"

"Heaven." He gave a little grunt of a laugh, half shrugging his left shoulder. "Or maybe hell, in the case of Poppa. He liked gambling and drinking a little too much. No, I'm just joking. He was a great father. Crazy sense of humor. Taught me how to swim, hunt, play poker and blackjack. We had all kinds of fun."

"Well, how is it that your folks 'moved on' and you never did?"

"They were ready to go, I guess. I never even saw their spirits after they died. But I wasn't ready. I'm *still* not ready."

Anoki's scent came to me suddenly, clean and light. I glanced up, just as the red form of his body appeared beyond the curtained window.

He was half stooped, working at something on the ground. I looked quickly away before Aldo/Bertrand noticed my distraction.

"I didn't have a life, Myron," Aldo/Bertrand went on. "Not really. I never got a chance to have a girlfriend, dance at a prom, go to college, get married and have kids of my own. I missed out on everything." He gave me this long, pleading look. "Does that make sense? You understand what I'm saying?"

"I do, man. You have no idea how much I do." I pointed awkwardly at his chest. "But, I'm guessing that body you're wearing is not yours."

He huffed out that little grunting laugh again. "No. It took me almost ten years before I could make myself strong enough to communicate with necromancers. Those are people who can—"

"Yeah, I know what a necromancer is. Go on."

"Not all of them are willing to help a spirit move into a living body. A lot more years passed before I finally found one who would give me what I wanted." He pressed his hands to his chest. "This body might be dumpy and all, but I can live again in it, swim, run, feel the wind on my face, kiss a girl. I've done that since I got in here, you know, kissed a girl. That, and a whole lot more."

His smile made me jealous. I dug my claws into the wood floor. "So, once you got a body, one of the things you'd been anxious to do was get back in school?"

He didn't catch the sarcasm. "Heck, no. I had to get far away from Alexandria, which is where I got this body. Momma left all her money to Poppa. Poppa didn't have any living relatives, so he left everything to the University of Alabama, where he went to law school. I made a deal with a demon, who possessed the university's bursar, went into the bank, withdrew a hundred and fifty thousand bucks in cash, and gave it to me. It wasn't even a tenth of what my poppa left, and I figured I was entitled to *something* as his son. I just wanted to have fun, but every city I settled in, I kept getting stopped by cops wondering why I wasn't in school. That's the only reason I enrolled at Killebrew when I came here, but once I was in, I actually liked it. I missed school, having friends and all. Even ribbing on your creepy face in class was sort of fun." He looked at my half-buried claws and shuddered. "When you scratched me, in the gym, it was the worst thing I ever felt. It tore my spirit apart, and I almost came out of this body. That's why you're here, isn't it? To finish what you started."

My claws ripped free, and I raised my hands in a gesture of innocence. "Hey, until just a few minutes ago, I had no idea what you really are. Just chill. I'm not here to hurt you."

As I spoke, a subtle pressure congealed around me. It was as if something had suddenly pressed the air down in the room. Aldo/Bertrand sensed it too. He shot to his feet with a frightened gasp. "You said you weren't going to hurt me!" he wailed.

"I'm not."

"Then why are you trapping me in this house?"

The light in the room flickered twice. The curtain snatched itself away from the window, its rod clattering loudly to the floor. The window slid up with a shattering bang that sent flecks of plaster sprinkling down from the ceiling like snow. Aldo/Bertrand and I both jumped and turned our heads.

Anoki stood outside, about two feet back from the now uncovered window, looking in at us. His green eyes were icy and scary as always, but he seemed absolutely warm and fuzzy compared to the way he had been when he'd jacked me off barely fifteen minutes ago beneath the bathroom window of this place. I sighed passionately at the memory of his touch.

Aldo/Bertrand swiveled back to me, a what-the-hell expression burning in his face.

I swallowed to slow my heart rate. Then I made the introductions.

ANOKI didn't waste time or words. "Why was Pike Wexlar so upset with you after he picked you up at the hospital?"

Aldo/Bertrand was sitting on the mattresses, hands dangling between his knees, a haze of resignation in his eyes. "I told him Coach

Frieda was with me. It was the only way I could get him to the hospital. I had to get out of there. I thought he was going to strangle me when he got to my room and found out he'd been suckered."

"Does Pike know you're a spirit inhabiting another boy's body? Has he made any bargains with you?"

"No. I only know him because Coach Frieda used me as a gofer to take little presents and messages and things between the two of them." A little smile came to his face. "I didn't mind. She let me drive her car to do that stuff. It was a pretty nice deal."

"What was their relationship like?" Anoki asked. "Were they having any problems that you could see?"

"Not really. The coach was seeing another guy, but I don't think Pike knows about him. Pike's pretty crazy about her, and he'd probably kill the guy if he found out."

That was like a slap to my head. It wasn't enough that Coach Frieda was fooling around with a dude just barely out of high school. She was keeping another man on the side. I remembered all the lectures she gave in hygiene about the virtues of monogamy, responsibility, and commitment in loving relationships. So much for leading by example. "Who's this other dude?" I asked.

"I don't know." Aldo/Bertrand looked at me. "I never met him. I just heard her talking on the phone with him a couple of times. She seemed to be upset with him because he was being pushy with her about something they were supposed to do together. I didn't pick up any more of their conversations because the coach always sent me off when she realized I was eavesdropping."

"When did you last have contact with the coach?" asked Anoki.

"Last Thursday. After school. She sent me to take a plane ticket to Pike. I parked her car in her driveway and put the key in her mailbox like always. I could hear her TV. Everything seemed okay, and I left."

"And what necromancer helped you take possession of that body?"

"An old guy named Nathan. He wouldn't tell me the rest of his name. He came through Alexandria on his way to Miami, had this fella with him." Aldo/Bertrand pressed a hand to his own chest. "His name really is Aldo Farmer. At least, that's what Nathan called him. Nathan slapped the kid around a lot and had him doing things for him like a slave. I thought he was the kid's grandpa or something until he said I could have the kid's body in exchange for $50,000. Nathan was a really nasty old goat."

"Yes, I'm familiar with him. Maybe I'll have to pay 'Nathan' a visit again someday." Anoki gave a nod. "Thank you, Bertrand, for this information. Myron and I have to go now, and—"

Aldo/Bertrand heaved out a strangled cry. "Don't. Don't take me out of this body."

"I can't let you keep it. I know you want to enjoy a physical life, but what you're doing isn't right. Your time here is done. That boy you've taken is entitled to his own life, in his own body. He has family and friends who love him and miss him. You have to let him go. And it's time that you moved on. Your parents are waiting for you."

Aldo/Bertrand covered his face with his hands. His shoulders began to shake.

"I can and will exorcise you if necessary." Anoki said in a tone that was quiet and sympathetic but had a definite finality to it. "It would be better, all around, if you left voluntarily."

The tall redhead dropped his hands from his face and stood up. His eyes were wet, and his nose was running. Despite his hulking body, he suddenly seemed small, somehow, and much younger. He looked at Anoki for nearly a minute, then turned and looked at me. I was still sitting on the floor at the bedroom door. Aldo/Bertrand's long face hardened. For an instant, it was as if we were back in the high school gym. I could see him sizing up his chances of getting past me. Desperation and some of that old hatred we'd shared surfaced in his face, and it looked as if he were going to make a run for it. Even if he got past me, however, he'd still be trapped in Anoki's circle, and he had to know he would buy himself only a few extra minutes of life at most.

His shoulders slumped. He looked at Anoki again and nodded.

"Thank you, Bertrand. Do you have any of the cash left you took from the university's account?"

Aldo/Bertrand gestured at the half-filled garbage bag. "About forty thousand bucks. It's at the bottom, under the clothes."

"Good. Aldo will need money to get back home. The rest," Anoki said, and then he gave a sly wink, "we'll consider compensation for the time you used his body."

Aldo/Bertrand sighed. "Okay."

"Once you have left the body, I will release the circle and you will be free to join your parents."

Aldo/Bertrand sat down on the bed. He gave me one final, incredibly sad glance. Then his eyes rolled up and he slumped back onto the bed.

Bertrand Ray Nelson rose up from Aldo Farmer's body like a thin fog, tiny filaments of pale, blue mist that appeared to seep from every pore. The filaments gathered into a shifting mass above the bed. Outside, there was the rustle of grass and leaves. The pressure in the room vanished. The ghost boy took a wide sweep, passing through me and sending a tingling chill down my spine. It was the equivalent of a loud, wet raspberry, one last dig at me. I took a playful, retaliatory punch at the ghost. It zipped around my swing and vanished through the ceiling.

I looked at the body on the bed. Something had clearly gone out of it. The freckled face was pale and clammy, the heartbeat had slowed significantly, and its breathing was shallow.

Anoki stepped forward, leaning through the window. "Myron. We have to go."

"What about this guy? He's barely breathing. Looks like he needs a doctor."

"The boy will be fine, now that Bertrand's ghost is gone. His own spirit has been subdued for a long time. He'll need a while to recover. Here." He extended his fist to me.

I went to the window and opened my hand. He deposited a fistful of loose red dirt in my palm. "Ugh." I made a face. "What am I supposed to do with this?"

"Sprinkle it around the bed and make a circle. Weakened as he is now, the boy is vulnerable to possession by any spirit that comes along. The circle will protect him until he is fully recovered. Hurry."

I spread the dirt around the bed, forming the circle. After wiping my palm on the back of my pants, I grabbed the garbage bag and pulled out the clothes, revealing a mound of dark-green bills. I rolled the garbage bag into a nice, neat bundle around the cash, and then lifted the pale boy's arm, tucking the bag against his side. When I stepped out of the circle, Anoki gestured with his right hand. A vague dome of force rose over the bed.

"Let's go," Anoki snapped. "I have a feeling Pike is in trouble."

CHAPTER
TWENTY

WE FLEW along the dark, virtually empty stretches of Highway 54 at ninety miles an hour.

I clutched the base of the bucket seat. "Anoki, slow down." I was going to add that he was begging for a speeding ticket, if not arrest, but a car pulled out behind us with blue lights flashing before I could say it.

Anoki ignored me as well as the flashing lights and wailing siren. After a few minutes, the lights flicked off, the siren went dead, and the cop car pulled quietly off the highway, parking on the berm.

I turned to Anoki. His determined eyes never left the road ahead. I wasn't aware that something had left the car until it came back, a cold, vague presence that wrapped itself in a distinctly proprietary sheath about Anoki. I squinted but could not see it with my supernatural vision. Whatever this shade was, I realized now that it had been with Anoki from the moment I first saw him at the corner of Alabama and Macon yesterday morning. I shuddered.

Trying to take my mind off Anoki's personal assistant, I said, "What makes you think Pike's in trouble?"

"Something Bertrand's ghost said to me," he replied.

I tried to pull more details from him, but Anoki wouldn't look at or talk further to me. I stared at him, amazed at how strongly I was attracted to him. What would it be like to have a guy like him for a boyfriend? A guy who thought I was so sexy, he forged an unholy deal with some ancient being just to have me. A guy whose touch made my body come alive in ways nothing else ever had. What would it be like getting to know him and seeing what lay beneath his lonely sadness?

What would it be like to take off with him, to see where the road and life would take us?

But it was a waste of time to dwell on what would never be. I slumped down in my seat, folded my arms across my chest, and sank into other thoughts.

I felt good about myself at the moment. I had helped to free a possessed kid who would soon be going back home, while simultaneously helping a deceased soul take its place in the afterlife. That was something few people got, a second chance to leave a mark with their lives after wasting most of it the way I had wasted mine. My parents weren't big on church, but they volunteered a lot of their free time working with local homeless shelters and food banks. Even some of my friends got wrapped up in the reaching-out-to-others thing. Every Christmas for the past six years, Bette had collected toys and money for the annual Toys for Tots campaign. Garrett spent a few hours on Saturdays doing fundraisers for the March of Dimes, something his mom used to do. Other kids focused on getting themselves ready to make a difference, to become teachers, doctors, researchers. I wasn't going to have forever to do such things, as it had always seemed before now. If I could get Bette and that snake LaVelle back from whatever evil force had taken them, it would make up, in some small way, for the fact that I'd never done much for anyone other than myself.

The Wexlar farm was now looming ahead. I could make out the black hulking shapes of the barn and the house in the distance. A red glow off to the right caught my attention.

"Slow down!" I insisted, pointing.

This time, Anoki pressed down on the brakes, maneuvering his car into the right lane and coming to a stop behind Pike's truck. We were roughly a mile from the farmhouse, and the truck looked as if it had spun around, straddling the right lane sideways with its taillights still shining. The headlights were a different story. Something had smashed across the front of the truck, shattering both lamps and crumpling the old, rusted metal like paper. The driver's door was open. Pike was nowhere to be seen.

Anoki shut off the car's engine as his door flew open. "We're too late. He's already been taken." He mouthed what appeared to be a curse as he climbed out.

I got out of the car. The night air had cooled enough to make my breath mist. "Anoki, tell me what's going on," I said. "What did that ghost boy say that made you think something would happen to Pike?"

"Bertrand said that Pike didn't know about Frieda Blevins' other boyfriend. What if that boyfriend, however, knew about Pike?"

Oh, damn. I turned, my eyes sweeping the dark, endless fields around us. White fog covered the ground like a sprawling blanket. To the east, my vision picked up the faint red glow of a human body, rapidly moving away from us. "There he is!"

I kicked off my shoes and ran after Pike. The knee-high grass was cold and slick with dew. The claws on my feet chewed up the ground, giving me the stability I needed to build up speed. On my left, the Beemer hove into view, roaring across the field and quickly overtaking me. *Uh-uh, Anoki, no way.* I laughed wildly. The thrill of being on the move welled out of my brain and through my body like a wave of electricity, giving me even more speed, and I pulled ahead of the car. It was important that I get to Pike first. The dead smell on the air, and the rapidity of the abductor's stumbling gait, told me we were after the scarecrow again. Physically, Anoki stood no chance against that thing.

Oh, and there was also that little old desire of mine to rip the straw man to shreds.

I gained ground fast, getting close enough to see the thing. Its right arm was coiled about Pike's waist, half dangling and half dragging his limp body in its wake. The legs of the denim overalls were soaked, and bits of straw flew back at me, ripped away by the wind. The blue-gray light of the animating spirit pulsed dully throughout the flopping body. It did not seem to be aware of my pursuit until the instant before I hurtled into the cold night air. The head spun completely around just as I crashed into the thing with my shoulder, the perfect flying tackle.

The unconscious Pike went tumbling off into the darkness. The scarecrow made a loud, intensely satisfying crunch beneath me as we slammed into the ground. With no brain to stun, however, the crazy thing retaliated immediately. Its arms and legs bent up and around its back at me, wriggling like tentacles. It planted the stumps of all four limbs against my chest and heaved me twenty feet straight up. I dropped down, ready to tear into it again. The scarecrow had other plans. It delivered a right hook to the left side of my head that knocked me face first into the ground.

The blow scrambled my gray stuff, and for a moment I just lay there with my butt pointing at the moon. Some dim part of my mind wondered if I was still suffering the effects of whatever charm Anoki had used to dampen my emotions. All riled up at the motel, I'd cracked a metal door with my skull without feeling a thing, but damn it, without that anger high, getting slapped into the dirt just now had been kind of painful.

The roar of the Beemer's engine shot past me. I raised my head in time to see Anoki pull alongside Pike's motionless body. He jumped out of the car and knelt over Pike, probably to see if he was still breathing. Anoki didn't see the scarecrow bounding toward them.

I spat wet sod from my mouth and yelled, "Anoki, look out!"

He stood up, placing himself in front of Pike. He faced the scarecrow with a blaze in his eyes that would have sent any sensible person running to hide under the nearest bed. The scarecrow stopped its headlong rush and began to circle the car warily, anxious to get at Pike but clearly in no hurry to tangle with Anoki.

With its attention on Anoki, I jumped onto the scarecrow's back and began slashing at it with my claws. Its right arm snaked around my neck. It peeled me off its back and whipped me around like some kid's doll. The scarecrow's left arm clutched my body, pinning my arms at my sides. Hissing, the thing smashed me to the ground, tightening the grip on my neck until I couldn't breathe.

At first I panicked, an entirely natural reaction to having a haunted rag doll mercilessly squeezing the life out of you. Gradually, however, I realized my lungs weren't exactly screaming for air. The steadily building pressure on my neck was uncomfortable, but nothing more. Shit, maybe there really was something to all of Anoki's talk about my immortality. A certain detached curiosity came over me.

What would the thing do when it figured out that strangulation wasn't going to give it the desired result in this instance?

I never got an answer. With an angry shout, Anoki jabbed a finger in our direction. Some invisible power hit the scarecrow like a missile, punching it half a mile through the foggy air. The straw-filled limbs released me, but not before the force of the blow sent me rolling across the ground.

Once I came to a halt, I just lay there, waiting for my brain to clear. When I raised my head, I saw the scarecrow hurtling back and forth across the field, struck by invisible blow after invisible blow. The spirit Anoki had sicced on the thing wasn't giving it any chance to even think about coming back at Pike.

"Myron, get up!" Anoki called out. I looked over my shoulder. He had summoned a new spirit, this one so vague, its substance so thin, that I could barely see it even with my predator vision. It whirled like mist around the Beemer, and the engine came to life.

"Come, get into the car," Anoki shouted, sliding his hands under Pike's body. "We must get away from here."

As I scrambled up, the ghostly mist swirled under Pike's feet, which lifted slowly. This new spirit wasn't very strong, but it was making an extensive and totally unnecessary effort to help Anoki. Anoki scooped Pike effortlessly into his arms, and then he nodded at the car. The feeble spirit swept over to open the passenger door.

"Where are you gonna take him?" I asked as I hurried over to Anoki. It seemed we were just setting ourselves up for some endless chase, since the scarecrow was fast enough to follow the Beemer wherever we went. Better, in my opinion, to stay and fight.

"Back to his home," Anoki replied. "When we talked to him earlier, I sent a ghost to ward his house against spiritual intrusion. If we get Pike inside his home, the scarecrow won't be able to touch him."

It sounded like a reasonable plan. Too bad we didn't get a chance to execute it. While our backs were turned, the scarecrow somehow managed to get away from the powerful entity that had been slapping it around the field like a soccer ball. In a flying leap, that big straw doll swept between Anoki and me, plucking Pike's body out of Anoki's arms as it went. Its passage completely disrupted the essence of the little spirit that was still trying to help us, the misty form breaking apart and evaporating on the wind.

"Stop that thing!" Anoki shouted at the darkness beyond me. A wall of pressure sent us both stumbling when his mighty companion spirit (as I was beginning to think of the cold, ever-present force I'd sensed around him from the start) went after the fleeing scarecrow again. I followed close on the spirit's metaphorical heels.

Ahead of us, I detected a faint pulse of power, like the hum of electrical wires. Casting about, my vision settled on a circle, roughly six feet across, that had been carefully burned into the grassy field. Clutching Pike to its chest, the scarecrow dove into that circle and vanished. I jumped, my body arcing headfirst toward the circle. Instinctively, I folded my arms over my head, closed my eyes, and prepared to tuck and roll, figuring I would just hit solid ground as I had when I tried earlier to pursue the scarecrow through its personal little portal.

Hit, tuck, and roll I did, but not across old man Wexlar's soggy field.

CHAPTER
TWENTY-ONE

THE air was warm. The soil beneath me was loose, almost powdery, and even warmer than the air. I smelled sea salt, and lots and lots of fish. I heard the soft crush of gently breaking waves.

I slowly opened my eyes.

I was sitting on a long, narrow beach of sand so white it practically glowed. It was still night, but the sky here was streaked with streamers of gray clouds that mostly hid the moon and stars. The sea opened to my right, an expanse of flat, gray water that stretched out to meet the darker sky. About forty feet to my left, a wall of mottled rock rose up from the sand. The dead odor of the scarecrow floated on the wind, faint and growing fainter by the moment.

Behind me, the air suddenly turned cold, and then it filled with the soft, clean scent of Anoki. I looked over my shoulder.

Anoki came rushing up to me, his long hair flowing off to one side on the breeze. His expression was grim. I couldn't see his companion spirit, that unshakeable demiurge, but I knew it was there, clinging to his body like some great snake.

"How'd we get here?" I mumbled through a goofy smile, somewhat disoriented from the transition to wherever we were.

"My shade reached the circle and held the portal for us before the scarecrow could shut it," Anoki said impatiently. "Get up, Myron. Quickly."

The cold of his invisible companion flickered around me, yanking me roughly to my feet. "Easy, *easy*!" I protested as the spirit withdrew, using the phrase Anoki had used with it earlier. "Damn. What's all the fuss about?"

Anoki raised his right hand, pointing skyward. "That."

I looked up.

The scarecrow was scaling the cliff face above us like a giant bug. It used its arms and one leg to propel itself upward with inhuman speed. The other leg was wrapped around Pike's waist. Good thing Pike was unconscious. If he could see the height he was dangling from, he'd probably be puking all over us right now.

A knot of anxiety ached in my stomach. "What's it gonna do? Throw Pike off the top of the cliff?"

Anoki's eyes flared at me.

Something smacked the side of my head so hard I stumbled. "*Ow!*"

"It's taking him to the Killebrew necromancer," Anoki snapped. "She wants him alive. She wants them all alive."

I stopped rubbing my sore head, puzzled. "She?"

Anoki growled with frustration. "There's no time for this, Myron. We must not lose the scarecrow. Go!"

I didn't think, just gave in to my instincts. I leaped fifty feet up, claws digging into the cliff. Then I started climbing at a frenzied pace, racing up the wall of rock. Out of the corner of my eye, I caught a glimpse of Anoki, arms outstretched as he rose effortlessly into the air below me, lifted by his unseen "shade." Cool. But I was climbing faster than he could fly, and I got to the scarecrow first.

I leaped onto the scarecrow's back as it was pulling itself onto the top of the cliff. I plunged my clawed hands deep into its straw shoulders while I snatched Pike free from the scarecrow's coiled leg with my feet. Then my body did a tight, powerful flip, and the scarecrow went flying. It hit the ground with all the force of a tumbleweed and began to roll toward a large, three-story wood cabin that nestled among a stand of hollyleaf cherry trees. One downstairs window in the cabin was yellow with light. That was all of the surroundings I had time to take in at the moment. I placed Pike down on the billowing carpet of long, thin yellow grasses, well away from the cliff's edge. Then I went tearing after the scarecrow.

It rose up to meet me. Beneath the black baseball cap, which had been stitched onto its head and remained stubbornly in place despite our previous less-than-peaceful encounters, the blank straw twisted, contorting into a horrible grimace that practically burned with malice. No way would I let it touch me again.

The last time I clawed the scarecrow, I'd cut deeply enough into its shoulders that its arms should have dropped to the ground like branches lopped from a tree. The damned spirit had held its grass body together, however, through sheer force of will. It wouldn't be able to do so this time. I attacked in a fury of slashing claws and teeth, ripping through the scarecrow in a violent tornado of motion.

My mind went blank, or maybe I passed out for a few seconds with my body on autopilot. When I came to, I was crouched on all fours in the grass, bits of straw stuck in my teeth. Straw and tatters of cloth were strewn over the ground around me in a wide, irregular patch that stretched for dozens of square yards. My head sang with an overwhelming lust that urged me on, and an answering growl rumbled deep in my chest. There was no sign of the gray-blue force that had animated the scarecrow.

My eyes settled on the cabin. There were people inside.

I could hear them. Smell them.

They smelled… delicious.

"Myron."

I spun and leaped at Anoki, claws outstretched.

You'll be relieved to know that I never got close enough to touch him. His companion spirit slammed me into the ground so hard the impact gouged a bathtub-sized crater into the loose, sandy soil. The demiurge bore down, pinning me in the hole like some gigantic, invisible foot. Anger radiated through my body, and I started scrabbling at the ground with my hands, trying to get the leverage I would need to force my way free.

Anoki leaned over me, looking into my eyes. "Everything's fine, Myron," he said in a velvety whisper. "You did it. We're all safe. Rest now."

He went on talking, mouthing soothing words, and the rage slowly seeped away. Just as I began to slip toward drowsiness, the pressure on my body withdrew. Anoki reached out, but it wasn't his hand that took mine. Instead, his shade grabbed my arm and hauled me out of the pit, depositing me upright a good distance away from him.

Maybe it was just being protective of its master, but at that point, I was convinced the cold, spooky demiurge was still jealous of me.

"What about Pike?" I asked. His still body was several yards ahead of me, lying on the ground where I'd left him. "He okay?"

"Still unconscious," Anoki replied. "But he should be fine."

One of the scents from the cabin increased suddenly, just as light footfalls crunched into the sand. Anoki and I turned.

A tall, athletically built woman stood amid the scarecrow's scattered remains. She was barefoot, dressed in blue jeans cut off at midthigh and a big T-shirt that draped over her body like a dress. Her blonde hair was cropped shorter than I remembered, but her hazel eyes were still filled with humor, even as she scowled down at the shredded straw surrounding her feet.

Coach Frieda raised her head and frowned squarely at me. "I wish you hadn't done that."

The coach had not come alone. I could see three distinct spirits billowing around her in a pale-gray haze. Their misty forms were interwoven with long, thick ropes of black, decayed flesh. They smelled heavily of rot to me, although, given the advanced state of decomposition, the odor would be barely noticeable to the average human. None of them were as strong as the thing that traveled with Anoki, but they radiated a hatred so nasty it made me want to dive off the cliff into the ocean.

"How'd you figure out that the coach was the necromancer?" I whispered to Anoki.

"I knew the moment the ghost in Aldo Farmer's body said it had struck a deal to run errands for her," Anoki answered. "That, and the fact that the spirit in the scarecrow was abducting people important to her."

I was puzzled. "Why? So she could feed them to a demon or something?"

"Of course not. Get out of my way." Coach Frieda looked directly at me when she spoke, as if there weren't two dudes standing in front of her. She didn't acknowledge Anoki's presence with even a glance in his direction, which only made it more obvious that Anoki's being there worried her.

The coach knelt beside Pike and pressed two fingers to his neck, feeling for a pulse. "He's alive, thank God." Her eyes took a long sweep of the area before snapping back to me. "Did anyone follow you here, Myron?"

"Huh?" That one threw me. "You mean, you recognize me, Coach?"

"You may be halfway to demon right now, but there's still enough there of the student I know that I can see it." Her eyes flashed with impatience. "Once again, were you followed?"

I shrugged, nodding at Anoki. "So far as I know, he was the only person to come through after me."

The coach stood up. "Help me get Pike into the cabin," she said nervously. "I don't feel safe out here."

Anoki stepped in front of me, forcing the coach to look at him. "Yes, we should get inside," he agreed. "You and I really must talk, Coach Blevins."

Coach Frieda was a real hardass around school, so it was downright shocking to see her shudder under Anoki's gaze.

THE cabin had three levels, all served by a winding spiral staircase. Carrying Pike, I followed Coach Frieda up to the second level, which had a bathroom on one end and a bedroom on the other. The only illumination in the hallway was from a small night-light plugged into an outlet close to the floor. The coach knocked softly on the bedroom door, waited a second, then pushed the door open and held it for me.

The room was small, furnished only with a chest of drawers and metal-framed bunk beds. LaVelle lay in the bottom bunk, eyes closed, mouth slightly open, snoring raggedly through his nostrils. The night was warm, and he was stripped down to his boxers, a sheen of sweat glistening on his face, neck, and chest. Drool ran from the corner of his mouth into his left ear. I'd never seen him asleep before and hoped to God I never would again.

"Put Pike up there," the coach whispered, nodding at the top bunk.

Standing on tiptoe, I lifted Pike over my head with my inhuman strength and carefully tossed him onto the upper bed. He'd been knocked out for about an hour now, and he was probably going to have one hell of a headache when he came around. Otherwise, he seemed to be in pretty good shape. The coach reached up and placed a hand tenderly on his chest.

I focused my attention on LaVelle. Aside from a few well-deserved bumps and bruises picked up during his abduction, he looked fine too. That was wonderful. Now it was okay for me to be pissed at him again for the knot he'd slapped on the side of my head. I wanted to flip him out of the bed, but Coach Frieda was standing right beside me. Teachers intimidate me, even ones who're done up in tees, shorts, and bare toes. I settled for raking a glowing claw back and forth through the air over LaVelle's head, which left crooked swatches of melted hair around his cranium.

"Shame on you," Coach chided me, a naughty smile on her face.

I gave her an embarrassed grin. "Okay. Where's Bette?"

Coach Frieda inclined her head toward the ceiling, and then led the way up the stairs. We emerged into a narrow, A-framed loft that overlooked the living room below. It was furnished with a futon, a bookshelf lined with paperback romances, a coffee table, and a floor lamp. There was a small television perched on a shelf built into one of the sloping walls. Bette lay asleep on the plush mattress of the futon, which had been leveled into a full-sized bed. She wore what was obviously the coach's robe, a silk number that was too tight and too long on her body. A small ashtray, stuffed with crushed cigarette butts, sat on the floor just below her head. The air smelled strongly of burnt tobacco. Bette's mouth twitched, and her eyes were roving beneath her closed lids. Probably a bad dream. But she was unharmed.

I sighed, almost weak with relief.

"Now," said the coach, "are you satisfied that your little friends are all right?"

"Yes ma'am." I turned to her but avoided looking into her eyes. "Only, I don't get it. I don't get how you could take people you know and trade 'em off to ghosts who'll wear their bodies like overcoats—"

"Oh, shut up. You don't know what you're talking about." The coach glanced down at Bette, who stirred suddenly. Coach grabbed me by the arm and pulled me over to the other end of the loft. She peered over the rail into the living room below.

Anoki had stayed downstairs to enhance the protections Coach Frieda had placed around the cabin. I could see him standing outside the big bank of windows that lined the front wall of the place, his arms outstretched, eyes closed, mouth moving urgently as he called up ghosts or demons or whatever to stand guard.

The coach leaned against the rail. The three disgusting ghosts that were wriggling around her suddenly got still, locking their hollow, baleful eyes on me. The rotting flesh in their vaporous forms kept undulating, dead snakes looking for somewhere to rest. "You've got the wrong idea about me, Myron," the coach said, her voice lowered to a whisper, "but there are more important things we should talk about before I get into that. First, are you aware that your transformation is due to a curse that—"

"Yeah, I know. Anoki filled me in. He's been helping me keep it under control."

"I thought so. But he won't be able to maintain that control constantly. You're a danger to me and the people in my house. Nothing personal, but if you 'go postal' in here, I'm going to turn my ghouls loose on you. They'll distract you long enough for us to get away. They can't kill you, but their touch will make you wish you were dead. I thought you should know."

"Great. I'll make sure I send you a thank-you card."

She smiled at that. "Second, what do you know about this Anoki?"

"Not much. He's a necromancer. That's about it." I didn't mention my powerful, inexplicable attraction to him.

"No, he's much more than a necromancer. I'm very good at summoning and communing with the dead, but that boy's talent goes way beyond mine. He has tapped into sources of power that I wouldn't dare touch, forces older than the earth itself."

"And how do you know that?"

"Because something from one of those sources has attached itself to him." The coach shivered again, more violently this time. She wrapped her arms around herself. "I felt it the instant he came through the circle onto the beach. I've called up some pretty nasty spirits— you've seen the ghouls I have with me now, I'm sure. That entity with Anoki is worse than anything I've ever encountered. Such... darkness. Such a cold, empty, heartless thing. It's more than a ghost, more even than a demon. Anoki is desperate about something. He has to be to call upon a being like that. And the part that's attached to him is only a fraction of what it is. We should all pray that the rest of it never comes through."

Okay, that was terrifying. Really, really terrifying. "Why are you telling me this?"

"Consider it a friendly warning. I can see that you like this boy."

Shit. I hadn't been around the coach a good thirty minutes yet. Was it *that* obvious?

"He is a cutie," Coach Frieda went on. "But that thing believes it owns him, and that he owns it. If it ever decides you are threatening that relationship, your immortality won't matter a damn. It will swallow you whole, like a gumdrop."

On that heartening note, the door opened below. An awful iciness came into the cabin. "Myron? Coach Blevins?" Anoki called out.

The coach slapped me nervously on the back. "Showtime." She pushed me forward, and I led the way downstairs.

CHAPTER
TWENTY-TWO

ANOKI and the coach sat facing each other from opposite ends of a long yellow suede sofa. I sat on the floor with my back against the wall, well away from the two of them. The coach's ghouls didn't seem to like being so close to Anoki's shade. They remained attached to Coach Frieda's body, but their misty forms whipped and bulged out behind her as if driven by some pounding gust that was howling off Anoki. Anoki's shade remained invisible even to my vision, but I could sense the burning distaste it directed at the ghouls.

"I'm not the one who started the abductions in Killebrew four years ago," Coach said in response to Anoki's first question. "I grew up in Birmingham. I've been teaching at Killebrew High for almost ten years. Most of my family and friends are back home in Alabama, and none of them know that I can commune with the dead. I would never jeopardize my relationships or my livelihood by trading bodies off to spirits."

"Then who is the necromancer behind the abductions?" Anoki asked.

"I don't know. I realized his presence, of course, once he started summoning spirits and the first kid disappeared. I've been trying for years to find him and stop him, but he's very good at covering his tracks. I'm more subtle at what I do, so it was only a couple of weeks ago that he realized I was after him. That's when he started calling me and making threats."

"You didn't recognize his voice?" I put in.

"Oh, I recognized the voice on the phone, all right. It was LaVelle Spears."

I scratched the side of my head. "Okay. I'm confused. LaVelle is the necromancer?"

"No. LaVelle was possessed. The necromancer has been using students at the school as tools and bargaining chips. He demanded that I join him in a particular summoning or he'd send demons to kill me."

Anoki leaned forward abruptly. "What does he want to summon?"

"He didn't say. But I figure it must be something very big and very unpleasant if he feels the need for help."

"You are correct," Anoki agreed, settling back against the armrest. "He's trying to enlist the aid of Geryon. My fear is that he is after the Unwas."

The coach gave a low, sharp whistle. "He's either a master at this business or a fool."

"I take it you tried to leave town when the necromancer threatened you," said Anoki.

"No, I didn't decide to do that until I discovered that Pike had been marked. I was going to take him to Miami. I have an associate there, a very powerful practitioner, but LaVelle showed up at my house before I could leave. He was hysterical, begging for help, screaming that a monster was after him. I thought it was a trick, but then this demon shows up hot on his heels. I let LaVelle in and warded the house against the demon. I calmed him down, made him some dinner, and planted him in front of the TV while I tried to plan my next move."

"And while you were doing that, LaVelle jumped you?" I guessed.

"He was still possessed," the coach replied. "The spirit inside him had gone deep enough that I couldn't sense it, and once it was sealed inside the house with me, it overtook LaVelle's personality again and came after me. I work out every day, and I'm stronger than a lot of men I know. But the spirit in LaVelle was *damned* strong. I didn't stand a chance against it physically."

Another revelation hit me. "That's when you called in the scarecrow."

"The 'scarecrow' was actually a ghost the necromancer had used. It had been a drug addict in life, and the new human body it got didn't last long once it started using again. It was insane, it blamed the necromancer for losing the body, and it wanted revenge. Naturally, I thought I could use that to my advantage, but I wasn't about to give it another body. I put it in the scarecrow instead. And yes, Myron, I did summon it to help me fight off LaVelle. My house was warded, so I had to open a circle to bring the crazy spirit in. Once it got LaVelle off me, it carried me back through the circle. LaVelle followed us before I could close the circle, but I managed to lead him through another circle I have in the woods outside Killebrew and left him there. Then I came here."

"Where is here?" I knew I was risking Anoki's ire with a question that was probably irrelevant, but I was curious.

"This is my uncle's vacation house, a few miles outside San Francisco." There was a chime from the kitchen. "Coffee's ready." The coach had put on a pot when she came downstairs. One of the ghouls whipped off her body and swept into the kitchen. It came back seconds later, floating a tray over its head loaded with coffeepot, mugs, spoons, a sugar bowl, and a bottle of hazelnut creamer. Depositing the tray on the coffee table, the ugly spirit rejoined its equally repugnant companions. The coach reached for the pot. "Myron, would you like some?"

"Yeah, thanks." I scooted across the floor to the table. "Can I get it myself?"

She handed the pot to me. I filled one of the mugs, put the pot back on the tray, then proceeded to stir in eight teaspoons of sugar and a big dollop of creamer.

Coach and Anoki both cocked an eyebrow at me.

"What?" I said defensively. "I have to kill the coffee taste."

Coach Frieda smiled and shook her head. "Anoki?"

"I like mine black."

The coach filled a mug and handed it to Anoki. Then she poured a mug for herself, which she also began to sip black.

Coffee without cream and sugar has all the appeal of a cup of hot shoe polish. But *I* was the weird one here. Go figure.

"The scarecrow spirit knew where the necromancer made his circles," Coach Frieda said. "He preferred to use natural materials, like trees and stones. I sent the scarecrow out on missions to dismantle the circles and bring some of the material to me, hoping I could use it to trace a path to the necromancer's home. But he's no newbie at this. He knew enough to ward the material so he couldn't be tracked through it. But breaking his circles did slow him down, even if only a little."

"So this guy marked Bette too?" I asked. "He was gonna trade her off to a ghost or something?"

"No, she wasn't marked. That was one of those in-the-wrong-place-at-the-wrong-time scenarios. I had that crazy spirit stake out my house in Killebrew in case the necromancer or one of his flunkies showed up again. When Bette went there looking for me, the spirit grabbed her and brought her to me. I knew she wasn't involved with the necromancer, but with everything happening around the town, I thought it was best to keep her here for the time being. LaVelle and Pike had been marked, however, so I sent the scarecrow for them both. Once I got LaVelle here, I exorcised the spirit the necromancer had left in him."

"Did the spirit in the scarecrow give you the necromancer's name?" Anoki asked.

"Yes," said the coach. "It kept calling him 'Sweets'. It could be a surname, or a nickname. Either way, I don't know anyone by that moniker."

Anoki gave me a questioning look.

I shook my head. "The name doesn't mean anything to me, either."

Anoki turned back to the coach. "You said the spirit was insane. 'Sweets' may not be a name at all. It could be some characteristic that the spirit associated with the necromancer. "

The coach gave a humorless laugh. "Well, 'sweet' sure doesn't describe the guy's disposition."

There was a sound from above, very soft. A thump, followed by a creaking floorboard. I tilted my head back.

"What is it?" Coach Frieda asked.

"Somebody just got out of bed." I sniffed. "It's Pike."

The coach's face brightened. "Oh, good." She put her mug on the table and stood. "I'll go up and see how he's feeling. Excuse me just a moment." She started for the stairs.

Maybe it was the caffeine and sugar that did it. Out of the blue, my brain suddenly made a connection from all of the random facts floating around in my head. "Wait...."

The coach paused at the steps and then turned back to me. Anoki leaned forward again.

It couldn't be. It couldn't be *him*. "I know who the necromancer is. Oh, God. I know who it is."

The defenses Coach Frieda and Anoki raised had filled the cabin with the faint, otherworldly pressure I'd come to recognize as the confining, protective power of a magic circle. That pressure collapsed suddenly, leaving a sense of vulnerability in the air as glaring as if the walls themselves had fallen down. Anoki shot to his feet, flinging the mug of coffee away from him.

"Someone in here broke our circle!" the coach said.

I jumped up from the floor as Pike came down the stairs. There was a little smile on his face. His scent was the same, but it wasn't Pike Wexlar looking out through those bright, playful eyes at us. "Yeah, sorry about that," he drawled lazily.

"Who are you?" the coach demanded, scowling at her boyfriend's possessed body. "Name yourself, spirit."

I did it for him. "Benito."

The demon grinned. "You remembered, flower boy. I'm touched."

The door to the cabin opened quietly. A tall, thickly built guy stepped into the living room, dressed in baggy black sweats and big white sneaks. A guy I'd known since first grade. A guy who'd sent LaVelle back to Coach Frieda's house to cover his tracks. A guy who pulled something from his pocket and flung it my way as he entered.

Coop's diabetes was diagnosed a year ago, and he didn't take care of himself as well as he should. When his blood sugar levels got out of whack, he gave off a fruity scent—the same scent I'd picked up in the woods just before LaVelle bashed me in the head. The odor was muted now, a sign that he hadn't forgotten his insulin this time. Good for him. I didn't want to see him fall sick. He was my friend, after all. Because he was my friend, I didn't want to believe that he was capable of the evil that had brought Anoki to town and driven Coach Frieda from her home. Because he was my friend, I hesitated a second too long before reacting to the thing he threw at me.

It punched into my chest just as I tried to dodge, and I stumbled back against the wall, sliding down to my hands and knees. Something that felt like nails of ice began to scratch outward from my chest, radiating through my body so rapidly it made me shiver violently. The pain was maddening.

Everything went dark.

Dimly, I heard a distant, inhuman howl. And I knew that it was me.

CHAPTER
TWENTY-THREE

I FELT as if I'd been pumped full of nuclear energy.

Coop had tossed a small, brown cloth bag, sewn shut at the edges, its middle bulging. When it struck my chest, power crackled along my nerves, through my blood vessels, reaching into every cell, and my body responded with equally impossible speed. My arms, legs, fingers, and toes elongated, the claws on my hands and feet extending gruesomely. My vision sharpened, bringing the ghouls surrounding the coach into brilliant, distinct focus. Their vaporous forms appeared thick as paint and bright green, obscuring the ropy flesh within. Now I could see once again the thing that clung to Anoki, a dark, shapeless aura vague beneath the shield it had raised to hide itself from my sight.

A bottomless hunger, coupled with pure fury, erupted in my gut, driving me into motion. Coach Frieda was closer, but Anoki's shade—the demiurge—posed the greater threat, and instinct sent me leaping in his direction. The shade bulged outward, a massive, fast-moving wall of freezing force. It swept by, missing me entirely, and angled toward Coach Frieda.

The core of my being was fire. I willed the flame into my claws. Anoki's shade would not get a second chance to strike at me. I slashed through the sight-bending shield into its center, streamers of molten, white-hot light trailing from my fingers. The demiurge splashed apart, its unearthly essence spraying like black goo in every direction. An enraged scream, far beyond human hearing, cut through my head, and I screeched in ecstatic triumph as the shattered demiurge dropped helplessly around me.

Anoki fell back, eyes grim, summoning one of Coach Frieda's ghouls to his defense before the pieces of his shade even came to rest.

The ghoul wrapped its substance around me as I landed, crouching in the spot where Anoki had stood only a moment before. I swung toward the coach. With a loud, angry shout, Coach Frieda turned her two remaining pets loose on me.

The dead flesh the ghouls incorporated felt cold and slimy as it pressed through the fog of their substance, burning against my skin like acid. Their mouths gaped and, from the fiery green mist within, some very solid, very sharp sets of fangs erupted. They bit into my chest and shoulders. True to the coach's word, pain rolled from the wounds with crippling intensity. Ten seconds ago, it would have left me curled on the floor, screaming for someone to help me. In my present form, however, the pain only drove me further from what little remained of my humanity. Sinking my burning claws into their writhing forms, I wrenched the ghouls from my body and ripped them apart. The ghouls fared less well than Anoki's shade. The shade was incapacitated, shredded, but its scattered remains were already pulling together. In a few hours, it would be whole again. The ghouls' bodies dissolved. The torn, mummified flesh melted into greasy gray smears wherever it landed. The vaporous part of their bodies simply evaporated into nothingness.

Both Anoki and Coach Frieda were making frantic gestures with their hands as they fervently mouthed commands. Some part of my mind understood that they were summoning more spiritual guardians, which would arrive in a matter of seconds. I screamed out a monstrous laugh. In those few seconds, I would have chewed out their warm, pulsing throats. I crouched, baring my teeth at them. I didn't see them as friends, as people I respected and cared about. They meant only two things to me in that moment—sport and food.

A shiny object flew over my head and shattered on the floor between Coach and Anoki. Coach Frieda threw herself back, vanishing behind the cloud of vapors that burst suddenly into the air. Anoki coughed and collapsed amid the spreading smoke. I glared at his unconscious, helpless form. This was not the way I wanted to take them. Someone had deprived me of the hunt. Enraged, I whirled, ready to attack the others in the room.

Something small and soft hit me in the face. I looked down and spotted another cloth bag, this one red. That was all I took in before paralysis hit me and I dropped to the floor, the breath hissing from my lungs in a grunt.

Footsteps scampered eagerly my way. Benito/Pike leaned over me, peering down with amazed eyes. "I'll be damned... well, I'm already damned." The grin that spread across his face was unmistakably diabolical. "It actually worked!"

Coop's voice drifted across the room, deeper, more guttural than I remembered. "That spell will only hold him for a few minutes, stupid. If you're gonna take him, do it now."

The grin got even wider. "This is gonna be fun." Benito/Pike's face withdrew, and then a big, booted foot came crashing into my head.

The boot landed three more times before my lights finally went out.

IT STARTED with my mom.

The sun was setting, and shadows had gathered beneath the trees surrounding our yard. She was on the patio, nervously watering the scores of potted plants she cultivated there throughout the year, occasionally pausing to prune a dead bloom or a withered leaf. All the while, she pressed the phone to her ear with her shoulder, pouring out her heart to her friend, Katie Ruby, who lived in New York City. I'd never met Katie Ruby, a woman with whom my mom had shared a dorm room when they were students at Stanford University. In my lifetime, the two of them had not once made the cross-country trip to visit each other, but they talked on the phone at least twice a week.

Mom's hair was loose, hanging down to her shoulders. With her slender body, some of the guys at school considered her a "babe," a fact that filled me with pride and made me cringe at the same time. She wore a T-shirt and cotton pants and flip-flops, which seemed strange on such a cool evening. Home alone and in anguish over my disappearance, she had turned to Katie Ruby, rattling off all her fears of what may have happened to me. Her work on the plants wasn't attentive but careless and distracted. She was too upset to keep still. If she hadn't been fumbling around with her flowers, she would probably be pulling her hair out.

Between the conversation and the plants, Mom took no notice of the dark figure that slipped silently into our yard. I saw him, however. Somehow, I felt his malignant intentions, felt the anger and hunger, the insane yearnings that drove him. He moved from tree to tree, closing in on the patio, red eyes burning in his shadowed face, stalking her as she chattered obliviously away.

I wanted to yell out a warning, wanted to throw myself on the predator, but I knew I could do neither. Something more than distance separated me from the scene. Nothing I said or did would be enough to reach in and stop what was unfolding before me.

The stalker was lean, small, scarcely taller than my mom, but I felt the inhuman strength that curled through his limbs. Mom shifted her woeful attention to the pansies growing in a row of boxes on the window ledge, turning her back to the yard. The stalker moved to the edge of the patio, standing in full view now, curling his fingers at his sides in cruel anticipation, like the talons of some horrible raptor.

Mom, look out! He's right behind you!

She went on spouting off her worry.

Turn around! Get out of there! Oh, God, please get her out of there!

She started crying at something her friend said.

Then a ghastly hand shot out and closed around her neck.

Her eyes went wide and her mouth gaped as the crushing fingers dug into her neck. The phone dropped from her suddenly nerveless fingers, breaking into pieces as it clattered against the concrete floor of the patio. She couldn't draw in enough breath to even gasp.

The stalker turned her slowly, so that she could look into his face. The sight stunned her.

She died trying to speak my name.

DAD had been on the gymnastics team at his high school. When I was a little kid, he'd dazzle me by walking across the backyard on his hands. It was the most amazing thing in my world at the time. I tried it too, of course, but always overbalanced and wound up flat on my back in the warm, green grass, giggling like a maniac. It wasn't until I turned nine that I was able to travel short distances by hand. By that time, Dad had packed on a lot of pounds and could no longer make such trips himself.

It took a few more years before he got serious about trimming down. He'd jog through Century Park in the evening, after he got off work. That's where he was when Mom perished so violently. The center of the park was woodland, wound through with asphalt trails perfect for jogging, power walking, or pleasurable strolls. But Dad wasn't here for a jog or stroll tonight. One of our neighbors had told him and Mom that they had spotted someone in the park's woods who looked like me. Dad had left Mom at home to keep watch there in case I called or showed up, and he headed out to search the woods.

Dad had the trails all to himself tonight, hurrying along in his gray sweats and black sneakers. He was breathing through his mouth and drenched in sweat from his head to his waist. His heart pounded as much from anxiety as from exertion. He called my name occasionally, pausing to listen for an answer. The only response he got was the eerie whisper of the wind through the woods. Above, the stars were beginning to peek out and the full moon shone down, but the light couldn't penetrate the thick canopy of yellow and red leaves the trees stubbornly clung to.

No longer detached from myself as I'd been with my mom, I moved among those treetops, silently keeping pace with my dad. He was so slow, so unaware, that he hardly seemed worthy prey.

Let's make it more interesting.

I loosed a low, rumbling growl deep in my throat, a sound somewhere between human and animal.

Dad stopped on the trail. His heart rate increased slightly, and the sudden release of adrenaline into his body added to his already acrid smell. He visually swept the woods around him, never looking up to where I crouched over him, all but shaking with delight at his reaction. He saw nothing except darkness among the trees, and that only made him more uneasy.

He starting walking again, picking up the pace some, glancing around as he went. I followed, scrabbling swiftly from tree limb to tree limb without a sound. After a few minutes of this, I gave another low growl.

Dad stopped again. "All right, who's out there? This isn't funny." His voice had an edge of anger to it, but it was also shaky with apprehension. He reeked of fear.

It was a delicious smell.

He spared only a few moments looking around this time before breaking into a determined run. It was obvious that he wanted to get the hell out of the woods and back to his car. I kept up with him for a few paces before throwing myself down in a sudden, deliberate hail of broken branches and leaves, landing noisily on the ground just inches off the trail to his right.

Startled, Dad yelled. I rose up, a dark thing of red eyes, white shark teeth, and glowing yellow claws. Although I was only slightly more than half his size, I could have killed him in an instant.

But where was the fun in that?

Dad fled headlong away from me, terror bringing a series of loud gasps from his throat. I ran after him at what was barely a trot for me, closing on him more quickly than I wanted in spite of myself. He cried out once for help but, strained for breath, the cry was barely audible.

Not that it mattered, because there was no one around to hear him.

That was too bad. I would have loved it if someone had come charging to the rescue.

I was almost upon him. Dad turned abruptly. He realized he wasn't going to get away and apparently decided to make a fight of it. Fury actually overrode his terror in that instant, and he spat a curse as he charged forward to meet me.

Of course, he stood no chance at all.

MR. CHESS was next. He had pulled a double shift at his job, where he supervised a team of drivers who delivered shipments to restaurants and stores across the tri-state area, so it was late when he got in. Garrett had gone over to his granny's after school to help her fix a few things around her house, so he wasn't home.

But I was there.

I toyed with Mr. Chess some, letting him see me first and then chasing him down as he tried to make it to his bedroom, where he kept a gun under his mattress for intruders. I nabbed him before he could reach the bed. He was tall and brawny, which didn't help him one bit. I killed him fairly quickly. He wasn't my primary prey here.

I left his mutilated body on the bedroom floor and then hid myself in his walk-in closet. Nearly an hour passed before the click of a key in the front door's lock whispered through the house.

"Dad?" Garrett sounded tired.

I heard the door close. He kicked off his shoes and dropped his backpack, muffled thumps against the carpeted floor. He'd had dinner at his granny's, no doubt. He never went over there without her feeding him, but that wouldn't stop him from raiding the larder now that he was home. Sure enough, the sound of cabinet doors opening and banging shut came from the kitchen seconds later. A bag ripped open, followed by the sound of munching. The salty, fried smell of potato chips drifted on the air with his own musky scent.

I heard the soft padding of Garrett's bare feet as he walked down the hall. He bypassed his room, coming straight to his father's. "Dad? Where are you?" The palm of his hand thumped against the partially closed door, pushing it open.

I heard the sharp intake of his breath. Then, a moment of utter silence. After that, a soft rustle as the bag of chips dropped to the floor. A thud, as Garrett grabbed the door and shoved it hard against the wall in an effort to steady himself. Another, heavier thud, as he fell to his knees.

Since the death of his mother, nothing had frightened Garrett more than the thought of losing his father. I knew that as well as I knew my own name. For me, nothing in my life was as satisfying as the moment when Garrett—kneeling on the floor, barely two feet from his dad's bloody corpse—clutched his hands to his scalp, threw back his head, and bellowed out a long, loud scream of pain and horror.

I do believe the sight of his father drove him crazy. He crawled on hands and knees up the hall to his bathroom, where he curled himself into a ball between the toilet and the bathtub, sobbing so deeply he began to choke.

God, to drink in such suffering! It was making me absolutely giddy. I burst out of the closet, screaming with hellish laughter, and raced to the bathroom. I wanted more. A lot more.

I took my time in killing Garrett, dragging his death out for over an hour.

He was, after all, my best friend.

CHAPTER
TWENTY-FOUR

IN THE darkness, I moaned.

It was cold. So cold.

I couldn't see.

Let me go. Please, please let me go.

"Oh no, batty boy, not yet. Not ever, if I have my way. Let's see what else you've got in you."

THE woman parked her car in the garage and climbed out. She wore black slacks and a pale-blue blouse, a professional woman's uniform—manager, accountant, maybe a lawyer. She opened the rear door and unbuckled the carrier that held her sleeping baby, carefully lifting the precious bundle from the backseat, and then bumping the door shut with her knee. Her shoes clicked softly as she made her way across the garage. Keys jangling musically, she unlocked the door and let herself into the kitchen.

She put her keys and her purse on the table, and placed the carrier beside them. A small, thin woman, she sighed, grateful to be relieved of her burdens. She turned, crossed to the door again, and flipped the light switch.

The room remained dark.

"Oh, wonderful," the woman groaned. "A power outage."

I made the slightest of sounds, letting the sole of my foot whisper over her tiled floor.

The woman's body tensed, and she began to tremble. She tilted her head slightly, listening. Aside from her own, now rapid breathing, there was no further sound, but she knew there was someone else in the house with her and her baby.

She turned slowly. Her intentions were clear. Get the baby, get the hell out of the house, call the police.

Once she faced the table again, she jerked to a stop, her face blanching.

I was standing beside the table.

My left arm was extended toward the woman. The baby dangled upside down, confusion shining in the big circles of her eyes, her tiny right ankle clutched in my fist.

The mother's face registered horror, inspired in part by my shadowed, demonic form but mostly by the danger posed to her child. She made a desperate squeal deep in her throat. Then she made a lunge for the baby.

I raised my right hand in a flash to the infant's plump, naked belly, claws bared and glowing. The woman stopped immediately. She clasped her hands helplessly beneath her chin, as if she were about to pray. The baby squirmed, trying to get away from the heat rippling off my claws. She locked her eyes on her mother and began to bawl.

No!

"Do it!"

NO!

"Oh, you'll do it, all right, fruit boy. You can't help but do it. It's what you are."

No....

THE glowing claws struck.

The woman gave an anguished cry and collapsed into a heap on the floor, her strength drained in that instant. But her wild, grieving eyes never left my face. "How could you?" she wailed hysterically, her fists beating at the air. "She was just a baby!"

The sight and sound of the woman's pain set my heart racing. I threw back my head as joyous, monstrous glee spewed up from my heart. My howls, long and deep, shook the house. The woman clapped her hands to her ears, staggered to her feet, and ran screaming for the door.

I let her go. She would send the police. And that would be more fun for me.

OH, GOD. I didn't mean to do it. I didn't want to do any of it.

I'm sorry. I'm so sorry.

I don't want to hurt anybody else. Please.

Please. Before the police come, before I do it again. Just let me die.

I was lying facedown on a floor somewhere, my body heaving with sobs, afraid to open my eyes. I didn't want to see what I'd done to that baby, or the blood that covered my body.

Garrett's blood.

Mr. Chess's blood.

My parents' blood.

There was nothing left for me. No forgiveness, no redemption.

Someone, somewhere, was laughing.

A SPIKE of impossible coldness, deeper than the chill around me and strikingly familiar, tunneled into my head. It shocked my eyes open.

I lay on a downy rug in the cabin's dining room. Demon Benito, still wearing Pike's towering body, stood over me, head thrown back, eyes closed, a blissful look on his face. His laughter was broken now and again by soft, almost sexual moans of pleasure.

He was drinking in my pain, savoring it. Just as I had relished the pain of the people I killed. I was no less evil than he.

It was time to put an end to us both.

Benito/Pike stopped laughing suddenly and opened his eyes. "Oh, shit...."

He watched with mounting fear as I got to my feet. The skin on my arms and hands was still obsidian, and my claws began to burn with fire.

"Now wait, flower boy," Benito/Pike said, backing away. A big, rustic oak dining table took up most of the room, surrounded by six matching chairs. He bumped into one of the chairs and then sidestepped, trying to put the table between us. "Let's talk about this for a minute, okay? We could have a real sweet arrangement here. With Mr. Do-Good out of the picture, there'll be no soul-sucking demon to take you. You and me, immortal buddies, traveling the world, taking whoever we want, whenever we want. I'd make sure we always had the finest things—cars, houses. I'm very good at that, believe me. I could possess cute, hot young guys for you to fuck. Or eat. Or both, if that's your pleasure. It would be fun. Forever. What do you say?"

My answer came in a bellowing roar of pure hatred. I threw myself into the air, smashing the chandelier from the ceiling as I hurtled toward Benito/Pike. Benito's spiritual form stood out sharply, a dirty brown haze of shapeless energy, as he fled Pike's body in a single pulse and shot toward the ceiling. Pike's now senseless body fell to the floor. I passed over him, rebounded off the wall, and went after Benito's ghostly form.

The demon oozed through the open window like smoke. Tucking my head, I crossed my arms over my eyes and burst outside in an explosion of shattered glass and broken wood. I hit the sandy ground, rolled, and came up running, relentlessly following the vaporous form as it zigzagged all over the place in an effort to get away. Determination fired my inhuman senses and kept me close on the demon's figurative tail.

The demon became desperate. There was nothing else to explain the sudden turn it took toward the sheer cliff. I was a boiling ball of every raw, horrible emotion you could imagine—fury, grief, guilt, topped with a consuming hatred for myself and the nasty little spirit I knew only as Benito. Common sense didn't stand a chance in such a cauldron. My brain didn't process little things such as the fact that the demon was incorporeal, while I was very much a physical being. Chasing a spirit off a cliff wasn't the wisest thing to do. My head also pretty much ignored the fact that there was a small, dark body in the distance, slumped among thick clumps of three-foot-high grasses waving in the stiff breeze coming off the ocean.

The fleeing spirit plunged into the body, disappearing momentarily from my sight. I slammed into the body a second later, sending it flying over the cliff. Chest skidding along the ground, I slid to a halt. Staring over the rocky edge, I saw the demon slip from the plummeting form of the bronze-skinned boy it had inhabited when Anoki summoned it back through the other necromancer's circle. The brownish haze rose up several yards to my left and scooted back along the ground.

The demon was getting away.

But below, a kid was in trouble. A kid who had already suffered much, his name and body stolen by an evil that had taken him away from his home and family. Now he was falling to his death.

Because of me.

I got up. Without thinking, I did a back flip, braced my feet against the rocky edge of the cliff, crouched down, and then launched myself like an arrow after the boy. My powerful momentum caught me up to him in seconds, and I wrapped my arms around his unconscious body.

Below there was a wide band of rocks. Beyond that was a wider band of sandy beach, and then the foamy white wash where the ocean met the shore. It was obvious from our trajectory that we weren't going to hit anywhere near the ocean.

I had to find a way to protect the kid. Shifting our rapidly dropping bodies, I put myself between the boy and the ground, clutching him against my chest.

After that, I was fresh out of ideas.

CHAPTER
TWENTY-FIVE

THE dagger of ice that had moved into my head quivered suddenly, like a plucked guitar string. The night sky, with its ribbons of gray clouds and scattering of white stars, vanished from my vision, replaced by an incredibly sharp, incredibly clear image of Anoki and Bette.

The two of them stood side by side in darkness on a spread of thin, dry pine needles, each bound tightly to a thick, gray tree trunk with nylon rope. They were awake, but their mouths were gagged. They were two of the bravest people I'd ever met, so their wide, straining eyes upset me. This was no hallucination, no dream brought on by a brain desperate to avoid thinking about the rocky ground waiting below. It was an actual vision of Bette and Anoki's present circumstances. They were, without a doubt, in very real and imminent danger.

I was *not* going to let them be hurt.

I squeezed my eyes shut, then opened them again. The dark sky had returned above me, and I realized that I was now falling closer to the cliff face than before. I shot my right hand out, gouging my fingers deep into the rock, and my plunge came to an instant, jarring halt.

My body cushioned the boy, Benito, against most of the impact from the sudden stop, which otherwise would have snapped more than a few of his bones. Draping the little dude over my shoulder, I dug both feet and my left hand into the rocky wall. Fear for my friends sent me clawing my way up the cliff faster than a human could run.

I'd just about reached the top when Benito woke up. His reaction was exactly what you'd expect from someone who came to and found himself dangling over a seven-hundred-foot drop. He locked his arms and legs around me like a vise. A high-pitched scream ripped from his throat. And he pissed, a gushing, hot flood that spread across my chest.

"Fantastic," I growled between my teeth.

As I pulled us both over the edge onto level ground, Benito began to fight me. He pounded my back with his fists and kicked at my stomach with his feet. *"El padre, me ayuda!"* he screamed over and over in a pure panic. I didn't have time to try and calm him or explain what was happening. Keeping him in a tight grip, I ran back to the cabin, shoved him into the first-floor bathroom, and then slammed the door, breaking the knob off with a quick downward jab. The boy fired off a rapid string of words in Spanish, probably a mix of curses and prayers, banging on the door hard enough to make it rattle within its frame. There was no window in the room, and with the doorknob disabled, the kid would be safe for the time being.

I peeled off my wet shirt and dropped it on the floor. Moving back toward the front door, I peered into the dining room and saw that Pike was gone. He might have wakened and stumbled off on his own. More likely, that runty demonoid had come back and set up shop again in his body.

Or maybe not. There was a small, yellowish brown stain on the polished logs of the wall beside the kitchen door. It wasn't physical matter but spiritual residue, invisible to human eyes. I gasped as another arctic piece of Anoki's shade suddenly pushed its way into my head. This one had apparently remained behind in the cabin, as I now began to see what it had seen.

The dining room flickered and vanished. Replacing it in my vision was the same dining room, but slightly different. There was no stain on the wall, and Pike's body still lay on the floor.

The ghostly brown form of Benito's former demonic occupant came pulsing down through the ceiling, making a beeline for Pike. The dirty little spirit had indeed intended to take over the big guy again. A ghoul—this one wrapped entirely in mummified skin—came out of nowhere and smacked the demon right into the wall. The demon gave one tiny psychic yip of surprise, and then it was gone.

The ghoul was taller and thicker than Pike, with strength to match its size. It scooped the unconscious guy up in its too-long arms and carried him out of the cabin. The shade showed me where the ghoul had taken him.

I squeezed my eyes shut, forcing the shade's visions out of my head. Then I ran out of the cabin, hoping I would not be too late.

THE woods were mostly pine. They were half a mile beyond the cabin, the trees tall and thick and dark against the cloudy night sky. Of course, it was woods again. Woods make for optimal conditions when it comes to forging ritualistic circles.

I took to the treetops. There I could travel in silence more quickly and with less effort than on the ground. I reached the center of the woods in minutes, guided entirely by the voice that was happily, eagerly declaiming in a dead, centuries-old language.

Perched above the site, I peered down, studying the scene. There was very little light, but I could see well enough without having to use infrared vision. Bette was tied to the base of the very tree to which I was clinging. The tree was one of six that grew within a circle of white, softball-sized stones. Anoki was tied to the tree on Bette's left. It was no surprise to see LaVelle trussed to the tree on Anoki's left. Spotting Coop, however, sweating and bound to a tree across from Bette, shocked me. Like the others, he was muzzled and scared.

Pike was tied to the tree next to Coop. He wasn't gagged, however, perhaps because his unconsciousness meant that he wouldn't be able to disturb the proceedings. A brief, barely audible moan from his throat indicated that he was just beginning, finally, to come around.

Coach Frieda, standing in the exact center of the circle and surrounded by her captives, either didn't hear or care about the pained awakening of her boyfriend. From the look on her face, it was clear that whatever had existed between her and Pike was definitely over. Her eyes were closed, her head tilted back, and a triumphant, blissful smile spread across her face as the incantation of summoning continued to roll out of her mouth. The air within the circle was growing colder by the second, and something very big, very powerful, was stirring beneath the ground.

Okay, the coach had obviously taken Coop down at some point. But why was she summoning the very thing that she had feared Coop was going to call up?

A bolt of pain rocked through my skull, a sort of mental slap from Anoki's shade. I was missing something here, something the shade wanted me to see.

Of course.

In my head, most of the pieces fell into place. It had been Coach Frieda all along who wanted the Unwas. She had been trading off souls for years, slowly working her way up to an audience with Geryon. LaVelle, Pike, Coop, and Bette were all tools that she used, like the scarecrow, the ghouls, and the nameless demon that had possessed Pike and Benito, to get her to this point. She had used me too. Anoki and his shade were the greatest danger to the coach. Anoki must have figured out what the coach was up to. A circle of power could be broken only at the command of the person who raised it. The circle at the beach house had been raised by the coach and enhanced by Anoki. That demon in Pike couldn't have broken the circle to let Coop in unless the coach directed him to do so. That's why Anoki sent his companion spirit after the coach instead of me. The coach manipulated me into disabling the shade, and then set me up to be tortured by that punk of a demon, clearing the way for her.

Maybe everything hadn't worked out exactly the way she wanted, but Coach Frieda had won. Geryon was coming. I could feel it, feel his approaching presence, ripples of sheer, cold evil that radiated invisibly up from the ground.

I took all of this in within seconds after leaping into the tree over Bette's head. The coach didn't seem to be aware of my arrival. Too bad for her. My hastily concocted plan called for me to jump down and knock her unconscious. The still enraged part of me wanted to kill her. My parents, Garrett, his dad, and an innocent baby had died because of her scheme. But the coach and her little pet demon had just been the catalyst; *I* was the one who actually ripped away their lives. Ultimately, I was the one who'd have to pay for that. No, just put the coach to sleep. That would stop the summoning, Geryon would go back to wherever he hung out, I'd set everyone free, and Anoki would figure out what to do with the big, bad necromancer. Then I'd go to hell, and everyone else would go home. End of story.

Only it didn't work out that way.

I quietly pulled my claws out of the rough, scaly bark and thrust away from the tree, letting myself drop toward the coach. Garbled cries came suddenly from Bette and Anoki. I scowled, wondering why the hell they were trying to warn the coach.

Too late, I saw something big shoot out of the darkness. It plowed into me in midair, driving the breath from my lungs in a grunt. We crashed into the ground, the heavy thing on top of me and struggling to pin my arms. It smelled dead, and I knew it was the ghoul that had carried off Pike.

Twenty feet away, the coach turned her head and gawked at me. There was surprise, anger, and panic in her eyes, but she didn't break with the incantation. She stepped up the pace, the words flying from her mouth in a rush. She knew her ghoul wouldn't be able to hold me more than a few seconds.

It only took a couple of swipes with my claws. The spirit within the ghoul screamed and disintegrated, leaving a sack of dry skin on the warm ground. That was time enough for Coach Frieda to finish her entreaty. She dashed behind a tree as she did so, trying to give herself some cover in case I rushed her. As I jumped to my feet, darkness rose up within the boundaries of the circle, a curtain of sheer, unearthly blackness. The sounds of the woods and the shifting ocean, the cloudy sky, the warm, salty breeze, everything cut off instantly. Even the scent of pine was gone, replaced with an odor of sage, cinnamon, and other spices that was so strong it burned in my nostrils and made my eyes water. We were not, I guessed, in California anymore. Geryon had not come to Coach Frieda. Rather, he had brought everything within the circle to him.

His presence was prickly, scraping against my... soul. That's the only way I can describe it. I cringed, cowering down and scratching rabidly at my skin, trying to dig his foulness out of me.

In the center of the circle, the darkness parted for just a moment. I raised my head and got my first look at Geryon.

CHAPTER
TWENTY-SIX

GERYON of the Second Order twisted around, coiling slowly in and out around the trees where the five humans stood captive. His body was around forty feet long, with the same oily black smoothness of an eel's skin, and as big around as a semi's tire. There were thick, gray, chitinous legs, spaced in groups of four, along the length of the body, clicking nastily against each other as they nimbly moved his bulk about. Above the first set of legs, a big, hairy human torso rose up, sporting four arms. The upper set of arms was long, muscular and human-looking, the hands strong, broad, and perfectly manicured. The lower set was an even longer pair of boneless, wriggling tentacles that ended in sharp, two-pronged white claws. Balanced on a powerful neck was a head, human in configuration with a handsome face, but covered in tiny, gray, reptilian scales.

Geryon roved a bright-blue gaze over the collection of humans he had brought into his domain, and turned up his thin, scabrous lips in an amused smile. He radiated malice, his evil filling the space around us like some thick, oppressive fog. It made my stomach churn, and I found myself swallowing repeatedly to keep from throwing up. He turned my way, giving me the most casual of glances, and my insides suddenly boiled with the urge to tear into this monstrous, unholy thing, to shred it and devour every foul bit of it. Spontaneously, my body went into a crouch, and for an instant, the expression on Geryon's face froze. Then the cold of Anoki's shade hit me, flashing in my limbs like bright pain. I stumbled backward and sat down hard on the ground.

Geryon's eyes flicked away from me. He looked again at each of the captives, his gaze assessing them, before turning his attention to Coach Frieda.

"Well, little mortal." The demonic voice was deep and ragged, like the ripping of thick, dusty, rotted cloth. "You've spent the better part of your past three years trading back and forth through the lower orders to get an audience with me, and now you have it. Are you going to talk or spend the time hiding back there?"

The coach shot another wary look my way. I was struggling to get up, inhuman, frustrated growls bubbling deep in my throat. My limbs kept slipping out from under me as Anoki's shade moved from muscle to muscle, somehow disrupting the nerves carrying orders from my brain and literally crippling me. From the coach's perspective, I must have appeared drunk or something, and thus not much of a threat, because she smiled at my predicament and stepped out to face the demon.

She stood straight and tall as she looked up, her gaze squarely meeting the inhuman, azure eyes hovering over her. Even as she spread her hands wide and made a tiny, respectful bow, her fearless look gave the impression that she was on equal footing with this chimerical thing. "Geryon, great guardian of the Circles of Hell and master of—"

"Yes, yes." Geryon rolled his human right hand impatiently. "We can skip the ass-kissing. Get to the part where you tell me what you want."

Coach Frieda's smile got just a little wider, and a lot bolder. "I want a piece of the Unwas."

"Really?" Geryon said, his face twisting into some unreadable expression. It might have been amusement, or annoyance. He began to coil slowly around the coach, legs clicking obscenely. The legs changed suddenly, shifting to become the cloven-footed hind limbs of a goat. "You're the 247th mortal to come before me seeking that. Do you know how many have gotten what they wanted?"

"None."

"Exactly. None. Their offerings for such a magnificent prize were so insulting that not only did I refuse them, but I sent them straight down into the blackest bowels of the Inferno." He leaned down, resting his chin on Coach Frieda's shoulder. His smile was very pleasant. "Now, then. What have you brought to bargain with?"

The coach didn't flinch. She grandly waved her right hand, the gesture taking in every one of the captive humans. "These, Guardian."

"Hmm." Geryon rose up to full height, folding his human arms—which shifted to look like sparkling, watery crystal—behind his back, goat legs carrying him in for a closer look at the captives. "Human souls. You're only the 247th mortal to offer human souls." The demon sighed, clearly unimpressed. He looked over his shoulder at the coach. "Ah, well. They'll make nice pets. And there's always room for another fresh, scheming necromancer in the raging pits. Good-bye, fool of a woman." One of the tentacles snaked back to seize Coach Frieda.

"Wait, Geryon," she said quickly. "These are not just any souls. Take a closer look."

The demon paused, giving a bored sniff. "Very well, I will. But if I'm not pleased with what I see, I'll just tear off your arms and legs right here. Agreed?"

"Agreed."

Geryon moved in on the half-conscious, moaning Pike. The tentacles slithered over and around Pike's neck, head, chest, and shoulders. Geryon closed his eyes, the rest of his body going still. Moments later, he said, "Ah. A camouflaged agent of the Enemy, one so fresh he doesn't even know he's been drafted. Very good. Very good, indeed." He opened his eyes, smacking his lips hungrily. "Let's have another look at these others."

The demon didn't remove his tentacles, which kept coiling possessively about Pike's body. Instead, he sprouted two smaller, thinner tentacles from his forehead, one reaching out to Coop on his left and the other to LaVelle on his right. Coop and LaVelle were terrified, staring with wild eyes, sweat running down their face and necks, screaming hoarsely into their gags. They struggled desperately, trying in vain to rip free of their bonds as the tentacles slipped around their heads.

Instantly, Geryon sneered. "Pah! These two are only favoreds of the Enemy, each with a nascent spiritual calling to serve. Mere wannabes. Still, depriving the opposition of potential new recruits is never a bad thing, I suppose." He shrugged, and then he turned to Bette, who suddenly snapped her scared, furious gaze from the coach to the demon. "And what's special about this one?"

"Oh. Nothing, really." For the first time, the coach shifted nervously under the demonic gaze. "She was just too much of a snoop for her own good. Consider her a freebie."

"If you insist." Geryon's legs changed again, this time becoming sleek, bare, very shapely human female limbs that were soft-looking and pink. The toenails were painted bright red. The churning limbs carried him over to Anoki, his tentacles finally pulling away from Pike. "Well, what have we here?"

"Another necromancer, O Guardian," Coach Frieda sneered. "One who has been actively working to set back the agendas of certain colleagues of yours."

"Indeed?" Geryon gave Anoki an intrigued look.

The tentacles sprouting from his forehead lashed downward, the pointed tips of them piercing the skin on either side of Anoki's neck. Anoki didn't even bat an eye; he just stared back at the demon stoically. Unable to speak, I screamed inwardly, my heart ablaze with a sudden fear that briefly overwhelmed the fury in me. Nothing must happen to Anoki. I couldn't stand it if anything happened to Anoki.

Geryon coiled his body about the tree where Anoki was tied and froze suddenly. The demon slowly closed his eyes. His human arms morphed into thick, barren tree branches. "Oh, this *is* a prize we have here. This one is no closer to the Enemy's grace than I am, yet he risked the ire of no less than Azazel of the First Order by crushing the emissary that dark lord sent into the English prime minister last month. Foolish, but daring. Hmm." The little tentacles sank deeper into Anoki's neck. Geryon laughed, a sound much like shattering glass. "And he was the one who managed to behead that mass murderer Deumos of the Second Order inspired in Seattle last year. We haven't been able to find so much as a clue as to who did these things. How in Hell's name could this little one have hidden himself from us so thoroughly? Oh, this is a delicious one, indeed. So delicious, in fact that I can hardly contain myself. I must taste him."

Tiny, glistening beads erupted on Geryon's forehead and ran down over his face. At first I thought it was sweat, but the beads quickly formed tight, parallel lines that streamed down his chest and down the first pair of womanly legs. Then they began to march over the forest floor, crossing the short distance between the demon and Anoki, and I saw that they were living, silvery pieces of Geryon's spirit, crawling on multiple legs like insects.

They streamed up Anoki's legs, under his pants. For the first time, I saw his eyes twitch. He kept staring at the demon, his gaze a laser beam of hatred and anger. But his bound legs jerked, and he dug his fingers into his thighs. He gritted his teeth, a grimace of pain. The little things scrabbled out from his collar as they continued to spread, covering his throat, going to his face. They poured down his arms.

Anoki tossed his head from side to side, trying to fling the spirit bugs off his face. He gasped and grunted, his breathing suddenly becoming heavy. I could hear the racing beat of his heart. I could smell his pain, a hot, sharp scent that burned in my nostrils. The things were biting, eating at him, but they weren't tearing at his skin. They were chewing out his soul, piece by tiny, agonized piece.

Watching that infuriated me. "Stop it!" I shouted, the sounds coming out of my throat as unearthly screeches rather than words. There was something in Anoki that scared me more than the curse I carried, but there was also something in him that was beautiful and hurt and lonely, and I wanted very much to protect that part of him. I couldn't just lie around and watch him suffer. My struggles to get up grew fiercer, more frenzied, but that damned shade kept slithering though me like oil, making it impossible for me to even stand up, much less fight. I screamed. *"Get away from him!"*

The coach spared me a cautious glance before turning back to the spectacle at the center of the circle, but Geryon ignored me completely. His smile grew as he watched sweat trickle down Anoki's neck. The spirit bugs had covered Anoki, spreading through his hair, chewing out more and more of his soul. His eyes stayed full of fire, even as his groans grew louder.

Geryon laughed, a growl full of both anger and admiration. "He bears pain well. I'll definitely have to save him for last." The spirit bugs lifted off Anoki like smoke and floated through the air back to Geryon, swirling around the demon's head before vanishing back into his monstrous body. The tree branches became human arms again, and he trailed a finger lightly across Anoki's forehead. "Let's see what else he's done...."

The tentacles slid deeper into Anoki's neck. He moaned, grinding his teeth against the pain of the horrific intrusion.

Geryon's eyes rolled up thoughtfully. "Definitely no emissary of the Enemy here. This one is better suited to the service of the King Below." His eyes closed again. A sound almost like a purr rumbled deep in his throat. "Ah! This is wonderful. He's attempted fratricide. Twice! Oh, I'm actually starting to like this one. I wonder what other delicious family secrets he has to offer...." The demon paused as the tentacles went deeper still.

Coach Frieda's smile spread into a triumphant grin.

Suddenly, Geryon's eyes flew open. His mouth gaped. His face became a mask of shock and horror.

The grin died instantly on the coach's face. She instinctively stepped back, edging away from Anoki and the demon. Geryon recoiled suddenly, jerking the tentacles from Anoki's neck with a loud snap. He reeled away, his legs vanishing altogether as he wriggled backward like a panicked snake. He spun on the coach, fury twisting into the terror on his face.

"Fool of a woman!" he screamed. "Do you know who his *mother* is?"

The coach obviously had no idea what the demon was screeching about, but she just as obviously realized that she was now in the worst danger of her life. Like a gazelle spotting a predator, she bolted.

One of Geryon's tentacle arms shot after her, snatching her up by the neck before she had gone three steps. It whipped her around, bringing her face to face with the demon. "You brought this dark spawn before me, teased me with him." Geryon's entire body trembled violently, and it was impossible to tell whether that was from rage or panic. "Have you any idea what unspeakable things his mother will do... when she discovers that I touched him... that I *tortured* him? You stupid whore of a necromancer! You have no idea what you've done to me!"

The tentacle tightened about the coach's neck. She gave a choked grunt, digging her fingers into the appendage as she tried to pull it away. In only moments, it seemed, that tentacle was going to squeeze her head right off her neck.

As evil as she was, I couldn't let that happen to her. I started once again to struggle against the numbing power of the shade, but the coach, as it turned out, didn't need my help. She stretched out her right hand and quickly mouthed several words. Lost souls swarmed from the darkness that surrounded us, shapeless, jet-black smudges moving too fast for human eyes to follow. They smashed themselves back and forth through Geryon's body. The demon sagged under the assault, losing control of his limbs. The tentacle holding the coach loosened, and she pulled herself free, dropping to the ground.

"Damned fools. Back to the pits with you, filth!" Geryon lashed out furiously with his left hand. A wave of ghostly, gray energy swept the air, and the lost souls were hurled, screaming, back into the darkness. He turned again, looking for the coach.

He barely spotted her in time. Coach Frieda was already rising, and rising fast, carried upward into the air by another spirit she had summoned while Geryon was distracted.

"No, bitch, you will not be leaving us." Tentacles shot from Geryon's forehead. They stabbed through the spirit, cutting it into nothingness, then wrapped tightly around the coach's body. The tentacles snatched her down, slamming her into the ground with jarring force. The coach gave a shout, the smell of her hot pain hitting me almost instantly.

"You sought a piece of the Unwas, did you not?" Geryon went on, his eyes raging wildly with uncontrolled emotion. "Well, congratulations, stupid woman. You shall have the whole of it! You're going into the Unwas." His tentacles lifted the coach, giving her a wrenching, malicious shake before tossing her aside. Then he looked at Anoki, eyes bright with hatred. "And since I am already fated to suffer heinously because of this boy, he shall go with you, along with all these others!"

Geryon raised all four arms straight up, and then slashed them down in a great ripping motion. The air over his head split, and Nothing bulged out.

CHAPTER
TWENTY-SEVEN

NOTHING wasn't bright or dark, big or small, noisy or silent, rough or smooth, stinky or sweet. It was everything, and there was no describing it.

No one had to tell me what contact with the Unwas would do to us. I knew. It would not merely disintegrate our bodies into random, discorporate atoms. It would unmake us.

It would undo our very existence.

There would have been no Myron.

There would have been no Coop, no LaVelle, no Bette, no Pike.

And there would have been no Anoki.

We would all be Nothing.

That would seem to solve Geryon's problem. After all, human minds could have no memory of someone who'd never existed. Geryon, being a demon, wasn't bound by puny little concepts like linear time. He would remember anyone he threw into the Unwas.

But I suspected that whoever Anoki's mother might be, she would, in much the same way, also remember that she lost her son to the Unwas. And Geryon must have known he would not be the only one to pay the price for that. The rage and grief of Anoki's mother would be far reaching.

My being unmade would be a good thing. It would mean that the people I killed would be alive again. I wanted that more than I wanted my own existence. Likewise, Coach Frieda's unmaking wouldn't be such a bad thing. But the others deserved existence. In Anoki's case, keeping him a part of creation would avoid a gargantuan amount of suffering doled out by his mother. And I loved him. I had always loved him.

Those thoughts went through my head in maybe fifteen seconds. That's about how long it took for Geryon to sprout seven long, thick black tentacles from his torso. Five of them wrapped around Coop, LaVelle, Bette, Pike, and Anoki, trees and all. There were loud cracks as the tentacles snapped the trunks in two at the root and lifted the tree-bound people into the air. The sixth tentacle snatched Coach Frieda up by her ankle as she tried, yet again, to escape. The seventh tentacle reached for me, and a blinding bolt of rage shot through my head.

I went completely predator then. An atomic barrage of energy and emotion blasted through me. My clothes burned away in a flash, as if my body had suddenly become intensely hot. A tail sprouted from the base of my spine, long, slender but rippled with muscle and as black as the darkness of hell swirling around us. From the tip jutted a curved, black spike, the inner edge sharp enough to flay rock. That spike and my claws blazed with greenish flame. I tore myself away from that debilitating shade as if ripping through paper. Any sense of caring, about anyone or anything, was gone. I only wanted to eat. Geryon, being the biggest snack available, was my first target.

The demon shouted, "Away from me, halfling!" as he swept out both arms on his right side, trying to swat me aside. I was too fast for that. I smashed into his chest and latched on, digging the claws on my hands and feet into the hairy flesh of his back. Devil's Fire blazed into those wounds in the same instant my teeth tore into Geryon's neck.

The demon's scream shook the ground. He threw himself backward in an instinctive but futile effort to get away from me. He slammed against one of the remaining trees, partially uprooting it.

I could sense everything that was happening around me, even with my eyes squeezed shut in ecstasy at the taste of fiendish flesh. The tentacles uncoiled. Bette, LaVelle, Coop, Pike, and Anoki all fell to the ground, still bound to the trees. Coach Frieda fell free, too, managing to land in a catlike crouch. She whispered a command, trying to summon a spirit to ferry her away. Anoki's shade bopped her in the head, knocking her unconscious before she could finish. The shade then went to Anoki, wrapping itself around him and breaking the ropes that held him.

The demon's tentacles clasped around my arms, legs, and neck. A laugh bubbled deep in my throat at that. I dug my claws deeper into Geryon's back, biting deeper into his neck. The demon screamed again. His tentacles tightened about my body and ripped me away from him. Unfortunately for him, a big chunk of his flesh came with me, evaporating into a foul cloud of dust in my teeth.

Geryon howled, a blast of pain and fury as loud as a jet engine. He flung me toward the darkness. My tail stabbed outward, the spike punching deeply into the trunk of a big pine. I whipped horizontally around the tree, and then hurled myself back at Geryon. In that spin, the spike cut completely through the trunk. As I slammed back into the demon's chest, there was a loud crack, and the top of the tree toppled sideways.

Muffled screams came from Bette, LaVelle, and Coop. They stared up in hopeless horror as the tree fell toward them and the still unconscious Pike.

Anoki was running toward the rift Geryon had made in the air. The Unwas continued to spill out of that opening, spreading like fire, making nothing out of everything it touched. Anoki turned back at the screams. Eyes blazing with a silent command, he jabbed a finger toward the endangered trio who struggled desperately to free themselves from their bonds. His cold shade unwrapped itself from his body and shot backward. Invisible to human eyes, it unfurled its uncanny substance over the others. The tree fell into that substance and vanished completely in an instant, like a screen image when a television is switched off. Once the tree was gone, the shade swept down and snapped the ropes that held them all.

"Myron!" Bette took a step toward me, and then she hesitated. I was now clinging to Geryon's back, ripping away at his chest and shoulders with my claws as he hissed in rage and pain, his serpentine form sweeping this way and that. Her voice was filled with worry. Geryon's tentacles curled backward, slapping viciously at my invulnerable body. Bette ran forward to help me.

That was a very bad move on her part. My attention switched from Geryon to her. It made me want to rip her apart. I scrambled up on the demon's shoulders, only seconds away from leaping at her.

"Stop!" Anoki got in front of her, blocking her path. "You can't help Myron. Leave him to me." He pointed behind her at the small circle of rocks he had hastily constructed. LaVelle and Coop, dragging the dazed Pike between them, were already stumbling toward the circle. "Go with them," Anoki told her. "Get out of here."

Too late. Even as Bette turned to run, I sprang into the air, arms outstretched, claws extended and burning. She screamed as I hurtled toward her.

It was Geryon who saved her. Enraged, the demon's tentacles lashed around my legs and snatched me out of midleap. "Filthy halfling! Pay the price for attacking me!"

He slammed me face-first into a tree, and then into the ground. As my body was lifted, I spat a wad of grass and dirt from my mouth. Geryon pulled me close to him with his tentacles. His human-looking arms became clear diamond. Six-inch diamond spikes sprouted from his fists just before he started punching me in the gut.

The powerful blows knocked the wind out of me, but that was the extent of the damage they did to me. The spikes couldn't penetrate my skin. The wounds I'd inflicted on Geryon had healed within seconds. Although my attacks had hurt him, he was much too powerful to be destroyed by single swipes of Devil's Fire.

I was way too insane at the time to realize this. I flicked out my tail, and the spiked end wrapped itself around the demon's crystalline arms and pinned them together. Using my hands to pull free of Geryon's tentacles, I swung myself up and over his head and landed on his back once more. There I resumed my attack, determined to rip him into bite-size pieces.

Still holding Pike, LaVelle and Coop jumped through the smaller circle, followed by Bette. Condemned souls, sensing the opening to the physical world, swarmed out of the darkness, black wisps zipping through the air in a desperate effort to be free of hell even for a moment. Anoki's shade promptly sealed the passage before any of them could go through. The souls wailed, furious at being denied liberation. They wanted no part of Anoki's shade, however, and quickly melted back into the darkness.

Cursing, Geryon reached over his shoulder with one of his human arms and closed his fist tight on my head. "Little fool, I have had enough of you." He peeled me off his back. I sensed the insect-like legs sprouting again from his eel body. With incredible speed, he scuttled across the ground, intent on stuffing me headfirst into the dark pits of hell.

Behind us, Anoki quietly whispered a summoning. A piece of Geryon's own silvery spirit popped out of his forehead, then skittered down his neck and along his arm before sinking out of sight into his fist. The fist opened. I dropped to the ground and bounded into the treetops.

The demon spun on Anoki. "Wretch!" Geryon snarled, face twisted with hatred. "I will suffer no less under your mother's hand regardless of what I do to you now. So I think I'll visit some of that torment on you... for starters."

Geryon reached out for Anoki with his tentacles. Anoki raised his arms as if to embrace them. Like some great gust of wind, the cold shade swept upward, snatching Geryon up by those tentacles. In a powerful whirl, the shade hurled him toward the spreading mass of the Unwas.

Geryon caught a tree branch with one of his hands, stopping himself before he hit Nothing. But the Unwas pulled hungrily at him, like a magnet pulling at metal. Straining, he tried to gain holds on the tree with his other limbs. If he could anchor himself to the tree with his serpent's tail, that would leave his limbs free to seal up the Unwas again.

He almost made it. Just as he managed to bring the tip of his serpent's tail to within inches of the tree's upper trunk, the shade snatched up the unconscious Coach Frieda and threw her. Her body smacked Geryon flat in the face, the demon lost his grip, and they both slammed into the Unwas. And they were gone instantly, made into Nothing.

As if it were a freshly stoked fire, the Unwas started swelling faster. In perhaps thirty seconds, it would eat up everything left within the confines of Coach Frieda's circle. I was too crazy to care about that. I sprang at Anoki, the only target left to me. The shade reopened the smaller circle Anoki had made, and Anoki dove through it. Then the shade went through. The circle remained open a couple of seconds more, just long enough for me to follow.

I felt Anoki's circle snap shut, almost on my heels. My body met a hard, polished surface and began to skid. I came to a halt, crouching low on my hands and feet. A giddy rush went through me. Anoki was somewhere just ahead of me. I could smell him, and I was damned hungry.

I bared my fangs in a horrible grin.

CHAPTER
Twenty-Eight

Anoki stood about twenty feet away. I'd be on him in an instant. The muscles in my legs tensed.

But I didn't leap.

I was on a round marble dais that was maybe ten feet across.

A circle. A magicked circle. My body sensed the pressure at the last second. I hunkered down on the marble surface, tail curling around my feet, and glared ravenously at Anoki.

He stood well away from the dais. He was turning a large silver coin over and over with his hands, staring at it as if he was surprised to have it. The shade snugged around his body like a cat around a litter of kittens. Somewhere, buried deep beneath my inhuman hunger, jealousy burned in my soul.

We were in a large, mostly bare room. Aside from the dais, there were thick, velvety-looking blue curtains over the window, and ornate crown molding decorated the edges of the ceiling and the hardwood floor. The walls were covered with weird runes, like the ones Anoki had carved in the trees when he first summoned a demon to take me. Wherever we were, it had to be night. The room was dim, lit by stands of flickering candles.

Anoki tore his gaze away from the coin, slipping it into his pocket as he looked at me. He walked forward, closing perhaps half the distance between us. I could smell the rich hotness of the blood in his veins, the herbal scents in his hair, the thin sheen of sweat on his muscled arms. So close. So tantalizing. My skin literally burned with the gluttonous need to tear into him, to bite into that tall, bronze body. Devil's Fire flickered over me in rolling, silvery-green flames.

He must have realized the effect he was having on me, because he started to step back. What little bit remained of my sanity slipped away then. Bellowing, I leaped at Anoki.

"Stop—!" he cried, his warning coming far too late.

I slammed headfirst into the air over the edge of the dais and stopped as abruptly as if I'd smashed into a steel wall. My body hung there, suspended by the force that formed the circle's powerful barrier. The unseen force crackled through me. Black ichor—the stuff of my spirit—started to seep out of my body, streaming from my scalp, eyes, nostrils, mouth, fingertips, chest, everywhere.

I screamed in pain and panic.

Anoki shouted something in a language I couldn't understand. It could very well have been English, but my mind was completely fogged with agony. He swept his arms over the edge of the dais, breaking the circle, and I fell hard to the ground.

I lay crumpled on my side, eyes shut, gasping raggedly for air, too weak to move. Anoki knelt on the dais, scooping me into his arms and holding me to his body. His fingers stroked my face, wiping the spiritual blood away. He leaned down, putting his forehead against mine. He brushed my skin gently with his lips. He whispered something in my ear.

I felt his words, rather than hearing them. They spread through me like a balm, covering and then erasing the terrible ache from my body, easing my heart and lungs, calming my soul. My arms and legs grew strong in the same moment their flesh shifted. All of this seemed to take a long time. Finally, I opened my eyes and lifted my head from Anoki's shoulder, looking into his face. I smiled at the frantic worry in his cold green eyes.

"I'm okay now," I said slowly, my words a bit slurred. Leaning forward, I rubbed my nose against his. Then I kissed him. It was tender at first, just my lips brushing lightly over his. He went still, closing his eyes, not kissing me back. I stroked the sides of his face and kissed him harder, forcing his lips apart, skimming the tip of my tongue over the smooth hardness of his teeth. The cinnamon smell of his breath and body excited me.

I slid my hands down and under the hem of his jersey, then pulled it up to his chest. I pressed my fingers into his broad, hard pecs.

"Myron," Anoki whispered. "I will most likely be as selfishly out of control as I was before when we mated. Are you sure you want this?"

"Yes. I want you, I *want* you," I replied eagerly. "Where's your shady friend?"

"In what's left of Geryon's domain, taking care of something for me."

"Good." I yanked up the jersey again. This time, Anoki raised his arms, and I hauled the jersey off him.

He slid his hands slowly down my back as I squeezed his chest. I was naked. My clothes must have ripped or burned away altogether when I fully changed into the predator. The chill in the air tingled against my skin. Anoki reached down and grabbed my whole butt with one big hand. He squeezed so hard I was sure the muscles in my ass would rupture. We both groaned, the sounds like the rumbling growls of two angry beasts.

I grabbed a fistful of Anoki's coarse hair and tugged his head back, exposing his throat. I bit down on the side of his neck, nipping sharply enough to leave bruises. Anoki hissed with each bite. He dug his fingers even deeper into the flesh of my ass.

He tore himself away from me suddenly. Getting to his feet, he stripped the clothes from his body. His huge, erect cock speared out from his groin with the foreskin peeled back, the exposed head of it only inches from my face. He pressed his dick to my lips. I opened my mouth and let him shove it in. The head of it hit the back of my throat, making me gag. In a panic, I planted my hands against Anoki's thighs and started to push away from him. He clamped his hands around the back of my head, stopping me before I could pull my mouth off his cock.

Holding onto my head, Anoki pumped his dick in and out, slipping its hot, rubbery length back and forth between my lips. The thrusting was intense but not so deep as to choke me. My brain started whirling in blissful dizziness, reeling at the feel and taste of this man's dick in my mouth. My hands reached around to clutch Anoki's flexing butt.

Just as my jaws began to ache from the pounding, Anoki yanked his cock out of my mouth. He sat on the edge of the dais, then reached over to grab me around the waist. I pushed myself up as he lifted me, and I straddled him. He held up his right hand and mouthed a silent entreaty. Droplets oozed out of the very air, coating the first two fingers of his hand in golden oil. He maneuvered his hand under me and shoved those two slick fingers into my ass.

The penetration made me gasp, my mouth hanging open. He stared at my face with raw lust. His fingers twisted and pushed, loosening me up. Seconds later, he pulled his fingers out and grabbed his dick, still wet from my mouth, and positioned the head of it at my lubricated hole. He thrust his hips upward sharply. My ass swallowed the length of him hungrily.

I cried out, squeezed my eyes shut, burning with pain and with pleasure. He didn't pause even a moment for my body to adjust to the invasion. Clutching my waist, he rolled his hips beneath me in a relentless grind, pounding brutally into me from below. I wrapped my arms around his shoulders, buried my face against his neck, and held on as my butt bounced helplessly in his lap. Time took on that odd, undefined quality again. It seemed that Anoki fucked me for an eternity, and for only an instant. When he came, I felt his entire cock swell even bigger, followed by the gush of his cum spreading deep through me in a hot spasm. My dick, squeezed and caressed between our bellies, erupted almost at the same instant, my cum spurting thickly over our skin.

Breathless and sweating, we held onto each other desperately, long after our orgasms faded, shuddering together. My heart raced, but not just from the exertion of frenzied sex. Something in me wanted to hold onto this man forever. I still longed to fuck him. My dick began to harden again just at the thought of it. Even as I wished that this time it had been me inside of him, I was glad—grateful—that things worked out the way they had. I had a part of him in me, a part of him that would stay with me.

At the same time, I could feel his lips against my ear, whispering in that ancient language I could not understand. Yet, I somehow knew what he was saying. I knew how deeply he wanted me, and how much it hurt that he could not stay with me. The connection between us was undoubtedly one forged of more time than the single day we had spent together. Somehow, somewhere, there had been a lifetime shared between us. He knew me better than anyone else in this world, was closer to me than even my parents. There was no denying it. I loved this man. And I never wanted to let go of him again.

A thundering coldness bulged suddenly between us, and I knew Anoki's shade had returned. It sent pain ripping along my nerves, far worse than what I felt when I crashed into the barrier of the circle. The agony flashed throughout my body in an instant, nauseating me and making me scream. I hurled myself away from that cold rage, away from Anoki. It must have repelled him as well, because he gasped loudly and shoved me from him at the same moment I rolled off his lap.

"I'm sorry... I'm sorry...," he muttered again and again in the dark.

The sound of his voice was soothing enough. I curled on my side, lulled by his apologies, and settled down to wait for this new pain to ease.

"Myron?"

I opened my eyes slowly. I raised my head, trying in my mind to place a face with the voice. "Dad?"

"No. It's me."

My arms went out before me as I stretched. My skin was its usual light brown, and my fingers ended in squarely trimmed, dirty nails instead of flaming claws. There was dried blood on my hands. Gray daylight filled the room, filtering though the drawn curtains.

I was lying on my stomach, naked. The marble was cold and hard beneath me. My body felt chilled and drained. I sat up.

Anoki stood at the edge of the dais. He had changed clothes, dressed now in navy cargo pants and a black jersey and black sneakers. I couldn't sense his shade now, but I was sure it was still with him.

Anoki had never looked lonelier.

I wanted to hug him, but he was standing outside the circle, and the circle had been restored. I tried not to think about what that meant. Instead, I gave him a smile. "I was dreaming about my dad." The dream itself escaped me. But as I tried to recall the details, another memory surfaced. "Oh, no. I killed him. And my mom. And Garrett…!"

Anoki raised his hands, shaking his head firmly. "Myron, calm down. Listen to me. You didn't kill anyone. Those were thoughts that demon calling himself Benito put in your head to torture you. Do you understand? Your parents, your friend, everyone is fine."

"They are?"

"Yes. I promise you."

Relief swelled through me, and it left me weak. "What about Bette? Coop, LaVelle—?"

"Bette, LaVelle, Coop, and Pike are all back home. They don't remember any of it, because with Frieda Blevins now a part of the Unwas, none of it happened. At least as far as they're concerned. You and I should be so lucky."

That was an attempt at a joke. I smiled. "Do they remember me?"

"Of course. At least, your friends do. Pike never met you. This morning, your parents posted a $10,000 reward for information as to your whereabouts. Bette and Garrett are participating in search parties. Coop and LaVelle are distributing flyers with your picture on them. You are very much missed."

"What about the Unwas?" My voice cracked with sudden alarm. I couldn't remember what that stuff looked like, but I still knew what it would do to creation if it spread uncontrolled.

"Sealed up again," Anoki answered confidently.

That seemed… unlikely. "How?"

"I believe that is another of those things you are better off not knowing."

"Yeah." I wrapped my arms around myself. "Can I get a blanket or something?"

"You won't be cold much longer."

"Right. Not where I'm going. Ha ha ha."

"I didn't mean—"

"It's okay." I sighed, dropping my chin to my chest.

"Myron?"

I looked up at him.

His hair was tied back from his face in a ponytail. There was something so sweet in his eyes, so vulnerable. "Thank you. I could not have saved these people and stopped Geryon without you. Your parents and your friends are very lucky to have had you in their lives. And I am very glad that I got a chance to know you. Thank you."

There was one more question for him burning in my mind. I wanted to know why a horrifyingly evil spirit, only a step down from a fallen angel, had been terrified of his mother. But I didn't ask the question. I feared the answer would bring nightmares worse than the one that was about to rise out of this circle to embrace me.

Anoki's smile was shy and sad and hurt. It thickened the pain in my chest. We exchanged looks for several seconds more, and my mind struggled to make sense of the strange mix of emotions in Anoki's face. Then, just as he turned away, I got it.

He loved me. Maybe as much as I loved him. So I didn't imagine all that stuff about the connection binding us.

In another life, who knows what could have happened between us. Or what *did* happen between us. But all we had now was this life, and I was about to leave it forever.

"Don't cry, Myron. Please." He turned back, taking a step toward the dais.

I swallowed the hurt in my throat and wiped my eyes. "Can you hold my hand until… it's over?"

The question seemed to stab at him. He shook his head. "If I reach across the circle, it will break, and that will leave the demon free to go anywhere he chooses once he comes. And if I stand with you inside the circle, I'll be at the demon's mercy."

"Okay. Okay. I guess I already knew that, but I had to ask…."

"I will miss you, Myron. More than you can possibly know."

"I'll miss you too." I didn't say anything else for a moment, hoping he would go ahead and summon the demon. The waiting was making me so nervous I wouldn't be able to stand it much longer. But he just stared back at me reluctantly. I dropped my eyes from his. "Anoki, hurry up and do it. I'm so scared."

"Myron. Look at me."

I raised my head again.

His gaze was suddenly intense. "I will find the person who cursed you, him or his heirs. This curse will be lifted, and you will have your life back. I *swear* this to you."

I believed him. The conviction almost seemed to radiate from his body like a glow. I nodded.

Anoki shuddered. After a few moments, he caught himself. He sighed deeply. "Are you sure you're ready?"

It took everything in me to answer. "Yes."

He closed his eyes and whispered the summoning.

I felt the demon rising beneath me, the pressure of it seeming to push the dais upward. There was something anxious about its coming, as if it wanted to make sure there was no time for Anoki to change his mind again. Its evil preceded it, flowing up around me like stifling, clutching waves of heat. "Oh, damn." I quailed, unable to hold back the terror that exploded in me. Panic brought me to my feet, ready to run despite that fact that there was no getting away. My eyes frantically swept the dais, trying to see the coming nightmare.

Finished with his invocation, Anoki opened his eyes. "Myron. Myron, look at me."

I forced myself to meet his eyes. His face was serene, full of reassurance and caring. Full of love. It calmed me enough that I could hold still as the demon came up through the dais.

I didn't look at it. My last sight was of the fiercely determined, adoring smile on Anoki's face.

Then the darkness took me, but I wasn't afraid any longer.

I knew Anoki would be coming back for me.

Get a sneak peek at the sequel to *Brown-eyed Devil.*

RED ROGUE

CHAPTER
ONE

ANOKI was not prone to sentimentality. Nothing in his life had conditioned him to it. He had lived 119 years, and in that time, he had never known the reassuring touch of a father's hand on his shoulder, had never experienced the comforting warmth of a mother kissing away his worries. As far as he knew, he'd had no childhood. For all of his life, he had been exactly as he was now, a tall, muscular man of Native American heritage who appeared to be in his early twenties. He knew he was more than he seemed. And he knew that he had a mother and a father, although he preferred not to think of them.

He was a man of reason and logic, not emotion. In the summer of 1940, he had watched scores of people die when the Luftwaffe bombarded shipping centers, homes, and railways in Germany's doomed effort to pound Great Britain into submission. He was on the Caribbean island of Martinique in May of 1902 when Mount Pelée erupted in a devastating explosion that sent seething waves of superheated gas sweeping outward in blazing black clouds that moved at horrific speed. The town of Saint-Pierre was wiped out, and some thirty thousand people burned to death in a matter of minutes. He visited the scene of a New York City subway accident in August of 1991 when a drunken and demon-possessed operator crashed a train, killing five people and injuring hundreds of others. In all such situations, Anoki did everything within his power to save as many souls as he could. But he was as emotionless as a robot in doing so, enduring the screams of the dying and injured without even a flinch.

He spent much of his 119 years in the ether, a realm of the spirit that existed within and around the physical world. There were beings in the ether that were powerful and voracious and evil beyond imagining. Yet Anoki lived in that realm for months at a time without fear. Part of the reason for that was that he was fairly powerful himself. And those things that did not fear his power feared his mother. Anoki was afraid of his mother, too, but he kept his terror under control. He kept all of his feelings under control. That was the only way he could maintain his sanity as he struggled to fight back the horrors in the ether that periodically tried to plunder the human world. Moreover, emotion powered his necromantic abilities, and letting those abilities run wild would raise the dead by the thousands and rip loose the barriers that divided the ether from the earth. And so, in 119 years, Anoki was never ruled by emotion.

Until he met Myron Mitchell.

Anoki had a passion for young, strong, well-built human men. Over the first eighty-seven years of his life, he bedded soldiers, construction workers, athletes, actors, and even priests: handsome men full of swagger and brawn whose size alone was intimidating. Many of them fell helplessly in love with Anoki, but he told himself there was no place for romance in his world, and he moved on with neither regret nor a backward look. Still, if he were going to love a man, he thought it would be someone more his equal in size and strength.

Myron was at least a foot shorter than Anoki, a slip of a man with a slender build who had only come of age a few months ago. It was the activation of a shape-shifter curse that drew Anoki to Myron in the little West Tennessee town of Killebrew. Anoki went there with the intention of dispatching Myron to the ether where a demon would imprison him forever, the only way to ensure that innocent lives would not be lost to the murdering creature Myron would become. But then Anoki laid eyes on Myron, and all reason left him.

Aside from an appealing face, Myron possessed none of the physical qualities that attracted Anoki. Yet, when he looked through Myron's bedroom window on that cool, cloudy night in March and saw him for the first time, Anoki thought the blood had suddenly frozen in his veins. He was taken instantly by a sensation of love so powerful that he had to fight back a scream. It felt as if he had found a vital piece of his life that he hadn't known until that moment had been missing.

But that was impossible. Myron, who had only lived eighteen years, was nothing like the men Anoki had once pursued. And surely Anoki would remember if he had ever been so stupid as to let himself fall in love with a human, especially a cursed one. And there was his shade, of course, the great, ancient demiurge that had bound itself to him in its own twisted love, so desperate for his heart that it had not allowed him the physical pleasure of another man for the last thirty-two years. Yet, Anoki was so deeply smitten in that first look that he couldn't force himself to open a portal and drop Myron into the foul arms of a demon as planned. For seven months, he surreptitiously followed the pint-sized youth, sneaking in forlorn stares and mentally kicking himself for his stupidity. He was being completely irrational. Myron could have transformed at any moment and begun killing the people around him. Anoki put lives in danger because his foolish heart burned for someone he certainly could not have loved or even known before. It was only after Myron became the predatory creature and slaughtered a pack of wolves that Anoki finally moved to trap the deadly young man in the ether. Even then, he let Myron talk him into a one-day reprieve.

Because of love.

Anoki stood before an empty round dais of black marble in a large, mostly vacant room that had once been a dining hall. Only moments ago he had watched as the demon Abaddon reached eagerly up through that dais and dragged Myron down into its murky realm. Anoki did not endure the sight dispassionately. Anguish exploded within him. He wanted to scream. It was as if the demon had plunged its claws into him and pulled every vital organ out of his chest (something Abaddon, a spirit too insane to know fear, would have happily done if not for the barrier Anoki had raised to stop the demon from moving beyond the dais). But he couldn't let his heartbreak show. He had to be strong for Myron. And he couldn't let his possessive, jealous shade know just how deep his feelings were for the little man.

He stared at the dais, fighting to keep himself from diving through the portal and attacking Abaddon with all of his power to free Myron from the dark angel's horrible grip. *Not now, not yet,* he told himself. *There are other things you must do first.*

The room was lit with candles. Thick, decaying blue velvet curtains and ornate crown molding were all that remained from the days when Anoki had dined here with other luminaries from the world of thaumaturgy. They had covered the walls with runes, creating a place of power. Anoki hadn't lived here since the end of the Second World War. The house was on the summit of Snaefell, a mountain on the Isle of Man. Outside, the afternoon was cold and rainy. Wind howled around the house, making Anoki feel even more anxious. He drew in deep breaths, steadying his emotions. If he was going to free Myron from the shape-shifter curse and bring him back into the human world, he had to be in complete control of his feelings.

It took almost fifteen minutes for him to fully calm himself. There were three ghosts who haunted the house. All three of them hovered around Anoki, pale, gray, shapeless forms drawn to and mesmerized by the vitality of his soul. Anoki pointed at the candles and the ghosts immediately leaped to do his will, sweeping along and dousing the flames. Next, Anoki reached over the rim of the dais, breaking the circle of power as he willed the portal to Abaddon's domain to close. With a sweep of his hand, he willed another portal to open. As a reward for their service, he paused and allowed the ghosts to briefly touch his body, letting them feel again the wonder of life. Then he closed his eyes and stepped onto the dais.

When he opened his eyes, he was standing in the woods outside Killebrew. He had come here through a circle that another necromancer, Frieda Blevins, had made by clearing out trees in a big, round swath. Making a circle in such a manner took more time, but it was worth the effort because it yielded more power. With Frieda Blevins' existence undone, Anoki now claimed this circle for himself. He strode off through the woods. It was 10:03 a.m. here, and the sun was shining, although the rays couldn't penetrate the thick treetops. That gave time for his eyes to adjust to the instant change from dark to daylight. He headed straight for the Mitchell house.

He wore navy cargo pants, a black jersey, and black sneakers, clothes suitable for his apparent age. His long hair occasionally rubbed "older" adults the wrong way, and he had tied it back. He didn't want to draw any suspicion. His first step, he had decided, would be to talk with Myron's parents. He had to trace Myron's curse back to its origin. Because it was a legacy curse, Anoki thought Myron's parents would be better able to identify the ancestor who had drawn the ire of the thaumaturgist who laid the curse.

As Anoki rounded the corner onto the street that led down to the cul-de-sac where the Mitchells lived, he saw several vehicles parked in front of the Mitchell home, including a gray-and-white Killebrew police cruiser and a van from News Channel 3. His shade, which was coiled around his waist like an invisible python, tightened its grip suddenly, a signal that it didn't want Anoki to go down there. Anoki ignored it and pressed ahead, walking faster.

Several people waited outside the house, among them a cameraman who stood off to one side on the sidewalk, filming a reporter who was speaking into a microphone. Some of the people were neighbors, milling about on the lawn, looking despondent. He recognized the neighbor who sat on the steps with his head down, a tall, lean African American youth. That was Garrett Chess, Myron's closest friend, who should have been in school at this hour. Locking down his emotions, Anoki went directly to Garrett.

"You there," Anoki said, stopping at the steps.

Garrett looked up. Recognition flickered through the tears in his eyes.

"I'm here to see Mr. or Mrs. Mitchell," Anoki said. "Has something happened to them?"

Garrett shook his head. "No, not to them. They're in there talking to the police. It's their son, Myron. He's been missing, and he was found dead early this morning."

Anoki was more curious than shocked, wondering how this particular rumor had come about. "Dead?"

"Yeah. He disappeared almost two days ago. We've been looking everywhere for him. And this morning, his mom looked out into their backyard and he was just lying there next to the patio. Dead."

"That can't be," Anoki scoffed.

"It's true, man."

"Is the body still back there?"

"The medical examiner had it taken to the funeral home until she can get a van to take it to the county morgue." Garrett squinted at him. "I've seen you around town. Who're you?"

"No one you need remember." Anoki nodded, and his shade wiped the memory of the encounter from Garrett's mind. Garrett lowered his head and resumed his quiet weeping.

Anoki turned and hurried away. McQuarran and Sons, the only funeral home in Killebrew, was at the eastern edge of the town. That was roughly five miles from here, and he would have to walk the distance. He cursed himself. He had left his car in a field at the Wexlar farm, which was even farther away. With a brusque mental command, he ordered his shade to go manifest itself as a human being and drive the car to the funeral home. The demiurge tightened its grip even more, reluctant to leave. At Anoki's insistence, it released him and departed.

He was sweating heavily by the time he reached the funeral home. It was a wide, one-story building with brick walls painted white. There were only two ghosts present, lingering because the bodies they had recently exited were stashed inside. They came out to Anoki as he walked up and tugged open the glass door of the main entrance. He immediately struck bargains with them both, sending them forth to possess the people he was about to encounter and make those people see what he wanted them to see.

The receptionist, a woman in her midthirties dressed in a white blouse and a long black skirt, rose from the elegant oak desk where she had been reading a magazine. She put on a practiced sympathetic smile. "Good morning. I'm Catherine. How can I help you?"

"I'm Charlton Mitchell," said Anoki. "The medical examiner had my son, Myron Mitchell, brought here this morning. I want to see him, please."

Thanks to the ghost residing now in her head, the receptionist was immediately agreeable. She saddened her smile appropriately. "Of course, Mr. Mitchell. If you'll come this way...."

She led him through a door at the back of the reception area and down a hall. They stopped at the door of a large office, where a middle-aged man in a black suit, with thinning, graying brown hair combed neatly back from his forehead, sat at a desk that was an exact match of the one in the reception area, reviewing financial records on a computer screen. He looked up at them.

"Mr. McQuarran, this is Charlton Mitchell," said the receptionist, gesturing at Anoki. "His son was brought in earlier this morning. He wants to see him."

"Oh, of course." McQuarran rose at once, buttoning his jacket. He crossed to the door and extended a hand to Anoki. "I am so very sorry for your loss, Mr. Mitchell."

"Thank you," Anoki said, shaking the man's hand impatiently.

"Follow me, please."

McQuarran led him to the back of the building and into the embalming room. It was large, the walls and floors covered in white, yellow, and green tiles that would have given a cheerful air to any other room. There were four stainless steel tables along the rear wall beneath a bank of high, narrow windows that admitted thin shafts of sunlight. Behind the tables were cabinets and sinks and equipment, the purpose of which was no mystery. The room had a distinct antiseptic chill to it. McQuarran veered to his left, toward a wall that bore a bank of twelve mortuary refrigeration units. He reached down and grabbed the handle on the door of the unit at the bottom right corner.

He looked up at Anoki. "Do you need a moment, Mr. Mitchell? To prepare yourself?"

"No," Anoki said. "Open it."

McQuarran pulled the drawer open and Anoki gasped.

The body in the drawer looked exactly like Myron. It had the same short, straight black hair, the same slim build, and the same tan skin, although the coldness of death had emptied that skin of all vitality. Anoki knew this was not his Myron. No, he had sent Myron's body and soul into a demonic domain not much more than an hour ago.

What he was seeing here and now could not be any part of that Myron. But Anoki's heart was already broken, and even seeing an obvious doppelganger of his love lying dead was more than he could take. He staggered back a step, reaching out for something to steady himself.

"Mr. Mitchell!" McQuarran closed the unit and quickly reached out to take Anoki's arm. Anoki shut his eyes. He couldn't breathe. He let himself be guided away.

"Here. Sit down."

He sat and leaned forward, putting his head between his knees. He tried to breathe but couldn't seem to get any air into his lungs.

"Cathy! Bring a bottle of water. Quickly!"

He heard and felt motion around him. A cold plastic bottle was pressed suddenly into his hand.

"Mr. Mitchell, are you all right? Here, take a sip of this."

The bottle disappeared from his hand and reappeared at his lips. He sat up and took a swig of water. *It's not him. It's not him in that drawer....*

His heart steadied, and he could breathe again. He drew in a deep breath and sighed heavily. He opened his eyes.

McQuarran was next to him, holding the bottle of water in one hand, looking at him anxiously. They were sitting on one of the pews in the funeral home's chapel. Catherine, the receptionist, hovered nervously in the doorway.

"Mr. Mitchell, are you okay?" McQuarran asked. "Do you need us to call someone?"

Anoki stared straight ahead for a moment at the large white cross mounted on wall over the choir stand at the front of the chapel. Then he buried his face in his hands, and for the first time in his life, Anoki cried.

He didn't know how or why, but someone had gone to a great deal of trouble to make people think Myron Mitchell was dead. In doing so, the perpetrator of this hoax had made a huge mistake, because he or she had added to Anoki's already considerable pain.

For that, there would be hell to pay.

EVAN GILBERT lives in Memphis, Tennessee, a Southern boy through and through. He thinks writing is a pretty neat way to make a living. When he's not writing, he enjoys, in no particular order, swimming, going to the movies, reading, long walks in the country, working out, and spending time with family and friends.

Also from EVAN GILBERT

http://www.dreamspinnerpress.com

Also from EVAN GILBERT

UNWRAPPING
THE PRESENT

EVAN
GILBERT

http://www.dreamspinnerpress.com

Read more from EVAN GILBERT in

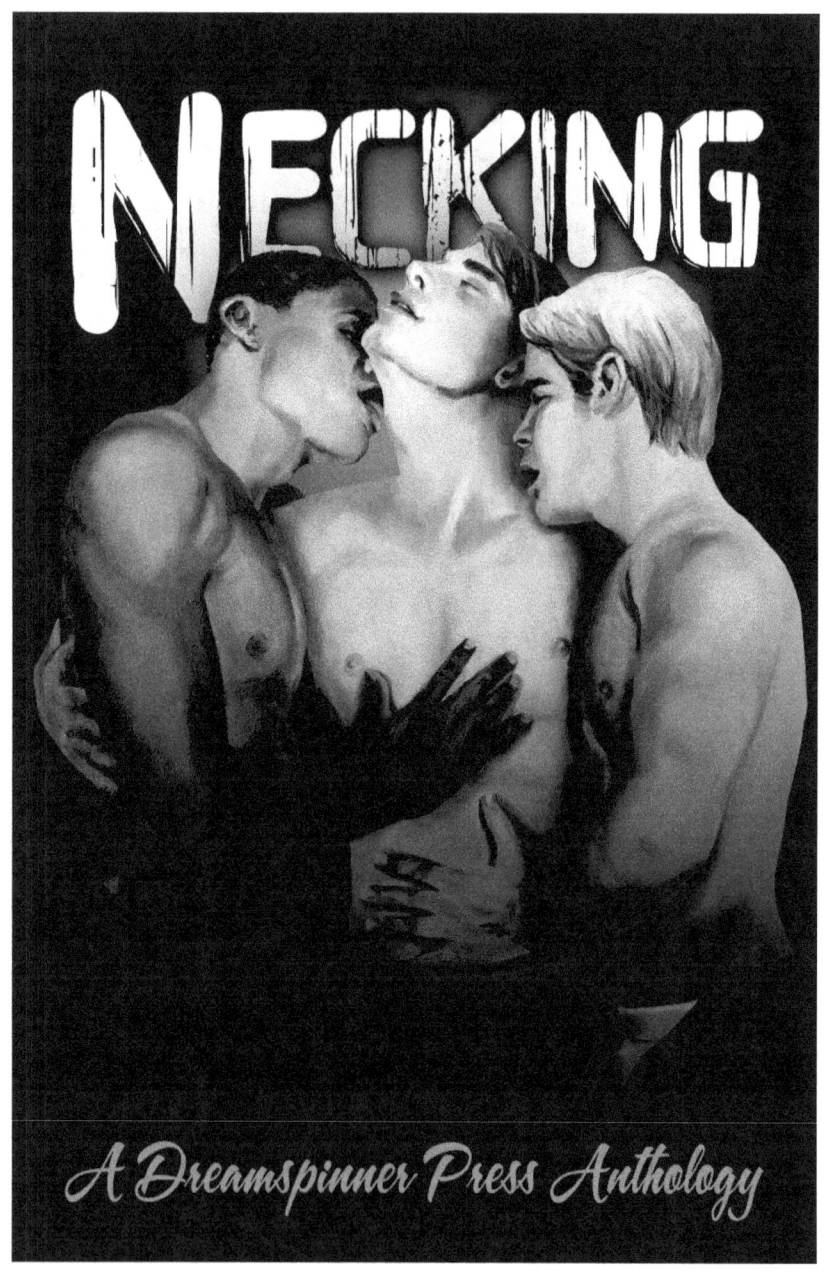

Also from EVAN GILBERT

http://www.dreamspinnerpress.com

www.ingramcontent.com/pod-product-compliance
Lightning Source LLC
Chambersburg PA
CBHW070112260626
47160CB00004B/1438